Fantasy book 2025

The Godless Void

Kim Teibio & A.C. Aerie

The Godless Void
Kim Teilio & A.C. Aerie
© 2024 Oxford eBooks Ltd.

Published under the sci-fi-cafe.com imprint.
www.oxford-ebooks.com

The right of the authors to be identified as the author of this work
has been asserted in accordance with the
Copyright, Designs and Patents Act 1988.

All rights reserved.
No part of this publication may be reproduced, stored in a retrieval system, or transmitted, in any form or by any means, electronic, mechanical, photocopying, recording or otherwise, without the prior permission of the copyright owners.

This is a work of fiction. All the characters and events portrayed in this book are products of the writer's imagination, or are used fictitiously.

sci-fi-cafe.com

About the Authors

A.C. Aerie and Kim Teilio met on an MA Writing course. Kim Teilio is the writer of *Into Dust*, and A.C. Aerie is the writer of *A Sun Going Down*. Kim Teilio can be reached on Bluesky and Twitter

FOR YASMIN, FOREVER AGO

There hadn't even been a whole hour since I had claimed a table at Howard's Tavern and already they were tossing additional sawdust onto the ground to soak up some more spilled blood. It had been caused by three apprentice sorcerers this time – the game of cards they had been playing came to a violent end when it was realised there were at least seven Aces in the deck. Being the kind of people that they are, they clumsily hacked at each other with daggers that had previously been concealed, certain the impending hangover could see them sleeping through the most painful part of regrowing severed limbs.

Howard's always had attracted a *certain* kind of people. Misplaced travellers on dark nights could see the welcoming lights of burning candles behind the grimy windows, but they would soon turn direction on hearing the noise from within. The laughter and the jeers would be as the sound of the damned to many a man, and that's because it was exactly that.

Women at the bar stroked the necks of drunken men and whispered promises of desire into their ears as they slipped a free hand into their pockets to relieve them of coin. I smirked at that, but it stopped being funny the moment I thought back to Yasmin. She may have cut the deepest, but that would never keep you from forcing the knife back in her hand and lowering your defences.

I shrugged it off as if someone were watching me – someone fully aware of my hateful thoughts aimed at any unknown man making her happy – and brought the tankard of watery alcohol to my lips. Things hadn't been that bad between us – at least not to me, anyway – and trying to convince myself otherwise wasn't going to benefit either one of us… Wherever she was now.

Cold air filled the room as the door was flung open and for a moment, I expected to see one of the bloodied sorcerers returning in search of a body part, but I wasn't so lucky. It was Joseph and Arthur, the Yorn brothers. Twins, but nowhere near identical. Arthur was so ugly, the most popular joke to make once he was out of earshot was that his parents had welcomed a wild boar into their marital bed on the night he was conceived.

The room was bright enough for me to see how each brother had blood on his hands, his clothes. Joseph was shouting about the elk they had supposedly killed before he had even reached the bar, but I knew there was most likely the remains of a lone traveller nearby as soon as I saw him pull the fat purse from his pocket.

Howard wouldn't mind, and he wouldn't question, because it was his rule not to. His establishment was known for welcoming bandits laying low for fear of running into wardens or bounty hunters. Many had even planned their next foul deeds here, while they waited for the dust to settle on their previous crime.

The door had almost swung shut before another figure entered and the second I set eyes on him, I knew he was a revenant. He had pulled the hood of his cloak up, but I caught enough of a sight of his glassy eyes and pallid skin to know exactly what he was. Despite the many years placed between now and then, my mind raced back to the Battle of Mealand and every long and ugly scar masking my face began to tingle as I instinctively reached for my own blade.

But I took a breath and returned my hand to the table, reminding myself of just how long it had been, and of how things had surely changed between us and *them*. Understandably, it wasn't enough for me to look away from him. Bringing my drink back to my mouth, I sat and watched, and I tried my best to ignore how those nearest him hadn't noticed or simply hadn't cared what he was.

Like I said, things change.

He surveyed the room slowly and as I was wondering if he had possibly been called from his grave to enact bloody revenge of his own or for somebody else, his eyes stopped on me. I felt his cold, milky-white eyes hover over me for a moment. Watched his thin lips tremble as if he were muttering something and, right as I was preparing to reach for the blade a second time, watched him turn and head back out of the door.

I only noticed how each and every noise of the tavern had disappeared when they came crashing back down and, looking to those nearest me, accepted that no other person had paid him any attention at all.

So why had it meant so much to me?

I finished what had remained of my drink and headed for the door. When a hand took a tight hold of my elbow, I was a heartbeat from freeing my blade and having a demand for more sawdust being called out.

It was Gricious who had taken a hold of me, and I couldn't really hold it against him. The once feared assassin of the land had lost an eye to the self-proclaimed Emperor of Shadows, and now he couldn't rely on his depth perception.

"I'm getting a crew together," he slurred, rocking on his heels as if we were standing on a boat crossing turbulent seas, "and I could do with a man like you."

I grinned and took to prying his fingers off of me as quickly yet as gently as possible.

"No one could ever need a man like me."

"Don't be," he insisted, "don't be so hard on yourself. It's like I'm always telling people – it's not your fault you let your king down!"

I gave him his hand back, patted him on the shoulder and smiled. "You got it all wrong, it was the king that let me down."

His fingers tried to find a hold on my shoulder as I moved for the door, but they slipped away quickly enough.

Outside, the night had grown darker, and the moon was as a sliver of silver against a starless sky. Removed so suddenly from the stench of unwashed men and burning tobacco of a low quality, the faint smell of wet earth went unnoticed. The revenant hadn't gone too far; I watched him shuffling along towards a black, horse-drawn carriage waiting at the side of the road, the burning torches at its front almost blinding in the dark night.

The dead man stopped at the vehicle and gently pulled the door open – then he turned and stood looking right at me. The two of us stood staring at one another for a moment, both of us silent until he reached the conclusion I didn't understand, and he made a brief grunt in an attempt at having me come closer.

"It's okay," I said with a smirk. "I enjoy the walk."

The light of the torches allowed me to see the look of confusion taking hold of his facial expression. With no idea of what to do in the current situation, he turned and looked into the darkness of the carriage. He moved away quickly as an irate-yet-well-spoken voice emerged from the impenetrable gloom of the compartment.

"You really are useless, aren't you?" the passenger said, climbing out of the carriage. An old man, immaculately dressed and clearly not used to things going the way he hadn't intended them to. He almost lost his balance on setting foot on the wet ground, and I almost laughed because of it. With his composure quickly regained, he locked his eyes on me and took measured steps forward.

"Raen Caleb," he said. "I had long believed you to be dead."

"Not me, but I can't be so sure of your companion."

He took a moment before deciding on humouring me. "Ha! My companion's name is Kain," he said, and the reveal was enough to have the revenant grunt and pull his eyes from me for a moment, just so he could glance to his master. "I can assure you that he is the most loyal of all the men in my employ."

"Sure he is," I said, "just watch you don't cut yourself shaving when he's around."

He didn't even need a moment to smile at that one. "You served under me a long time ago, although I don't recall us ever meeting before now. Lewis Castle," he said, and my mind immediately raced back to good men falling at the hands of bloodthirsty revenants because of terrible orders.

"Charles Burroughs—"

"*Sir* Burroughs," he said, making himself as tall as he could manage. I'd never heard of his death over the years, but I had sure hoped to.

"It would be an idea to keep your voice down," I advised him. "This far north, you won't find many a man pledging allegiance to the king or dropping to the knee for men of your title."

He smiled. Something I said had lightened his tone, just as easily as I had first darkened it. "Yes," he said, observing Howard's, "this is quite an unexpected place for a man like you to be. Well, to some, maybe."

"You should see the place in summer, it gets to looking real pretty. Anyway," I said, turning to head back indoors, "I better get moving along, before—"

"You were known as being a brave and just man, before and after the Revenant War. I'm curious as to what, exactly, made you leave such a reputation behind," he said, "only to settle here."

"You can't beat a little peace and quiet," I said, and the noise coming from Howard's instantly turned louder as two drunken men came staggering out of the door, both trying to beat the other unconscious. Burroughs positioned himself onto his tiptoes for a moment, eager to take a good look. I looked to Kain and saw how the smell of blood must have caught in his nostrils. He grunted and, for a moment, looked ready to charge forward. Whatever it was that held him back, it wasn't physical.

"Where were we?" Burroughs asked, looking back to me, already bored of the spectacle at my back. "Ah," he said, "now I recall. Your services have been highly recommended, and I happen to be in need of a man of your talents."

His lips were moving, so it was easy for me to see he was lying.

"Thank you for considering me," I said, determined to make it back to the warmth of Howard's despite how two regulars were still rolling around in a violent struggle, "but someone is already paying for my time."

"I'll more than double whatever it is you're currently being paid," he said. It wasn't enough to stop me. He could quadruple it, but the sum would still be non-existent.

"You turn your back on me, despite the cruel waters I travelled to reach this place?"

"Moreso." I grinned and said, "My days of crossing waters are yet another distant memory."

"I leave at first light, should you change your mind," he called as I stepped over the men fighting in the mud. "You will find us in Harlow."

I didn't grace him with a final look back on returning to the tavern, where the heat created from the bodies of crowded drinkers clawed at my throat upon my entering; the noises these people made were almost overwhelming. My table had not been claimed during my absence, and so I sat back in my chair and called for another tankard. A smile had come to my face before the drink was brought over. The troubles of those upon these lands were rarely enough to gain my interest, and so the troubles of men across water were little more than faint echoes now strenuous to understand.

"Burroughs," I muttered, signalling for yet another beer and being almost drunk enough to regret not cutting him down when he had stood before me, leaving him to be devoured by his pet while his life continued to bleed out from his body. Such a fate would have surely been most deserving for a man who had killed more of the living than the risen army they had stood against, but it would be the decision of any one of the gods or goddesses for this to occur.

"A room," I at long last called on getting back onto my feet, "and no company." I added before Howard could insist upon the companionship of a woman. He knew better than to try and change my mind, granting me my own company and a chamber on the floor above. There was a pathetic cot with a pan beneath it and nothing more – not even a chair, but that was always more than enough for men such as me. Unsteady on my feet for both alcohol consumption and exhaustion combined, I stood my blade against the nearest wall and fell atop the covers heavy with the stench of men. Once the flame of the candle had been extinguished, sleep claimed me almost as easily as darkness had done so the room.

*

It was the groaning of a floorboard that brought an end to the silence and, before I could bring my tired body to reach for my sword, the weight of another man came down upon the cot in which I had been sleeping and a blade was pressed against my throat.

"I know who you are," he almost cooed into the darkness, his warm breath and the stench of alcohol finding my face. "I wonder if you would recognise me?"

I cleared my throat and said, "There is a candle beside me. Light it and let us see if I remember your face, and perhaps we can—"

He increased the pressure of the knife against my throat.

"No," he took much pleasure in responding, "I have no interest in seeking reason with you, Raen Caleb. You were a warden, and you apprehended my brother and me both. Because of your interference, I lost my only kin to the mines.

"Your silence is enough for me to know you realise how desperate your situation is," he continued, "but there is still more for you to know. You were with Liberty Jaxe when you brought us in," he laughed, "and now it is Jaxe who shall reward me for your death."

Jaxe, I thought, *of course you would still be alive, and of course you would still want my head.*

"My weight in silver, and he will accept you dead or alive. I think I would prefer to take you in somewhere between the two," he laughed, "but do I really want the hassle of tying you to my horse? No… No, that would be far too tiresome. But what if I removed your ugly face from your skull, and brought that to him? Perhaps you would still be alive when he took it from me? Perhaps you would still be alive when he came here, wanting to finish the job?"

Had I grown so old and careless, or was the alcohol

to blame? Years of training and schooling, and for what? The end felt a lot nearer now than it had done during the Revenant War. The man could have killed me, and taking pleasure in the moment is all that had stopped him. I hadn't woken to the sound of him coming up the stairs; I hadn't woken as he moved along the landing and now, it was only his gloating keeping me from drawing my last breath.

I said, "Howard isn't going to like this… Who's going to pay for a room here, once word gets out how it'll only make you a sitting target? You come to me when I'm at the bar, that's a different story. But creeping up on me when I'm asleep? I don't think anybody is going to be pleased with that."

"You think I care what other people think?" he hissed. "If Howard wants to cause a commotion, then Howard can get it next! All that matters is you're mine. Between the two of us, I'd just as happily gut you for free."

"Well, I'd sure get the payment for it if I were you. You get to work on me in here, and there's going to be an awful mess. Sheets will be ruined. Probably the whole cot. Howard will want payment for those," I said, "probably payment for all the nights the room is out of use. Howard—"

"For crying out!" he yelled, and he was so angry at my lack of fear and abundance of logic he was trembling. It caused the cot to shake with him. The blade kept right against my skin, but even that wasn't so steady now.

"You sure like the sound of your voice," he said. "Maybe we should see how much you like it when I've sliced your lips off? Or maybe—"

"You put that blade down and stand up," I heard Howard demand from the doorway.

"I've got a bolt pointing right at you and I won't be telling you again, Menyz."

Menyz! I almost let out an embarrassed groan. Of all the people to get on me like this, it had to be Menyz?

"You stay out of this, Howard," he said and now that the voice had a face I could picture, I regretted the idea of getting him loud enough to bring Howard along. Howard couldn't even hold his own water. Come nightfall and a whole lot of new customers, everybody would know about this.

Menyz! Had things really gotten so bad, or does every damned fool get one chance to shine in life?

"This is my tavern," Howard reminded him, "and I've worked a long night, and I really don't know how much longer I can go on holding this bolt back."

"Let it go," I said, "you've given him his chance."

"You're in no position to make suggestions," Menyz snapped back at me.

"Menyz—" Howard growled and that was the final straw. My would-be-killer, angered all the more on feeling his prize slipping from his fingers, got to his feet in a rage and shouted out a curse to any and all of the gods and goddesses that could have been watching this little performance. He was still hollering as I jumped up from the cot and onto his back, wrapping my arms tight around his own.

That seemed to both confuse and upset him. He turned in a quick circle, but I held on because it was my life that was depending on it. He managed a quick step or two forwards before he lost his balance and dropped to his knees with me as good as standing behind him, arms still keeping his pinned to his side. He was quiet, and I could feel him shaking. It felt a lot like he was crying.

"Menyz," I said, "if I let go of you, will you drop the knife and talk with me like a man?"

Nothing. Just more of that gentle shaking.

"Howard," I said, "get us some light in here, would you?"

Howard struck a match against a worn fold of striking paper, and the flame lit up the room like a comet in the night sky. I knew there and then that he had been lying about having a crossbow, but it wasn't something for me to hold against him. Once my eyes had adjusted, I let go of Menyz and took a step back. Freed of restraint, he rolled onto his back and stared up at the ceiling, gasping for air. Blood was pumping out of him. The handle of the dagger he had put to my throat was now sticking out of his chest.

"Menyz," I said, "look what you've gone and done to yourself."

He didn't look to me. His eyes remained on the ceiling, his mouth open and closing like he was a fish pulled from the stream.

"By the gods," Howard said, shaking his head and taking the match to the bedside candle, "this is going to take some tidying up."

"Nothing I could do about it," I said to try and save face, "he handed me a drink earlier, I thought it just tasted a little off, but he must have drugged me. But I'll tell you what; any coin he has on him, it's all yours."

The last part was all to try and buy his silence. Or at least have him saying Menyz had drugged me before getting so close.

"At least the cot isn't too damaged," Howard said, sounding like he was almost ready to give it all up.

"You get some soap and water on here and there won't even be any stains on the floor."

"Yep," Howard nodded, "yep… You are going to help me move him, aren't you?"

"Afraid not," I said, reaching inside my pocket for the smoking pipe and pouch of tobacco within. I kicked the bottom of Menyz's heel to try and get his attention, but he kept his eyes on the same spot on the ceiling. "Where is he, Menyz?" I asked, thumbing a little rolling tobacco into the bowl, "Where's Jaxe?"

"Man isn't going to give much conversation," Howard said as he put his hands at his hips, "I reckon he's already facing judgement. Anything he has to say right now, he's saying it to something more powerful than we could ever dream of becoming."

"Could be you're right," I said, bending down to pull the dagger from Menyz. The blood took to spilling out a lot faster once the blade was free. I wiped it clean against his shoulder and slipped it into my boot, happy to know there was one less weapon to be held against my throat.

"Why'd you have to go and do that?" Howard said, "You've gone and made it all worse."

"Just don't give it the time to start drying," I said, turning to collect my sword. "Go wake a couple of girls and get them in here with scrubbing brushes and hot water, they're already known for doing their best work on their hands and knees, anyway. I'd stay and help out, but I have to get moving on."

"Yeah? Where you heading at this hour?"

"The sea," I said with a smile. "This all has me in the mood for a little fishing."

It had been a long time since I'd had a horse of my own, but it was safe to say Menyz wouldn't be needing his. As I looked over the horses in the barn, I knew it was likely I'd claim another's by mistake, but getting to Harlow before the sunrise seemed a whole lot more important than separating a man from his animal. There was no bad feeling as I claimed ownership of the horse that looked best and charged it out onto the treacherous dirt road.

It wasn't like I was running scared of Jaxe; I just knew I wasn't in any position to face him. It had been years since we had gone at one another, and years more since we had been friends and even equals. I had spent too long drinking and working any job that wasn't too difficult, and I had no idea what he had been doing during that same time. He had offered men their weight in silver for my head, so it was safe to assume he had money and money brings a lot of influence and a lot of men willing to do your bidding. I had no money, and I certainly had no friends, but I had time. If Jaxe could be forced to reveal his hand during my absence, then I could learn more of what I was up against.

Between towns, I spotted two wardens on patrol, faces hidden by the hoods of their fur-lined cloaks. The quick glance I stole was still enough for me to guess they were young and inexperienced, and it was either too late or too early for them to pay any interest in someone with a face like mine. They didn't say a word, didn't even try and follow me from a safe distance. Truth be told, they were most likely waiting to collect a bribe.

*

It was a good horse; it looked ready and willing to run until its heart could take it no more, and I would have allowed it to do so. Upon the horizon, the rising sun was already lightening the sky. If I were to make it to the boat in time, I could not risk being merciful to the animal so desperately claimed.

I smelled the sea before I heard it and heard it before finally seeing it. At long last arriving in the port town of Harlow, the waters appeared still despite the noise they produced and looked as nothing more than a darker patch of land ahead.

Burning torches remained in place, guiding those travelling the road, yet the men standing sentry paid me no heed. As the horse took us further into the town, I could see how there was only one vessel in sight and that was far out at sea. The all too familiar feeling of disappointment reared its stupid face, but I managed to keep from looking right at it. There was just as much chance that the ship was coming as it was going – it was just too far away for me to tell. It had been a long time since I had any reason to be here, but I still knew my way around.

"Come on," I said to the horse, "turn here," and the lightest of kicks had him do as I'd asked, and soon we were approaching the inn. The carriage old Charles Burroughs had travelled in was outside with a giant of a man dutifully cleaning it. Once he could hear the approaching horse, he took a break from wiping the carriage and turned to look at me. He may have looked dumb, but he was most likely guaranteed honest work until he died.

"You tell me what room Burroughs is in?"

The man tilted his head to one side and replied with a simple, "Uh?"

"*Sir* Burroughs," I said, hoping to aid him before my temper failed me. "That's his carriage you're cleaning."

The man looked to the carriage, then back to me and shook his head. "This here is property of the inn," he said. "You can rent it, if you like?"

"Do me a favour," I said on dismounting the horse, "keep an eye on him, won't you?"

"I been told to clean—"

"This won't take a minute," I said, as good as forcing the reins into his hand.

"But I've been told—"

The overall structure was exactly how I remembered it to be – a spacious room with carved arches and a bar stood at the far side. Stone stairs leading up to a landing with rooms for rent. The only thing was, the last and only time I had been here was during the war. It was funny, seeing so many fellas sat drinking at the tables with pretty working girls beside them in a state of undress. I couldn't help but wonder how many coats of paint it had took to cover the blood on the walls.

"You run here?" I asked, approaching the bar. The

man was sweating as if we were in the hottest day of summer, but he sure wasn't moving much.

"I do," he said without taking a good look at me. "You want to wait here for the next boat to arrive, you got to at least buy a drink."

"I'm looking for someone."

He looked to me and smirked. "With that face of yours," he said, "I sure do pity 'em."

I smiled back at him, and only because I knew how easy it would be for me to cut him down, and any man he had working security here.

"Distinguished fella," I said, "has a pale companion."

The smile fell from his lips and he gave an audible gulp. You have to wonder what the world is coming to, when a man with extra coin is more imposing than a man with a sword.

"Of course, sir," he said, lifting a trembling hand to point out the sealed double doors of solid wood across the room. "The conference room... Could I tempt you with a drink? The company of an adventurous lady, perhaps?"

"My horse is outside. I want it looked after for as long as I'm gone."

"Of course," he said with a nod to show he could understand.

If any of the other patrons had watched our little back and forth, they didn't acknowledge it. They were all too tired, too relaxed, and must have known this was something they didn't want to get involved in. And as I made my way over to those sealed doors, I began to wonder if I really wanted any part of this. My hand had instinctively come to be upon the hilt of my sword, and I could fully understand why. Last time I had been here, we had been barricaded on the other side of those doors. A whole bunch of us, wondering how long the door would stand against the bloody army wanting to get through to us.

But neither one of the doors had a single mark on it. Not now. Not a single scratch. A part of me wondered if it had been easier to replace them than it had been to sand them smooth.

Being a courteous kind of man, I stopped and knocked at the door.

"Come in." Burroughs responded from the other side.

I turned the handle, gently pushed the door open just enough for me to enter. There was a brand-new table in the centre of the room, which was all too understandable, and Burroughs was sitting at it in a brand-new chair, parchment spread out in front of him.

"Raen Caleb," he smiled before getting up on his feet, "you've no idea how glad I am to see you."

My eyes scanned the room. There was nobody else – or *nothing* else – with him.

"Please," he said, "come in and close the door, so that we won't be disturbed."

I stepped further in and closed the door behind me with a gentle click. "Where's your companion?"

"He won't be too far," he said in a failed attempt to set my mind at ease, "and he'll be back in time for us to depart."

"You're sure it's a good idea, letting him go wander on his own."

Burroughs stood perfectly still for a moment, looking right at me, and his smile changed. Only a little, but enough for me not to like. The smile was the kind he clearly gave to people he felt were lacking in intelligence.

"You know, we have made some fascinating discoveries, since the war," he said. "Did you know that, in smaller numbers, revenants are really quite docile, and able to follow simple instructions?"

"I already knew that. It's why so many took to burning their dead, and it's why I think it's a good idea to behead any you see that avoided the flames."

The smile changed to one of pity, and that somehow made it even worse.

"I understand your reluctance," he claimed. "You only witnessed them at their bloodiest."

He was right. I saw them up close as he gave the orders from his guarded posts, far removed from the action.

"We have been unable to uncover what caused them to return from death," he said as if already bored with the discussion. "Although," Burroughs smirked, "we learned why they do not talk. It seems they devour their own tongues!"

Despite his potential boredom, it was me that yawned. My disturbed rest, followed by the long journey here, was clearly catching up with me. Burroughs seemed to look to me with a newfound interest because of it, but I went on as normal.

"The popular explanation was that a sorcerer had been responsible," I said, though he must have already known of this. "Throughout the war, a lot of magicians were apprehended for questioning… Even those that had volunteered to fight alongside us."

"Yes," he nodded. "Many were hanged or drowned, no matter how insufficient the evidence. I doubt their kind would have been permitted to continue, were it not for changes made to the law. But anyway," he smiled, "why waste time with discussing such history, when it is an interest in the future that has certainly brought you here?"

I looked Burroughs up and down without subtlety, then I smiled. "Could be I am," I said, "could be I'm more interested in here and now. King Selborne had you as one of his closest advisors and then it looked like you had simply disappeared, only to turn up in a part of the country that doesn't favour titles or rulers, and in need of someone like me."

"As I have already explained to you," he said with a smile, "you were highly recommended."

"By whom?"

"The name of the person wasn't given to me," Burroughs said, "it wasn't important."

"Maybe not to you, but it is to me."

"And what do you intend to do? You raced all this way to arrive on time," he said, "now you are going to turn back, without another word?"

"That depends on what questions you can answer."

My ultimatum put him at such ease, it's a miracle he didn't drop to the ground.

Smiling, he allowed himself to sit back down in his chair and acted like a speck of dust on the table had caught his attention for a second. "Please," he said encouragingly, "ask freely, and I will answer all that I am capable."

"I know whatever it is you're after, you won't be paying for my services out of your own reserves."

"Not once did I claim I would," he said. "I told you I was after a man of your talents and that I would pay you handsomely. That was all you needed to know."

"No," I said with a smile of my own, "it wasn't. Someone ordered you out here and you came with nothing but a dead man to keep you company. You didn't even come with a carriage, because you didn't want to risk their insignia being seen. All this, along with crossing the sea? You want me to do something that goes against King Selborne, don't you?"

Burroughs took a leisurely breath and released it. "You are aware of Lord Stoneisle, are you not?"

I was aware of him. A long time ago, this country had six kings claiming to be the true ruler and, eventually, it would be decided on the battlefield. Kyif Stoneisle was one of the five bettered rulers, and he took to the sea with those still breathing and loyal to him, claiming a small island he gave his name. Things may have changed throughout the long years, but there was always a Lord Stoneisle ruling over that island.

"I'm aware of him," I said.

"One of my great grandfathers advised his," Burroughs said, "until he decided to devote himself to a new king, and so I was raised to advise the ruling Selbornes. Of course, I would have gladly continued to do as such, if only the king were capable of listening to opinions not entirely his own."

"Careful," I said, "you might bring a tear to my eye."

"Perhaps you don't care for history," Burroughs said,

"perhaps you don't even care for this great country, but surely you care for the living?"

"When we were at war," I said, "with the revenants, it was Lord Stoneisle that was making excuses for them… Saying we should try and understand them. Even now, he had one of them travel with you."

"His studies helped us understand how, in small numbers, they can be controlled and are of little threat to us. And King Selborne's response? Yes, he ordered we burn our dead or, at the very least, sever their hearts. But what followed? Taxes for burning the dead and a man under his jurisdiction to be paid for ensuring the heart was indeed severed!

"We were certain the dead were rising on the commands of a great sorcerer," he continued, "and he followed my advice on apprehending those capable of any level of sorcery, but what came after a small number of public executions? The king founded academies for the teaching of magic, in a clear attempt to have the most powerful swear their allegiance to him and no other. King Selborne cares for nothing other than his own throne and your decision to remove yourself from those loyal to him only proves you are aware of this."

"Then let me guess," I said, "Lord Stoneisle is planning for a great return. He will cross the sea with a great army to reclaim what was his, and all I have to do is find enough men willing to support him and to cause trouble for the great pretender?"

"That would be impossible, and it is not my responsibility to achieve the impossible.

No," Burroughs said, "Lord Stoneisle has no

intention of ever coming here, at least not to cause turmoil and bloodshed. And why would he? He is adored by all those upon the territories long claimed by his ancestors, and his rule is without challenge or complaint."

"That sounds delightful. Why would he need to bring me into it?"

"Because he has been told of an almighty weapon," Burroughs said, "that would claim victory for whomsoever should possess it, no matter the numbers that should oppose him. Lord Stoneisle does not want to risk such a weapon falling into questionable hands, nor does he want to risk the temptation of possessing it to consume others. Remarkably, there is currently an understanding of peace amongst all major countries, and Lord Stoneisle wishes for this to prosper. That is why he has set me the task of having the weapon – should it exist – destroyed."

"Then why waste time coming here to ask me to do this?"

"I explained it could not be a man of Stoneisle he sends – for, if another knows of this weapon and should happen to see a man searching for it upon order of his lordship, it would appear that he had an interest in claiming it, and then the lands of his fellow rulers. A war unlike any other could be declared, and all because of a simple misunderstanding. When you were recommended, it made perfect sense."

"Why is that?"

"Because you were there at Lewis Castle and Mealand both, and you lived,"

Burroughs said, "so do not think for one moment

that I could think of one man capable of bettering you. And once I learned that you had renounced your king and all those that served him, I was certain you would not want to risk such a weapon falling into the hands of any other undeserving man."

"And what if I decide I'm a deserving man?"

Burroughs struggled not to laugh at that one.

"You could use it to claim a throne," he said, "but you would then be responsible for the citizens beneath you. And how long do you think it would be before another army should decide to challenge you? And another? Every ruler and every man of desire would want what you had claimed and although they may never relieve you of it, you would never know peace.

"But were you to see it destroyed? Lord Stoneisle maintains the wealth for a great kingdom still, and you would be richly rewarded. Lord Stoneisle is in favour with many a nation, and he would be indebted to you."

The doors to the room creaked open and Kain sloped in, blood smeared across his lips and what remained of a rabbit or maybe a cat held tightly in one hand.

"The sunrise nears," Burroughs said as he moved quickly onto his feet, "and with it comes our departure. You must decide if you are to come with us, or if you will remain here and leave me with the troubles of finding another man for the task."

A part of me doubted that such a weapon could possibly exist, especially one that wasn't commonly heard of, but I remembered how the dead had first taken to crawling from the dirt and I thought of all the secrets and knowledge kept by those of magic.

"Who told Lord Stoneisle of this great weapon?"

"A traveller," Burroughs said, "a man of magic. He remains on Stoneisle."

"I'd need to speak with him."

"Then we need to leave," Burroughs said, "and quickly."

*

It turned out that a number of men in the inn had arrived with Burroughs, and it turned out the boat I had seen earlier wasn't coming for them. They had arrived by longboat, which had been hidden behind the building. There was room for Kain to curl up and be covered by sheets in the centre of the boat, then a little free space at one end for Burroughs and me to sit while the other men worked the oars. The sun was still rising as we set off, all silent apart from the controlled breathing of those rowing, and I stared back at the lands I no longer recognised nor claimed to belong to. Three wardens came riding over the hill, heading towards the small town we had just departed, as local sentries took to extinguishing the flames of burning torches.

"Your king grows increasingly paranoid," Burroughs said, "do you see?"

"I don't recognise any man as being my king."

"Then may you never have to."

I turned my back on the lands and looked to the sheets covering the revenant. With next to no breeze to disturb them, they were completely still. You would never have guessed that there was something resembling a man concealed beneath them.

"Is he going to stay like that?"

"I should think so," Burroughs said. "He has feasted, and so he should remain at peace until he grows hungry."

"And if we removed those sheets that are covering him?"

"His skin may possibly blister, but he will not awaken during the daylight. Does his presence bother you so much?"

"He shouldn't take it personally."

*

The sun had reached its highest point, and my hangover had taken me to my lowest. There wasn't any land in sight and the skies above didn't hold a single cloud. We sailed an endless blue sea, and there was another hanging above us.

And I was hungry, and I was exhausted but every time I was ready to surrender myself to sleep, the sheets covering the revenant seemed to stir and my grip would tighten upon the sword and all tiredness would desert me.

Of course, the revenant hadn't moved. It was my own imagination – my own caution. Burroughs, on the other hand, had no such concern. If anything, it was my fidgeting being responsible for him remaining awake. For a man who had experienced years of unrivalled privilege, he appeared comfortable enough.

I figured the journey to Stoneisle could take anywhere between three and five days.

Regretting the decision I had made, I sat upright and took to filling my smoking pipe.

Burroughs said, "You never become aware of the stench caused by that pastime until you have replaced it with another."

"Don't worry, I have no intention of stopping."

One of the boatsmen had lowered his oar and was pulling a net through the water. He caught a fish and removed it from the sea, placing it with a couple he had already caught, before returning the net to the water. Cold fish. My stomach grumbled at the thought of it, but I doubted I'd be able to hold anything down. Pulling smoke deep inside of my lungs, I gestured toward the covered revenant and asked, "Is he guaranteed to stay like that?"

"Once we take to eating, the smell of blood could possibly awaken him," Burroughs said. "You'll enjoy it; Kain will be looking to each and us all, in the manner of a pleading dog."

"If he gets hungry, it's probably a wise idea to feed him."

Burroughs laughed. "You don't want to spoil him," he said, "and you want him to remember his place."

"Would that be underground, or scattered to the winds?"

"You should accept that the war was a long time ago and things have changed. We are in control, and these creatures have proven useful."

"They've also proven dangerous."

"I compared Kain to a dog, and that was foolish," Burroughs said. "I can assure you that you will never be in any danger around him. Yes, they become savage in large numbers, but the revenants' behaviour is very much a reflection of how it was in life."

"I'm thirsty," I said, "I don't suppose you have anything for me to drink?"

He smiled and reached under the bench of the nearest oarsman, retrieving a jug constructed of black clay. "Water, for now," he said, passing it over. "But I can assure you that there will be a great feast in your honour."

I drank greedily at the contents of the jug, forcing myself to stop once my chest felt as if it were swollen. It was difficult for me not to pour all that remained over my head.

"You told me how a traveller spoke of a great weapon," I said, handing him the jug.

Burroughs took the lightest of sips and nodded before responding.

"I did," he agreed. "If there is anything you would like to know about him, I'm afraid to say I can tell you very little."

"How did he arrive at Stoneisle?"

"He was carried back. One of our ships was returning, and a member of her crew spotted him in the waves. They pulled him aboard, where he slept until brought onto land.

There he awoke and, without first being informed of where he had come to be, insisted upon an audience with Lord Stoneisle."

"And this was granted?"

"Eventually," said Burroughs. "When it became apparent that this man was a dream-reader, Lord Stoneisle requested we bring him to him."

"What made you so sure he was capable of magic?"

"He spoke of things only those present would know of, and then he insisted upon an audience with Lord Stoneisle. Of course, we kept him under watch while this was discussed and, eventually, an advisor granted him his audience. What the traveller was entirely unaware of," Burroughs said, "was how an imposter would be in the chair of our lord, and Stoneisle himself would be standing amongst the crowd."

"And the traveller declared there was an imposter before him and singled out the true man of nobility? It's an impressive trick," I said, "especially if you've never seen it done before."

"Indeed, it is. But I beg you, do not assume our ignorance. Stoneisle may be far removed from your great capital city and citadel both, but you forget a lot of your knowledge is our own. We too know the way of the charlatan," he said, "and, being so isolated, we have had many arrive at our land since the first of the revenants began to walk, believing we will have come susceptible to their ways."

I smirked, then apologised. "Please," I said, "carry on."

"The traveller, delivering an entertaining display to Lord Stoneisle, was granted time with both him and his counsel. It was then he told us of a weapon long hidden, capable of wiping out any that should stand against the man wielding it – but how ownership of it would haunt the soul of this man, and darkness would surely devour all light in the world. He insisted Lord Stoneisle send a great warrior to retrieve it, so that it could be destroyed before it was found by another."

"Let me guess," I said, "and that was when you decided to come and find me?"

"No, not quite… A member of the counsel was most displeased at this man arriving and issuing demands, and he called for him to be thrown in a cell – which he quickly was. Of course, we had no way of knowing how this would only worsen things. The following morning," Burroughs said, "the goats and the cows produced foul, bloody milk, and the hens of Stoneisle laid eggs that were filled with black tar. That same night, the traveller was seen dancing through the fields, though he vanished without trace before he could be apprehended and was found back in his cell, much amused."

"You think he cursed you?"

"Is it not obvious he did just that? We offered him his freedom, yet he refused to leave. He insisted on a great warrior retrieving the weapon. When it was explained to him that Stoneisle's strength is its defensive terrain, how we may have archers impossible to be bettered, but not a great warrior as he may wish for, he told me of you… How you had walked from Lewis Castle and Mealand both. I had heard such claims, of course, but I had believed you long dead. He told me of the very night, and where, I would be able to find you."

The hangover made it impossible for me to cover my frustration. It mightn't have been a bad thing, given what he had just said.

"This isn't what you said when we first met. It isn't what you said at the tavern."

"No," he said, and I almost believed he was ashamed. "The traveller told me you would not listen if I tried to convince you that fate had summoned you. He told me if I could just tell you of my waiting in Harlow, then you would come. But he also told me of how this truth would be revealed, and he wished for you to know something that will make you certain you are meant to be here, and you will benefit from this deed."

"And what's that?"

"The traveller wanted you told that, through him, you will find freedom."

I snorted at that. "My freedom?"

"Yes," Burroughs nodded, "you will find *liberty*."

I stared at Burroughs for a while, and he looked like he was not only out of things to say but he had no idea of the relevance of what he had just said – I was certain of that much. I took in one last lungful of pipe smoke before emptying the burning contents of the bowl into the sea.

"What are you thinking?"

"I'm thinking I'm tired and I'm hungover," I said, "and I'd like to try and get some sleep. If Kain starts moving before me, wake me up."

"He truly has no desire to hurt you."

"I truly wouldn't give him the chance."

*

I dreamed of snarling, bloody faces and towering flames. I witnessed the death of good men all over again, and I felt the struggle to pull my blade free of bodies. I dreamed of slipping through the smooth hands of Death.

Rest had dampened the worst of my hangover,

but I was still tired. Still hungry and weak. The sun had moved across the sky, but we still had plenty of daylight ahead of us.

Whether we had travelled a great deal or remained on the same spot, it was practically impossible for me to tell. All I knew was there had come to be something other than salt to smell in the air. A smell of butchered fish and nameless spices.

The oarsmen had left their places and were gathering around the one who had been charged with catching fish. He had a rusted pot in front of him. I can't tell you where he had kept it, but the dents it held showed he could have surely taken better care of it, and was breaking the flesh of the fish he had caught apart, mixing them in with the herbs he must have brought with him. Only Burroughs had remained in his place. Burroughs and Kain, actually. Kain was still motionless beneath the sheets, the men all around him as if they didn't even care he was there.

"Are you feeling any better?"

I looked to Burroughs, to see if he was being funny, but he looked serious enough.

"No," I said, and I took to filling my smoking pipe. He waited for me to say something else and only started talking once he realised how I had no intention to.

"I am tired but find it difficult to sleep during the daylight," he said. "It's as if my mind refuses to grant me peace if night is still to come. One thought follows another, until I eventually give up."

"How long would you give Kain to wake up," I said, "before deciding he wasn't going to?"

Burroughs laughed.

"I can't say I have ever thought of it," he said. "But he has eaten, and he should understand that while we remain on this boat, there is nothing for him to see done. I very much doubt he will awaken before we arrive at Stoneisle."

"You think he's that aware?" I said, lighting my pipe. The smoke that rushed down into my chest felt too heavy, because of the little sleep and lack of food.

"If he were to remain as he is now, never to awaken," Burroughs said, "I would not mourn him, if that is what you wish to know. He has been loyal, and he understands what is expected of him, but many of his kind are. Kain could be replaced and with little difficulty."

The cook among us decided the meal he had prepared was ready, and I hadn't known exactly how hungry I had become until I pushed that first morsel of fish into my mouth. He hadn't made anything memorable, it tasted like nothing more than the sea, but we all kept returning our hands to the dented pan until there was nothing left to be taken.

Feeling a lot better, I sat back and went to smoking my pipe. Most of the men pulled pouches of tobacco from their pockets and dug pieces of paper out from the dried leaves to roll cigarettes. It wasn't too long before every one of us looked pretty relaxed and content. Burroughs instead kept dipping his fingers into the sea to get the oil from them, so he wouldn't have had much luck with a match anyway. Watching the repetition of his movements was enough to have me lost to my own thoughts.

Burroughs looked to me and said, "Have you spent

much time at sea?"

"No. Bit of fishing here and there, but that was about all. I was a warden," I said, "Selborne has a whole load of sailors and a large navy, and they all managed to get by without me."

Burroughs nodded like he could understand, but he couldn't. He took a breath and said, "I always find it most relaxing, being away from land."

"Not me. You don't know what's down there, not really. You put a man in deep enough water, and he can be attacked from any angle."

Burroughs smiled at that, but I wasn't in a particularly playful mood. I emptied the contents of the bowl into the sea and lay back as best I could, closing my eyes. "Wake me if the revenant stirs," I said.

"Back to work," Burroughs said to the others, "we still have some way to go."

*

There was the lapping of the waves, and there were loud voices calling over them. I woke. The sky was deep blue and filled with stars. The oarsmen had stopped rowing and had all taken places behind a man, standing with a burning oil lamp in his hand. There was a large ship coming right for us. Lanterns burning from up high made the men looking down at us appear as ghostly silhouettes. Getting up on my feet, my joints were stiff but I prepared to reach for my blade and stood beside Burroughs. I said, "You know them?"

"Yes," he said with a nod. "They have come to take

us the rest of the journey."

"That should shave a day or two off."

"Yes," he said. "Better food and a more comfortable space to rest."

I glanced to the sheets covering Kain and realised he still hadn't moved. The man at the front of the boat carefully lowered the lantern, reclaimed his oar and insisted the others do the same. They fell back into place without hesitation and took to guiding us to the side of the ship, where the men onboard were already hanging ropes over the side for us to attach to the longboat.

"They'll pull us up," Burroughs said. "It will only take a minute, but it would be a wise idea to sit back down."

Pulled aboard the ship, the captain was quick to introduce himself. His name was Elias Lyons, and he took much satisfaction in revealing he was the third of that name. I would have told him I had never even heard of his predecessors, but he was quick enough to say how there was a hot meal waiting for us and that was enough to keep me polite. The men Burroughs and me had travelled with fell back quickly enough, disappearing amongst the other, less valued men. This meal was fit for only the captain and his two special guests.

*

It was a large room with plenty of candlelight. The banquet that waited for us filled the entire table, which was something in itself. One of the men closed the door behind us, ensuring our privacy, and Captain Lyons joyfully told us we could sit. The smell coming from so many cooked meats was enough for me to sit without needing to be told a second time, my stomach rumbling despite the fish I hadn't long eaten.

"Wine?" the captain asked on reaching for a jug. It seemed funny, having such a display and having no one to serve us, but I doubted this was a regular occurrence. The other men would most likely devour what we hadn't touched, as well as the scraps of what we had.

"Please," Burroughs said softly. Believing himself back to civilisation, he took to speaking a lot quieter. "Your timing was perfect, Captain."

"I know these waters better than any man," he said, handing Burroughs a drink. He looked to me and he kept his smile in place, just like he kept the jug high, but there was suspicion in his eyes. He didn't like the look of me, and I couldn't blame him. It was probably considered unlucky to even bring somebody with a face like mine aboard.

"No," I said, reaching for the cooked chicken.

The captain filled his own glass before lowering the jug back onto the table. "You don't drink?"

"I drink," I said, removing tender white meat from the bone, "I'm just not thirsty."

It was a lie. Of course, I was thirsty. But if I started drinking now, without being expected to give coin in exchange for it, I probably wouldn't stop until I had to.

The captain looked to be nothing but smiles, his face red in the candlelight. He finally looked back to me and said, "You're the first person of Sundeberg to ever sit at my table." It was peculiar, because I hadn't considered myself as belonging to Sundeberg, or anywhere else, for a long time. "Were you born in the capital?"

"He was not," Burroughs said, "although he was one of many brave souls to defend it during the war."

The captain solemnly nodded and lowered his glass. "Such a ruthless, bloody part of recent history… I pity the countries of such great numbers. The population of Stoneisle must only be in the hundreds of thousands, the combined population of Sundeberg many times that, and we ourselves were overwhelmed for such a time. Your survival," he said, "is surely down to the wishes of the gods."

"No," I said, "the blade is responsible for the survival of many, I can assure you of that."

Captain Lyons cleared his throat and kept his eyes down as he reached for his glass, clearly fearing that he would be judged by the gods for my supposed blasphemy if he even dared look at me too soon. Burroughs took a sip of his wine and said, "The blade and the planning of our attacks and how we defended our posts. I can assure you that I prayed for guidance from many a god and goddess when it came to doing this."

"I prayed for the dead to crawl back into their graves."

The captain spoke quickly, certain the mood would sour all the more if he allowed Burroughs and me to go uninterrupted. "This banquet is delicious," he said, "we are lucky that the traveller has not entirely cursed our livestock."

"Did you pluck him from the sea?"

"No," the captain said, eager for me to believe him. "I like to believe that I would have sensed something was not right, and left him to the mercy of the waves, but I can't be certain I would have done so. Tell me, have you ever found yourself so far from land, and entirely at the mercy of the waters as your vessel sinks beneath you?"

"No," I said, reaching out for more chicken, "not once."

The captain chortled and said, "Then I will pray that it remains as such, my friend. I can assure you that the souls of the damned must experience something similar to it."

I knew Captain Lyons had clearly been lost at sea. I knew Captain Lyons wanted me to ask him all about it, but I didn't. I carried on eating. Even Burroughs helped himself to more from the table. Silence resumed and silence, I came to realise, was not appreciated by the good captain. Eventually, he smiled and puffed out his chest. "I have had business dealings with many men over Sundeberg," he said. "Where were you born? I may know someone from that place."

I shrugged my shoulders. "I can't tell you where I was born," I said. "I was one of many children handed over to the citadel, and I was taught how to read, and how to fight, and I had the one name until I was claimed by a nobleman. He continued my education. In time, I proved myself worthy of his name."

"The fate of the Calebs was a tragedy," Burroughs said before sipping at more wine.

"You honoured them with your bravery, and your very survival."

The captain nodded and, eager to please, raised his glass. "To the Calebs," he said, "may they go remembered."

Burroughs merely nodded in approval before returning his drink to his lips. I sucked the grease from my fingers and got to my feet. "I'm tired and I'm full," I said, "and I was assured that I would have somewhere to rest."

"Of course," the captain said, standing, "I'll have you taken there, now, if you're sure that is what you wish?"

"It is."

"I will see that you go without disturbance."

There was a cot, and there was a table and chair, and that was more than enough. I slept soundly and only left my cabin when I was hungry. The captain seemed embarrassed that I had had to do so.

"I told them not to disturb you," he said, "but I thought one of them would have had the sense to see if you wanted something to eat."

"I'm glad they didn't," I said. "I do have one request, however."

"Please," the captain said, "allow me to see it taken care of."

"I would like Kain to be brought to me, as soon as he rises."

"Kain?"

"The revenant," I said, letting him know there had been no misunderstanding. "Can you do that?"

"I can… Yes," he said, "is there anything else? More food? Some drink, perhaps?"

"No, that's all," I said. "Until then, I don't want to be disturbed."

I managed to ignore the sounds of other men behind the walls and rats scurrying beneath the floor. I focused on my own silence. At times, my thoughts were all I needed, and this was such a time. I noted the movements of the sun as it moved across the sky and watched it disappear into the waves. It grew quiet as the night advanced. The time came for there to be a knock at my door. I moved forward, unlocked the door and pulled it open. Kain stood facing me, Burroughs planted behind him.

"Come in," I said, and the revenant obliged without question. "Not you," I said as Burroughs stepped forward.

"I was told you requested an audience."

"Yes," I said, "with the revenant. Don't worry – I'll send him back to you."

I moved to shut the door. Burroughs pushed a foot forward and kept me from doing so. I looked down at his foot, then I smiled and looked at him.

"Your foot is in the way," I said.

"What are you doing? Why must you insist on my remaining out here?"

"I'm not," I said, "you can wait wherever you want," and I gave him a gentle shove back and closed the door. "That's far enough," I said, turning to see Kain taking slow steps toward the table. It was more than a little surprising to see him stop right there. He didn't turn back to face me. He just stood, looking right ahead, as if waiting for further instruction.

"Aren't you an obedient one," I said, passing him

by without taking my eyes from him for a moment. I took the chair out from beneath the table, turned it around and sat facing him. He went on standing there, eyes never really focusing on anything, mouth open. It was interesting – horrifying, maybe – to see he still had his teeth. Burroughs could talk about how Kain had been domesticated, but I'd still not take the chance. Up to me, I'd have had all his teeth removed. Maybe his entire jaw. No, that's not right. Up to me, I'd have him burned down to ash.

"I saw a lot of good men fall to people like you," I said. "Then, I saw them stand and become people like you. How much can you understand? Could you stomp your foot to show you understand me… Nod your head? No… I guess Burroughs hasn't gotten around to teaching you anything like that – yet."

Taking a breath, I took the smoking pipe from my pocket and filled the bowl. It could have been the precise movements, it could have been the smell of the tobacco, but Kain's eyes suddenly moved to my fingers with interest. He may have even smacked his dry, dead lips together.

"You used to smoke? A part of you remembers, is that it? Do you remember the war?" I asked him, "Were you even wandering around back then, and do you remember feeding on people like me, if you were?"

His eyes kept on my fingers until he blinked. His interest was gone just as suddenly, and his cloudy eyes went back to moving aimlessly across the room.

"I've seen revenants do a lot of unexpected things," I said, bringing the flame of a match to my pipe, "but there is something I never expected to see one doing, and I saw you do it. When you came looking for me, at Howard's, it sure looked like you were talking to yourself. Was that you, or was the mysterious traveller I've heard of responsible? Is he in there now, paying close attention?

"I don't like how it feels," I said, bending forward to slide the dagger from my boot, "if I think I'm being played. I don't like it when I believe there's even a chance somebody is playing me."

I held an open hand toward the ceiling and pressed the blade of the dagger against it.

One quick movement and my blood would spill. The revenant's eyes were sure on me, now.

"You think I'll be able to retrieve this powerful weapon for you, if I've been fed on?"

Those eyes were on me, but the body didn't move. I kept my eyes on him for a moment, then considered I might have been acting out of my mind. And why shouldn't I, after all that had happened in so little time?

"Get out of here," I said, slipping the dagger back inside of my boot. "Go on – get."

The revenant turned and made his way back to the door.

"Trust works both ways."

Kain opened the door. Burroughs had remained outside, waiting for him. I wasn't surprised.

*

It was the sound of glass breaking that woke me.

I sat upright, but the room felt quiet. My eyes struggled to adjust to the darkness. Nothing seemed to be moving, but I cautiously felt for the matches I had placed beside the bed and struck one, surveying what I could of my surroundings as I guided the flame to a beside candle.

Nobody, but that wasn't enough to satisfy me.

Swinging my legs to the cold floor, I got to my feet and slowly moved forward. The sound had been real, I was sure of it.

It took a number of slow steps with the candle held in front of me, but I found the cause. A mirror I hadn't paid much attention to lay broken along the floor, the pieces resting in a shape resembling a crescent moon. I looked to the wall and examined the hook it had been depending on. It looked fine and it wasn't loose. Kneeling back down, I moved my fingers over the shards of glass and told myself we could have just taken a particularly forceful wave. It didn't feel quite right, but it was all that I had at that time.

We spent another day on the waves, and I managed to keep my own company throughout it. The sun had long set, and the winds of the night were in full flow before there was a knock at my door. A young seaman had come to tell me we were nearing Stoneisle.

The air was cold and damp. I felt the salt it carried settle on my skin. There was the sea, and there was the night sky, and there was Stoneisle. It looked to be nothing more than a daunting rockface, climbing into the heavens solely to challenge us. The kings of Sundeberg had sworn to protect the waters of Stoneisle for generations, and it was easy to see why.

Stoneisle would be a perfect place to launch offenses or retreat to. Anybody coming here with plans to conquer would find the land itself against them.

A member of the crew was sending a message of some kind by covering the light of the lantern he held at brief intervals. I tilted my head back, eyes climbing the wall until I saw a small speck of light responding. I said, "What are they saying?"

The captain turned to me. He didn't look too pleased. "I can't take you much further," he said, "we're going to have to lower the longboat."

"And how do you expect me to climb up there?"

He seemed pleased to know the answer to that one.

"There's a ladder," he said as he pointed at Stoneisle, "and it leads up to that platform," he explained, but I couldn't make out any platform. "Platform takes you to the grand stairway, long carved into the stone. They'll be plenty slippery, but there's a rope running alongside them. Just be sure you keep hold of that."

Burroughs emerged on deck, the revenant beside him. It was the first time I had seen either one of them, since I had insisted on Kain's company, and a less-observant man wouldn't have noticed that Burroughs was still upset about it. He rubbed his hands together and surveyed the imposing landscape.

"Here we are," he said, "may you bring an end to our misfortune."

*

I insisted on trailing behind Burroughs and Kain, and no one could ever blame me. Burroughs went first because he knew the land well, meaning I could watch how he went up the rockface and try imitating it. Then Kain, who I wanted to keep an eye on. The revenant needed little instruction on how to scale his way to the top, but that didn't surprise me. If I had learned one thing during the war, it was that the dead won't let locked doors or high walls keep them from what they want.

Come the time we reached that last, treacherous step, I was dripping wet, and it wasn't all down to moisture from the air. The palm of my hand was tender from how tightly I had kept a hold on the rope hammered into place alongside the stairway. Sweat burned the tender flesh. I would have gladly sat down to take a breath, but there was already a carriage waiting for us with a little welcoming party of three men in leaf mail as poorly fitted as it was maintained. Even their blades looked dull.

One of them bowed and said, "Sir Burroughs, how glad we are that you are back. And you must be Raen Caleb."

I'll give him his due, he looked right at me and didn't show any hint of revulsion. One of the men beside him wasn't quite as well reserved. I wouldn't say he was struggling to keep down his evening meal, but he was certainly interested in how a man could ever have survived the injuries I had.

"You three must all know about the man you're keeping in a cell," I said, easing my pipe from my pocket. My breathing was ragged, but I like to think it didn't show quite how much the climb had taken out of me.

"Yes," the same one of them said with a nod. His eyes were wide now, hopeful. He seemed to honestly believe that I was here to rid them of some great dragon.

"You know where he is," I said, filling the bowl, "and he must sleep... Why haven't you just gone in there and killed him?"

His face became a mixture of hope and shock, like they hadn't thought of giving that a try.

"Men approached him with flaming torches," he said, "and the flames died at his command! They approached him with swords and rope, only to drop to their knees, vomiting until they could crawl away from him! They—"

"Did you witness any of this?"

He swallowed, looked briefly to Burroughs and then back to me. "No," he said, "but I know of men that were told—"

"These things did indeed occur," Burroughs said. "If you believe you can succeed where a number of others failed, you are welcome to try."

I nodded, brought a flame that struggled to stay alive in the winds to the tobacco and breathed smoke into my lungs. "Maybe I will," I said, stopping to look over the lands for the first time. It was as if plentiful fields and mountains had been placed atop of the impossible structure we had climbed. Small villages in the distance held quaint cabins, some with candles still burning at the windows.

"The driver will take us the rest of the way," Burroughs said, stepping closer to the carriage, signalling for one of the three men to get the door. "We shall rest and, in the morning, discuss matters with Lord Stoneisle and his council."

"Won't he want to discuss this right away?"

Burroughs smiled back at me from over his shoulder. "Would you have them all pulled from their chambers at such an hour? You are here," Burroughs said, "and you may rest. I can assure you that everything will be taken care of."

He climbed into the compartment. I looked to Kain, who seemed to be waiting for an order. "Go on in," I said, "I may as well take my time."

The revenant grunted and did exactly as I had asked.

It may have been dark, but it didn't keep me from spotting the dead man wandering the wheat field we passed. Burroughs looked to me and said, "Much better than a scarecrow."

"Has he got company?"

"There are others performing such tasks, but we know not to have too many in close proximity of one another," he said. "I can assure you that we have successfully maintained control."

"And what if a child goes running through one of those fields? How can you be certain one of your dead won't decide to have a little something to eat?"

The journey was long and uncomfortable, the inside of the carriage providing little luxury. Burroughs had placed his hands upon his lap and kept his eyes closed. Kain focused on me, as if awaiting orders, so I gave him what he wanted. I said, "Look somewhere else, won't you?" and he obliged. Still, I knew not to take my eyes off him for too long.

Despite the darkness, Stoneisle managed to look

pleasant. It looked to be all open fields and cottages placed close together; men I doubted would be much good under duress manned their posts in old leaf mail and carried swords like they had been given them for the first time at sunset. I thought of the skilled archers I had been told of and wondered where they happened to be. Sleeping? Could all the people of Stoneisle be required to practice archery, even those looking uncomfortable in armour, blade at their hand?

Eventually, as the sky began to lighten in the distance, the carriage came to a halt. Burroughs opened his eyes the instant a man opened the door for us. "Sir Burroughs," the man said with a bow, "you have at last returned to us."

"I am not one to shirk from responsibility," Burroughs said, almost reprimanding him. "Kain, see that my sanctuary is prepared."

Kain didn't need to be told a second time. Keeping his head down to keep it from hitting the ceiling above him, he quickly moved out of the carriage and walked out of sight, the figure at the door giving him the briefest of glances, as if to be sure those teeth weren't going to get too close to his neck. Burroughs returned his attention to me.

"Although your stay may be brief," he said, "I'm sure you will find Stoneisle House much more welcoming than the wretched tavern I found you in."

He climbed out of the carriage and I stepped out after him, because I was too tired to respond. Without looking back, he started walking along the path leading to what must have been Stoneisle House. It was a big place of wood and stone, with large windows, many of them decorated with stained glass. Bright flowers and stone statues complimented the surrounding grounds. And it was welcoming, I'll give Burroughs that much, but it paled in comparison to some of the homes I had seen in the capital.

The man responsible for opening the carriage door looked to me. My lack of movement uneased him, leaving him terrified he had overlooked some ancient custom or greeting. Eventually he cleared his throat and asked, "May I take your sword?"

I said, "I wouldn't advise it," and took to walking behind Burroughs. As we neared the large door it was opened from within. Another man presented himself. Tall and wearing armour he looked to have spent good coin having maintained and polished. The purple cloak he had flowing from his shoulders kept his blade hidden.

"Sir Burroughs," the man said with a pleasant smile, "how pleased I am to see you back. And you must be Raen Caleb," he added. A trace of the smile remained but it wasn't meant for me. His eyes moved over me. He didn't even try hiding the fact my appearance had captured his attention.

"Yes," Burroughs said with little interest. "I trust the back entrance is open? I have sent Kain to see my room is prepared."

The man looked to Burroughs and smiled all over again. "I insisted that be done the moment we learned you were back," he said. "Food is being prepared, but I'm sure they won't mind Kain coming through. I'm convinced one or two of the hands have actually missed him."

"As long as they don't spoil him with cuts of meat," Burroughs said, sounding tired.

"I'm sure you're glad to be home," I said, "and I'm sure you're glad he's home, but there are things I would rather be doing than standing out here all morning."

Our host looked to me like I had offended him, but it didn't make me feel bad, I'd hurt plenty of feelings over the years. Burroughs, wanting to defuse any potential situation, turned to me and quickly said, "How rude I have been, you must be as tired as myself. I will have a servant take you to your room, and—"

"That can wait," I said. "I'd rather go and see a certain new arrival to Stoneisle."

"You will see him," Burroughs said, "I can assure you of that. But first, you must speak with Lord Stoneisle and his council. I thought I had made it clear, and so I apologise if I did not."

"And why is that, exactly?"

"Because that is what they have insisted upon," Burroughs said. He looked to me like I was still an unclaimed boy in the citadel for a moment, but he tried to win me over with the hint of a smile on seeing how he wasn't about to intimidate me. "Forgive me," he said, "but I am tired, and you must also be tired, and it will do you no good, seeing him in such a state. You may be easy to confuse, or struggle to remember what he has to say to you."

I looked back at him. From the corner of my eye, I saw how the other man was watching events unfold with interest. I saw how one hand seemed ready to go for the blade should the need, or the opportunity, present itself. So I smiled at Burroughs.

"You're probably right," I said. "We'll all be getting together soon enough, won't we?"

"I'll have a maid wake you," he said. "Before that, would you like to eat, or shall I have you taken straight to your cot?"

"I'm not hungry."

"Then let me find someone to assist you."

Burroughs stepped into the building. I followed, taking the opportunity to give the other man a slight shove on passing him. Looking back over my shoulder, I smiled right at him. He didn't think it was funny.

A sweet, young thing escorted me to my room. She was beautiful, and she didn't stare for too long. As a matter of fact, she did her best not to even look at me. As she was fluffing-up my pillows, I was tempted to see just how far she had been instructed to go to see my needs met. I resisted the urge. She was bound to have someone local, someone deeply in love with her, and I doubted Stoneisle's ruler would appreciate my cutting down a lovesick fool, even if it was in defending my own miserable life.

Head bowed, she held her hands behind her back and stood beside the cot. "Can I be of any further assistance?"

I wanted to hold her close, but I knew a part of me would only count her imperfections on remembering Yasmin. Acting like she was of no interest, I walked to the window and felt the thick, purple curtains that kept the sunlight out of the room. "Who's the man downstairs," I said, "wearing a cloak?"

"You mean Hurley, sir?"

"If that's his name, yes."

"Forgive me," she said, "I only wanted to be certain… His name is Campbell Hurley. He watches over this place, and all those that stay here."

"Does he now…"

"Would you like me to take a message to him?"

"No," I said. "You're free to go. Just make sure you close the door behind you, and don't let anyone disturb me until your lord and his men are ready."

"Of course," she said. I listened to her walk out of the room and close the door shut behind her before allowing myself to turn around. Traces of her smell remained. It was a sweet, delicate smell, compared to everything else. The smell of stale sweat and bodily fluids hung onto everything. It's always the same in places like this. The more coin a man has, the filthier his habits. Bedpans remain unused as they relieve themselves out on corridors or stairways. I knew of one ruler who, tired of people using his priceless tapestry to wipe their greasy fingers clean after eating, said he would maim any man he caught ignoring his order.

Pulling the covers back from the cot, I wiped the few bugs I saw from the sheets before undressing and climbing in. Despite the time of morning, sleep claimed me almost immediately.

And I dreamed that Liberty Jaxe and I were young again, and we were back in the mountains. And I dreamed of great fires and bloody teeth.

A knock at the door brought me from such memories.

"Who is it?"

"Could I interest you in something to eat?" a softly

spoken voice said from the other side of the door. "I know you asked not to be disturbed, but Lord Stoneisle insisted we offer."

"You've talked with Lord Stoneisle?"

"Yes," the voice said, the speaker remaining out of sight. "He is preparing for the day."

Reaching for my smoking pipe, I said, "Bring me some cooked meat. And a bowl of water, so I can clean myself."

"What meat would you prefer?"

"Animal," I said.

I had eaten and washed and was smoking my second pipe before there was a knock at the door. I didn't answer. I carried on looking out of the window, to the lake outside and the birds gathered around it, waiting for a fish to come close enough to the surface. There was another knock before the door was pushed open and Burroughs walked in. He had changed his clothes. Being back here, he looked a little healthier.

"I apologise for how long you have waited," he said, "but some members of the council insist on being the last to arrive, no matter how serious the discussion to be had."

I kept him waiting for an answer and emptied the contents of my pipe out of the window. "Where's your companion?"

"Kain? He rests during the day," he said, "as is to be expected."

"I hope you didn't bury him too deep. But let's go," I said, "it sounds as if some of you have waited long enough."

It was a large room, with plenty of windows to make

the most of the sunlight. Portraits of the previous lords covered the walls, and the floor was covered in polished tiles. Eight men sat at a table with Lord Stoneisle, who was beardless, and not by choice, sitting in a throne at the end. Eight men and their lord looked to me with keen interest as I approached. Two chairs remained, one for Burroughs and one for me.

"Lord Stoneisle," Burroughs said, "esteemed men of the council. May I present to you Raen Caleb, of Sundeberg."

"If that's a present," one of the men muttered from behind his hand, "I have no intention of accepting it."

"It is my pleasure to welcome you," Lord Stoneisle said, getting to his feet, and all others joined him in standing. "Sir Burroughs informed us all of your acts of bravery throughout the Revenant War."

I smiled and said, "Forgive me, but I thought you didn't agree with the war?"

"I would be lying if I claimed to have ever supported the war," he said, and with that, he lowered himself back into his throne and the others were quick to follow his example. A servant rushed forward to assist Burroughs into his chair. I claimed my own without any assistance. We all of us remained in silence until the servant had left the room. Lord Stoneisle looked directly at me and said, "I hope you will understand that what we are to discuss shall remain in this room, between us?"

I looked back at the many eyes that had settled on me and nodded my head in understanding. Lord Stoneisle was pleased at that. "Believe me when I say that your presence here is much appreciated," he said, "and how every one of us here surely wishes your reason could have been of finer circumstance.

"In the dungeon below this place, a man sits in a cell," he said. "He allowed us to place chain and lock upon him, surely for his own humour, for he has been seen—"

I exhaled, loudly, and took to pressing the loose contents of my smoking pipe into the bowl. Lord Stoneisle fell silent and looked at me, just as the others did. Such a display was clearly unheard of.

"Forgive me," I said, "but I know all about the man you pulled from the sea, and I know he has told you that I will bring a great weapon back here for him to destroy. Do you all believe what he has told you?"

A member of the council was not impressed by how I had responded. Dressed in expensive robes, his head was shaved bald, and he was without eyebrows. Golden rings ran down his right ear. He was most likely castrated at a young age. It's rare, but you still get some men in power that do it, believing it will prevent the needs of the body from corrupting their logic.

"He told us you will fetch the weapon for him, and he will destroy it," he said. "He told us he will leave this place, once this has been achieved just as you will, on accepting payment."

I struck a match and guided the flame to the bowl. "That sounds a lot like a prophecy," I said. "A great weapon that can corrupt, a man sent to fetch it for a sorcerer of some kind… What's to stop someone within this room from deciding the weapon, whatever it may be, belongs with them?"

Lord Stoneisle smiled. "Your own king promised to protect my waters, for he fears my forging an alliance with any other country. If I so desired," he said, "I could encourage your king to form a deeper alliance with me, so that we could launch an attack on any such country. Stoneisle is a strategic point for many. If I had a desire to conquer, I could have already done so."

"And you can be sure that each of these men feel the same as you?"

The members of the council revealed their contempt at such a remark. One man brought his fist down on the table. "How dare you say such a thing? How could a clear nomad—"

He fell silent on seeing Lord Stoneisle raise his hand. The accusing whispers around the table ceased.

"My people are my true concern," Lord Stoneisle said, "but I wish for all peoples to know uninterrupted peace in their lifetime. Perhaps this is all but a game for the amusement of a great conjurer, but I daren't take any risk. I want for you to bring him what he needs, so that we will be free of him. We already have a ship prepared to take you from this place… What else would you have us do, to prove that you can trust us?"

"That's easy," I said, "you could grant me an audience with him."

"Forgive my interruption," another member of the council said, "but trust surely binds us. Can we be at all certain that, on possessing such power, you won't decide to make yourself ruler?"

"This is not a man with a desire to rule," Burroughs

said for me, "nor is this a man with need to be worshipped. He will accept the generous payment we will offer for his work, and then he will return to the life that he knows."

I blew a couple of smoke rings up at the ceiling and nodded. "I've seen magic before," I said, "and I experienced it long before the dead took to crawling out of their graves. If there is such a weapon in creation, I would very much like to see it destroyed, before it can cause untold damage. That is why I need to speak with your guest… I want to hear him out, and I want to be sure we are on the same page."

The probable eunuch looked to me and gave a smile that wasn't too nice before addressing the others. "I suppose we should take our guest down into the dungeon. Any volunteers?"

"Actually," I said, "I would rather go alone. There's less chance of any confusion if it's just the two of us. No risk of anyone unintentionally reminding him of anything important. If I have your blessing, Lord Stoneisle, I will speak with him now."

The men at the table turned to face their lord. Sir Bald and Feminine tried to get someone – anyone – to look at him, so he could smirk and shake his head in disbelief, but he had no joy and eventually looked to the end of the table because of it.

"As you wish," Lord Stoneisle said.

*

The door was made of thick iron. One man stood before it, with a key on a chain hanging from his wrist.

He wasn't wearing leaf mail; instead, he wore clothes with plates of steel attached. Word must have reached him already, because he nodded and slipped the key into the lock of the iron door as I approached.

"There's only him down there," he said, turning the key, "we've ain't ever have much use for the dungeons."

"Have you spoken with him?"

"No," he said, quickly shaking his head.

"Have any of the other guards?"

"We remain here," he said.

"If there's nobody down there," I said, "how can you be sure to take the sightings of him in the fields seriously?"

He thought of that for a moment before he started to pull the door open. "Why would we want to encourage anyone to believe we couldn't keep a prisoner locked up? Lord Stoneisle insisted he be left down here," he said, "and no one should listen to what he has to say, in case he works his ju-ju on us."

I smiled, despite the fact the air rising from the bowels of Stoneisle House smelling worse than anything I had encountered in recent memory. Steep steps of damp-looking stone went into the darkness, the nearest light being of a burning torch in a long and narrow room.

"You'll hear me lock the door behind you," he said. "Procedure."

"You do what you have to do," I said, and I took my first step into the dungeons. Already, there was the sound of dripping water.

The guard was true to his word – I hadn't reached the fourth step before he closed the door behind me.

With the only light coming from the torch ahead, I took extra care on the steps and was glad I didn't miss the last one. Beyond the torch, an archway you didn't notice until it was right upon you. With nowhere else to go, I headed through. It was a cavernous area, with torches burning on four walls and even lighted candles here and there. The many flames did little to help. The floor was different – tiled, and not cleaned for a long time. There was the smell of wet, decaying hay, but I couldn't see any. Of course, it would be in the darkness beyond the locked gates – one on each of the four walls, with three of the gates being laced with spider webs.

As if to announce myself, I cleared my throat and stood still… Took to filling my smoking pipe. The sound of rattling chains came from behind the gate that had been put to use most recently.

"Raen Caleb," a voice, low sounding and quiet, said from the cell. I struck two matches, just as much to light my pipe as to try and see the lone prisoner as best I could. It might have been the darkness, but the prisoner could have just as easily been a young man as he could have been a young woman trying to pass as one. Sat with his back against the wall, he was covered in thick chains and thicker locks. If the light of the matches hurt his eyes, he didn't show it. He didn't smile, but I got the impression he was glad to see me.

I got the tobacco burning and dropped the matches to the damp ground. We simply looked to one another because I had no intention of showing anything.

"We have met before," he said at last with a flicker of a knowing smile that was extinguished as quickly as the matches I had held.

"I don't think we have."

"No," he smiled again. "I've met you in your past, and again in what could still be your future, and I know you well."

It was my turn to smile. "The guard knock you on the head a little too hard?"

"You want me to tell you where Liberty Jaxe is, and I am willing, but you will come to accept that confronting him will surely have to wait."

"And you want me to bring you a mighty weapon, all so you can destroy it, before it falls into the wrong hands."

"That is truth."

I nodded and smiled again.

"They tell me you were found in the water," I said. "You're pale, so you can't be from any of the hotter climates. Sundeberg, or just an unrecognised soul of Stoneisle?"

"I am no longer of this plain," he said, "nor any you could travel to. I am now without a land – as you are too – and I have returned only to prevent a great catastrophe."

"It mustn't have been easy," I said, still grinning. "You missed dry land."

"Despite how this world is in constant movement, I missed Stoneisle by a mortal heartbeat."

"Funny," I said, "I can't feel the world moving."

"Then you do not know how lucky you are."

We went back to simply looking at one another, and I took a leisurely pull on my pipe before speaking. "If you can travel so well, why would you need me to retrieve this weapon you're interested in?"

"It has come to a place I am unable to enter."

"Convenient," I said.

"At this time, you doubt me. But there may be a time when you confess to me how your dreams of blood and fire do not trouble you, not like your dreams of *her*."

It briefly felt as if a trapdoor had opened directly beneath me, but I didn't show it.

"I can't see that happening."

"Then we shall both have to wait and see."

I laughed.

"Where is Liberty Jaxe?"

He stood up and the chains dropped to the floor, allowing him to approach the bars with ease. It wasn't a sight I had expected to witness, but I didn't let it show.

"He holds men of influence in the citadel," he said, "and so his touch can be felt throughout the whole of Sundeberg."

"I can believe the part about the citadel, because Jaxe would have made a better Caleb than I ever could... But where is he now, or where will he be, should I retrieve this weapon for you?"

He smiled at the question, ran his tongue over his lips, like he had waited a long time to be asked it.

"Jaxe is preparing to make his own journey. He intends to claim that which I would have you bring to me."

"Convenient," I said again. "And how did Jaxe, surrounding himself with lawmen and scholars, happen to learn of this great weapon?"

He smirked, turned his back to me and took to walking back to the far wall of his cell, stopped, looked over his shoulder at me and smiled. It wasn't a smile you could ever like to see. "What do you remember of The Brothers of Aeternal?"

"Corruptive men of magic," I said, "following questionable texts. They were the first to blame for the growing number of revenants, and they were dealt with."

He smirked again, stayed silent until he was back on the floor of his cell, securing the same shackles he had easily discarded back onto his limbs. "Oh, you and the others certainly handled the loudest, the sloppiest, of them. But have you never wondered *who* truly encouraged the idea of academies for magic to be taught? The most cunning of the Brothers survived, and they are in the citadel, or they're sat close to rulers, and they are still doing as they so desire.

"And Jaxe knows one of these creatures, and they have told him all about the weapon, and the power it could grant the man that claims it.

"Liberty Jaxe already prepares to set sail. Liberty Jaxe prepares to rule without question, nor challenge. Liberty Jaxe, alongside those Brothers that have waited so long to reemerge," he laughed. "Did you not question why he suddenly wanted you dead, after all this time? He intended to see one part in the story of his life brought to an end, so the next could truly begin."

"Where is it he's going?"

"Allsen. Liberty Jaxe has gone to retrieve the weapon from Allsen."

Of course, it would have to be Allsen, where the worst of men go to die, and the best fear to tread. I looked back to my most recent years, and even some long before, and wondered which of the two I happened to be.

I blinked, then I asked him, "Who are you?"

He looked to me and smiled, as if he were finding his own words to be foolish.

"I was a Brother, so very long ago, and I escaped the blades of men such as yourself. I hid alongside the rest of them, and we listened to the tales of our supposed – but not utter – demise, and we spread ourselves over the land to prevent our true obliteration.

"But the losses we had endured drove some of those I had loved into the darkness we had foolishly been associated with… Influence over power was no longer enough, all their plans were of but vengeance and destruction, and missing texts were sought for – and, regrettably, found. The forgotten history of the gods that had loathed us, despite our loving them in return, was uncovered. As they eventually tired of witnessing our lives, and approached the end of their own, Victor, the God of War, whose maul was used to shape the continents, decided to leave his weapon behind as he left for another realm, knowing the influence it would hold once it was eventually discovered.

"That was his last act – his final joke… For man to one day find it and bring our time to a dark end.

"And we learned that it had already been found long ago, by a religious sect long forgotten. A religious sect wise enough to carefully cover it in sacred cloth before touching it a moment too long. Once it was covered, they buried it on Allsen, longing for it to remain hidden. When those I had considered my true family planned to retrieve this weapon for their own gain, I protested, and they allowed me to believe they had listened.

"One moonless night," he said sadly, "they performed two rituals, the first being that I could neither touch nor approach the weapon of Victor – not unless it was willingly brought to me. The second ritual, and the most spiteful of them both, was to cast me into another realm, for they saw me as a great betrayer. I witnessed long-gone years and potential futures both. One day within that realm was as one hundred years! And eventually, I found a gateway that would return me to these lands.

"There are two outcomes I did witness. In one, you did bring me the weapon, and I destroyed it with the knowledge I have returned with. And in the other," he concluded, "you remain on Allsen, to confront Liberty Jaxe, and all is lost because of it."

He stopped talking. The silence that returned allowed me to hear the flickering flames of the torches. The sound of my own breathing. I heard rats moving within the old hay of empty cells. Eventually, I had to ask him the only question left.

"How will I know where to find it?"

He smiled. "Those that first took to building upon that cursed island felt something they knew to be divine at one particular spot. It was the call of the hammer of course, but they did not know that. Where the call was at its strongest, they built a small place of worship, believing that there they could hear the gods, and the gods would hear them in return. If you enter this place of worship, you will unearth what you must bring to me."

"There is no place of worship there," I said, and I laughed at the sudden absurdity of it all. "There is nothing but a prison!"

"A prison containing cells," he agreed, "and rooms for the jailers – and a place for them to worship. You must enter the prison to reach what is needed. It will be no easy task, and that is what makes it a great one."

*

The Mascis was a trading ship. There was absolutely nothing remarkable about it. It set sail from Stoneisle as the sun was setting, and I was aboard it, hidden within the darkness of a crowded cargo hold. Another trading ship, The Honourable Highsmith, was to follow. We were to get as close to the prison island of Allsen as we could, and I was to search for the relic of an absent god. If we were spotted, the crew of The Mascis were to claim difficulties had caused them to stop there, and the crew of The Honourable Highsmith had come to assist. In case those aboard any other vessel turned a little too curious, a number of skilled archers were ready aboard the Highsmith.

I knew it was unlikely we would encounter any such ship. No one had any reason to get close to Allsen. Before the Revenant War, ships brought prisoners alongside food and other supplies. After the war, we learned the cursed island had also experienced the dead rising in their numbers. We were told Allsen was overrun with revenants. And now, I was going there.

I struck a match to light the tobacco waiting in the bowl of my pipe. In the complete darkness, I hadn't been aware of the rat. It had been close to my foot. I looked at it. The rat looked back, then scurried beyond the reach of the light. Once the tobacco was burning, I blew out the flame.

I woke. My body was as stiff as stone. I stretched then I made my way above. It was dark. Clear skies without a single star. The moon was fat and full, and close to the water. Only a few of the men remained awake, and I hadn't even met the captain. Breathing in a little cold air, I looked back and saw The Highsmith trailing behind in the distance. There was no sight of any other ship, no sign of land. I stopped a sailor heading in my direction. I said, "How much longer?"

"Good weather," he said, "we could get there for nightfall."

"Nightfall," I said back to myself, taking the pipe from my pocket. I wondered just how many revenants could be there. Looking back to the Highsmith, I wondered if those skilled archers had been instructed to fire on any revenant that got too close to me.

"We're going there because of the mage," he said, "aren't we?"

Even the crew didn't know about the war hammer. It was understandable. At least one of them would be tempted to claim the weapon... To take any throne of his choosing, instead of risking his demise to the waves.

"We are."

"And this will get rid of him?"

"It's all he has asked for."

The sailor nodded, then looked to his feet. I left him to his own thoughts. When he was done, he nodded again as he looked back to me. "You ever seen Allsen?"

"From a distance."

He smiled. "It's true… What they say about it. It looks like it's almost entirely made of iron. I'd never seen anything like it… You see the occasional patch of earth, the occasional tree, but there's nothing else. Nothing that could survive alone. Just," he stopped to briefly laugh. "The rocks are all that same iron! It's like the gods put it there just to show us something we could never understand.

"We were carrying a prisoner," he said, "a man without any other emotion but anger. He started begging us to take him back once we took to walking to the prison."

"Guards included, how many men would you say were there?"

He briefly looked down at his feet again. "Into the hundreds," he said. "Easily."

"Did you ever set foot inside the prison?"

He laughed again. "No," he said, "not once… There are things in my past, and I was always scared a guard would recognise me and decide, because I had never been punished, that I should stay there. The place makes all men feel like that… You worry you've arrived there, because of something you have done, no matter how small the act was."

I tapped at my teeth with the stem of my pipe. The sailor looked at me, waiting for me to say something. When I didn't, he took a breath and started again.

"You look like you were in the war," he said. "Was it as bad as they say?"

"You wanted to die," I said, "but you refused to, because you didn't want to become one of them. You never thought that's exactly what they were doing… Refusing to die. We fought the most basic, most savage part of ourselves."

He took one last look at me and said, "Can you be sure you didn't die?" before walking away.

*

I dreamed of Yasmin. I dreamed she was scared of where I was going, and why, and I told her that I was doing it all for her.

The hold was pitch black when I woke. In the bowels of the ship, it was impossible to know whether it was day or night. I brooded in the cold darkness until sleep claimed me all over again. It had been a long time since I had done something like this, so I paid close attention to the demands of my body. If it felt like it needed more rest, then it would have it.

Even when I went to find something to eat, the rooms I walked through were dark, lit by candlelight. I couldn't hear many men, only the waves. The cook seemed a little nervous. I could understand why. He gave me a few slices of meat and offered me a little wine. I took the meat and refused the wine, claiming a little goat's milk in its place. As I turned to head back to the hold, the cook quickly cleared his throat. When he didn't take the chance to speak, I turned back to face him.

"Say what you have to say."

He certainly didn't want to ask, but he did anyway.

"You've faced those things before, haven't you?"

"More than I would have liked to."

"I've heard claims of how they can't cross water," he said, "but I've heard stories of them coming from the sea… Can they…?"

"Claims and stories are the same thing, they're just told differently," I said.

"But water," he wanted to know, "does it keep them back?"

"I could lie to you. But the truth is, I only ever faced them on land. They never had a reason to chase me onto the waves."

I saw the movement in his neck as he swallowed. I hadn't given him the answer that he had wanted, but he still had some hope to hold onto.

"The ship's not getting too close to Allsen," I reminded him. "They can't risk it getting stranded, or hitting a rock. I'll be taking myself by boat."

"It's how they used to take the supplies over," he said, nodding enthusiastically, "prisoners, too. Used to have prisoners working the oars."

He laughed at that one. It was far from joyful.

"How long are we to wait for you?" he asked.

"You can turn right back, as soon as you see me fall."

*

I dreamed of Yasmin. She was upset. She begged me not to go to Allsen, and I told her there was no other choice. It didn't make her feel any better. She started to cry, and then she started to turn into stone. I tried to help her even though I didn't know how. Then I stumbled back from her, leaving her to become a statue that began to crumble. I was in agony. My smooth face was bubbling, becoming an ugly mass of scars.

*

I woke up. Someone was making their way down the stairs. I sat upright, struck a match and got my pipe burning before extinguishing the flame. It's always a good idea to have people believing you're constantly alert and needing little rest. The door opened. The man that stepped into the hold did so cautiously, holding the burning oil lantern ahead of him.

"Stranger," he said into the darkness, too far from it to see me, "stranger, are you awake?"

"Have we arrived?"

He looked in my direction, but I knew he still couldn't see me. "Almost," he said. "There's no sign of any other vessel. We could be able to do this, with no one else ever knowing we were ever here."

We. Even if he had been able to see me, I still would have smiled at that.

I got up onto my feet and realised how stiff my limbs were. The man could hear my movements. His eyes scanned the darkness as he tried to find me. Once I had walked close enough to step into the light of his lantern, he opened his mouth to say something but stopped. My face can do that to some.

"Whatever you were about to say," I told him, "say

it."

His lips twitched. Only the sight of me was keeping him from forming the words.

"This could be your only chance," I said.

He took a breath, swallowed, and looked glumly at the floor.

"Stranger," he said almost apologetically, "we've no idea what the prisoner has asked of you… We've been told it's best not to ask, even. But I beg of you, to reconsider whatever dark acts he intends to have you perform on that bastard of an island. Everything is such a game to him. You have to wonder, can he really be trusted?"

"Are you saying we should turn back?"

He didn't say a thing, and I couldn't blame him.

*

It was night when I got back on the deck. The skies were a deep, dark blue. Starless. The moon was still full, and closer than ever.

The crew were already rushing around. Some were getting ready to bring the Mascis to a complete stop, others were getting ready to toss the right powders into the burning lanterns to turn the flames red, the sign of a ship in distress.

Allsen wasn't too far. It was a darker shade of blue than the sky. The prison, too. A tall, square building. There didn't seem to be any windows. There certainly didn't seem to be any sign of movement, either.

What was I doing here? Did anyone know what happened to revenants without a steady food supply?

Did they die out? Did they turn to cannibalism?

I turned and made my way back to the boat. The crewmen, despite how rushed they were, quickly moved out of my way. Not one of them told me to watch where I was going. They were all careful to keep from knocking into me, because the last thing they needed now was for me to hurt a leg and say I couldn't take the risk of going to the island.

There was another ship out in the distance. Apart from that, there didn't seem to be any other on the sea. I turned to the nearest man and said, "Is that the Highsmith?"

He looked out to it and nodded, like he had the eyes to identify it from so far. "That's her," he said.

"What happens if another ship happens to see the red lights?"

He shrugged, said, "They wouldn't have to offer assistance. Crew would see the Highsmith has responded, and, unless we was sinking, sail on."

"What if they happened to be kind enough to offer assistance, anyway? Especially with us being so close to Allsen…"

He shrugged a second time and stared in the direction of the Highsmith a while. "So long as they didn't notice you coming from the island, it wouldn't be anything to worry about."

I smiled, turned to walk away, and stopped before I had even started. Despite the furs and the hood covering his face, I knew exactly who he was by his movements alone. No one had told me Burroughs was going to be joining us on the journey. Truth of the matter is, I was surprised he hadn't sent someone along in his place.

If I retrieved the war hammer, did it really have to be me that brought it to the unwelcome visitor of Stoneisle? I should have asked the question when I had the chance. If my throat was slit, could another simply claim it? Could someone torture me into handing it over?

My hand was already edging towards my blade. I took control of it and went for my pipe and smoking tobacco. Burroughs drew closer as I was guiding a flame to the bowl. He pulled back the hood of his furs, revealing his identity as quickly as he could. The man seemed sure that I would never have known it was him. "You seem to be spending a lot of time away from your lord," I said.

He brought his cupped hands to his mouth, blew into them, and shuddered. "Lord Stoneisle has insisted I observe the matter at hand," he said. "He would hear of no other taking the responsibility."

I grinned. It looked like Lord Stoneisle wanted him to keep an eye on me, and to keep one step ahead of me. He didn't want to risk me claiming the weapon and sailing away in the opposite direction with it in my possession. No doubt if it really could influence me, or if I took to influencing the men at sail with me, he would try and see to my immediate execution. And all of these things would only be possible if I made it back.

"Are you going to make the final part of the trip with me?"

"No," he said, and the look on his face was more than enough for me to know such a task was surely beneath a man of his stature. He quickly added, "But I can assure you that I will say a prayer for you."

"A prayer," I said, "now I feel foolish, for thinking this could be so dangerous. Speaking of dangerous, where's your loyal friend?"

He smirked at that. "I will assume you mean Kain? He has remained on Stoneisle. Allsen has always been a peculiar place," he said, "and now it could be overrun with savage revenants, I feared he could appear as some form of beacon for them to come to."

It was one of those rare instances where he had said something that piqued my interest.

"You've studied these creatures," I said, "can they cross water?"

Burroughs took a breath and looked out at the waters. Despite how far out we were, they were calm. The cold winds rippled over the surface. "I have witnessed them run through shallow depths, but the sea? I don't know whether some distant instinct would encourage them to swim."

The red flames signalling distress were ablaze shortly after, and the ship resembled a level from the Realm of Damnation because of it. The men were silent. Even once I was sitting in a boat so narrow it could have been a coffin, and even more so as they carefully lowered it onto the water with me in it. I wondered why I was doing this. I wondered why I hadn't gone out in search of Liberty Jaxe the moment I knew he had put a price on my life, and then I remembered Yasmin.

I took the cold oars in my hands and started rowing away from the Mascis and towards Allsen. The crew looked down, watching in deathly silence.

Rocks hiding beneath the surface scraped the bottom of the boat as I neared Allsen. The first time it happened, I pictured dead hands trying to take hold. As I neared the island prison, more and more rocks appeared from the water. They made it a little harder to control the direction of the boat, and constantly punched at its sides.

The damaged remains of another boat were caught between such rocks. I wondered how far out it had drifted to come here, and what had happened to the man aboard and the vessel he had left behind.

As Allsen came closer still, I saw how the moonlight shone against it. It was all true, the island looked to be made entirely of metal. The light of the moon glistened like undisturbed frost. And a little inward, the great jail itself. Now that I was so close, I could make out the arrowslits in the high walls. There was no hint of light coming from behind them. The whole place would be in complete darkness.

The bottom of the boat began to scrape along hard ground and slow down. I released the oars, jumped out and pulled it onto dry land, or at least enough to hopefully keep the sea from claiming it. It dragged along the uncanny surface of the island as I barely managed to keep myself from slipping, it was that smooth. It wasn't too different from walking across a frozen river.

And I spotted the first revenant despite the darkness. Then another, then another. I took my sword and cursed my decision to come here all over again. The dead didn't move. They were completely still...

Lifeless. I crept closer to the nearest of the bunch; stood over him and prepared for him to suddenly spring to life, but he didn't. The body remained motionless, its features sunken, mouth wide open. It looked like they really did die all over again once you removed their food supply.

That didn't mean I was going to take any chances.

I kept my eyes on them for as long as I could, then turned and hurried towards the prison. My eyes kept darting up to those same arrowslits. I pictured a lone survivor, long turned insane, seeing my movement and releasing a bolt because of it.

Then another lifeless revenant was presented to me, quickly followed by another. And another small boat, this one close to the building. I pictured a guard hurrying out with it when they were being overrun, only to fall to stiff hands and crimson teeth.

The prison towered over me. As I neared the large doors, I worried boiling oil would be thrown down on me.

It didn't happen.

I pushed the doors open. Now that it wasn't being kept out, the light of the moon found the first few feet beyond the doors. There was a lantern within reach. I quickly claimed it and fumbled around for my matches, constantly looking around to be sure there wasn't a revenant staggering in my direction. Despite the winds, the matches created a flame and the flame created another in the dusty lantern. After seeing what the light had to show me, I almost wished it hadn't.

A long running corridor; piled high with the bodies

of the dead. They were as still as the others I had already seen, but it wasn't enough to convince me this would be easy.

My hand took a tight hold of my sword. With the doors standing wide open, the winds rushed in and hurried through every corridor and barred cell to make sounds of tormented wailing. The idea that not turning back now was a sign of wanting to become acquainted with Death came to me.

I didn't have to explore every cell, every level of this forsaken place. All I had to do was reach an area used for worship. That would be at ground level, if they had really constructed it, sensing the power of a great weapon beneath the earth.

I slowly moved my arm sideways to have the light of the lantern brush against the dead. Still no signs of movement. As satisfied as I could be given the circumstances, I slowly moved forward. There was the smell of the sea, but it wasn't enough to cover the smells of a lot of other things.

Stale air and the dust that danced through it. Rotting flesh. The faint, metallic smell of spilled blood. The smell made when the men locked behind the bars of their cells had released their bowels as the revenants tried reaching them. The revenants looked to have starved, along with some of the prisoners.

More imaginative prisoners had found a way to end it all.

A wall opened up to the side of me. Waiting behind the veil of darkness, stone stairs leading into pitch black. I stood and waited a while, listening. The wind was still causing wailing sounds, but I knew that's all it was. There was no groaning from dead mouths, no whimpering from forgotten men waiting to be saved. I looked back to the bodies around me and slowly moved the light of the lantern over them once again. Not one stirred.

I moved forward. The corpses took to appearing in smaller numbers.

A door stood at the far end of the corridor. Solid metal, possibly even forged from the ground of the island itself. A large lock beneath the knob.

It was ajar.

The hinges made a scraping sound as I slowly pushed it open. There was a single body on the floor. Hands shackled in front of him. His mouth had been bitten clean off, revealing long-dried flesh and dirty teeth. One look and I knew he hadn't died clean, he had returned, only to die all over again.

There was hope that the second time had been even worse.

I tapped him with the toes of my boot. No response. I stepped over him and moved on. More steps leading into more darkness. I crept down them, walked a few steps into the underground and thought I had entered a chasm before my eyes adjusted and the light of the lantern revealed more of the room to me.

No, not a room. A place of worship.

Carved pillars looked to be holding the ceiling up, but they were mostly for show. White tiles had covered the floor. Now, they were stained by footprints and congealed blood. I moved on, through the tranquil air, and counted each decaying body as I saw them. There were seven of them in total. Nearing what must have once been the altar, I spotted another body and had an idea to who it had been by the furs draped over the broad shoulders.

I edged around the last body, shone the light over it to get a better look. It was exactly who I had expected it to be.

"Jason Keely," I said, speaking the dead man's name as if I expected a response.

A bite had been taken from his neck. Bite marks lined his exposed arms, the patterns made by the teeth of the dead being easy to notice. I stared at him a while longer. He looked to have died and remained that way. But what was he doing here? It felt as if the walls of the temple rose around me as it dawned on me that Keely had come in search of the sacred artifact. The broken boat I had seen could have been the same he had arrived in. And the second boat?

"Jaxe," I allowed myself to mutter.

I turned on my heels, sword high, preparing to deflect any surprise attack. But there was no one else moving in the darkness. When I kept still and listened, my breath was all that I could hear.

But Jaxe was coming, and I couldn't risk him getting his hands on the war hammer, not if there were any chance it held such power.

I hurried forward, desperately moving the lantern from side to side in search of a sign, and I found more than that. Keely had always carried a hammer of his own. It looked like it weighed a lot more than he should have been able to comfortably swing. He had been known for taking care of more than one man at a time with it, and there it was, exactly where he had dropped it.

Right beside a patch of tiles that had been broken to pieces. The ground beneath them wasn't much better. Keely had been working that particular spot well – right up until he had been overcome, anyway.

I knelt down, brushed my fingertips against the earth he had exposed. It wasn't like the ground of the island I had travelled to get here. It was cool, loose soil. But it was more than that. There was a tingling sensation at my fingertips, and a steady calm at the back of my mind for the first time in a long time. It dawned on me that the great war hammer could really be right here, right at this spot.

I swallowed; placed the lantern down beside me and looked to those dead figures that remained in the light. They were exactly how they had been when I first saw them.

I swallowed again, looked back to the soil and lowered my sword, so I could dig through the dirt with both hands. The tingling feeling almost became too much – it soon felt as if I had plunged my hands into the icy water, but I couldn't stop. The deeper I got into the ground, the more certain I was it was right there, waiting to be found.

I kept digging. Looking back, that's all I was aware of at the time. The feeling of my hands moving dirt out of the way. There could have been a revenant stumbling towards me, hissing and tripping over his own feet, and I doubt I would have noticed it.

My fingers felt old cloth around something solid.

The sweat on my brow was cold in the still air. I hadn't even noticed I was sweating. The taste of salt was on my lips. I swallowed, moved some more dirt and could finally remove the discovery from the ground, though the earth seemed reluctant to let it go.

Wrapped in cloth that had been covered in forgotten incantations, the maul was as light as air. Slender, too. I wondered how much smaller it would be, once the old and dirty covering was removed from it. I had expected it to have been a lot heavier and bigger than Keely's, but it wasn't. The two weren't even close.

I placed it on the tiled ground and slowly moved my fingers over the material that bound it, like I was desperate to remove the creases. There seemed to be a high-sounding note in the distance… A faint voice in my mind that wasn't my own. There was an urge to pull back the ancient dressing and to hold the hammer as it was intended to be.

The flame of the lantern began to flicker. Unusual, given how there was no breeze.

There was the sound of air struggling from a throat as dry as bones bleached under the summer sun. Keely was twitching. He made a short gagging noise, twitched a little more and sat upright. His eyes were still rolled to the back of his head, he wasn't aware of me. Not yet.

Quiet as a mouse, I took my sword and eased it into its scabbard. It had been years since I had faced a revenant that hadn't been tamed. There certainly hadn't been enough years for me to convince myself it had all been a lot easier than it had seemed at the time.

Keeping my breathing steady, I took hold of the lantern in one hand and the hammer the other. Slowly raised myself up onto my feet. Keely was still sitting upright. Still twitching.

More gagging, from multiple directions. The other dead bodies were following his lead and becoming more animated. I hurried in the direction of the stairs as quietly as I could manage, and that still didn't seem close enough. Their twitches became more violent. The noises they made became increasingly loud. The noises they made were far worse than I had cared to remember. Memories of defending confined areas from being overrun flooded my mind and I could *swear* the touch of the hammer was getting warmer, and it seemed like the best thing to do was to free it of its binding.

The second I set foot on that first stone step, I broke into a run. I raced up the stairs and out onto the corridor closing the door behind me. But the lock was broken. Any minute, they'd come charging up those same stairs.

Facing me in the far distance, the light of the night sky. Between us, a heavy darkness and countless dead bodies. I could already hear them moving. Could already hear plenty of them preparing to sing the old song. It dawned on me how I had forgotten just how these things filled me with fear. Every retreat we had made during the war, and every face I saw dying because of these animals, came back to haunt me. Why had I agreed to do this?

The first revenant to attack came running out from the shadows. I saw him early, thanks to the light coming from the end of the corridor. A quick, but clumsy, silhouette. Hissing. Reaching out for me, determined to tear me apart.

I panicked, swung the lantern and it broke against his skull. The impact knocked him off balance. His thin strands of hair caught fire and gave me a glimpse of his face. He was already trying to get back up. My heart was pounding like a war drum. I brought my foot down against the back of his head and wondered what had cracked, his skull, or the floor. It still wasn't enough, not to stop him completely, and I knew I was wasting time concentrating on this *one* for so long.

I clutched the war hammer in both hands and ran for the door. I felt hands grab at my arms from the darkness. Heard bodies fall at my back as they clumsily lunged for me. Another rushed out in front of me. I kept charging, swung the hammer. The weapon struck the revenant and sent it back into the shadows as if it were nothing.

The doorway was getting closer. I could hear the winds more than ever. I could hear the waves and feel moisture on the air.

I could feel how the touch of the hammer was getting hotter still. Logic told me that it was the dead symbols written all over the cloth that was causing the increasing heat, and that casting it aside would solve the problem. The only issue was, I doubted that it was truly *my* logic.

The instant I was out in the elements, a strong gust of wind tried pushing me back inside of the prison. The clear skies were darkening. Rain was falling from the black clouds. The droplets were as cold and as sharp as glass. The ground I had to travel shone all the more now that it was wet. It would take a miracle for me not to slip on that treacherous surface.

Almost a lifetime away, the Mascis awaited my return on troubled waters. I saw the vessel rocking against the crashing waves, the red flames signalling distress still burning. The Highsmith had gained plenty of distance.

A revenant came rushing in my direction. The winds had blocked my ears, I couldn't even hear the noise escaping from its dead mouth. It made the look of the thing even worse. We had always taken the noise of their attacks as being an advantage.

The second before I charged for it, I felt the fingertips of another revenant against the back of my arm. Heading towards the latest arrival, I had to accept that I wasn't just old and sloppy, I was finished. It was nothing more than a miracle that one of the monsters from the prison hadn't brought me to the ground, but I didn't take a look back to see him or whether he had disappointment in his eyes. I kept my eyes on the one coming forward to meet me, and I hoped more than anything that I wouldn't lose my footing.

Up close, I finally heard its cries over the winds. The stench of him was something new. If Allsen had a pigsty hidden away somewhere, this one had found it and been bathing in whatever fluids were still there.

I ducked under his outreached arms, came back up from behind to take a look at how many were now flooding out from the open doors of the prison. There were a lot. I didn't take the war hammer to the one in front of me, I kicked his feet out from under him, turned and kept running towards the shore. Even when it sounded like they were right behind me, I didn't look back. When I heard the sounds of one falling to the hard ground, I still kept my eyes ahead. The rocks were as slick as oil in parts. A foot would slide in a direction of its own choosing, but I managed to keep on my feet. Even when my breaths were ragged and my lungs were almost as hot as the touch of the weapon I carried, I kept moving.

The boat I had rowed to shore on was finally straight ahead of me. Relief didn't last. How could I be expected to take it back to the water, when I had so many bloodthirsty monsters at my back?

The answer revealed itself and my spirits lifted. I couldn't see the archers standing aboard the Highsmith, but I saw the row of arrows being lighted. I saw the flames move as the men got in whatever formation they had been instructed to take.

The small boat I needed to reach was getting within touching distance, and a single arrow was still to be released. I wondered what was taking them so long. I was about to call out a command for them to fire, when they finally came racing down from the ship like shooting stars. Some went by so close I felt the wind left in their wake. Not one grazed me. It was true, the archers of Stoneisle were something else. They had only released one and they would be preparing to release another.

I dropped the relic inside of the boat and started pushing it to the waves. The arrows were still coming, and faster now. The revenants must have been right on me, but I didn't look back. Leave the archers to their task. Looking back could cause me to panic, and that could lead to a mistake, and that would lead to my death.

I felt the heat of one arrow as it went by. The revenants were so close, I could hear the sound of the arrows that found them as well as the sound of the risen dead falling to the hard ground. A revenant stumbled at my side. An arrow pierced his skull and he fell out of sight. I kept pushing the boat forward until finally it was on the waves. I jumped in and started rowing as best I could, the waves determined to push me back onto land.

Splashing sounds as the dead came into the sea. I kept rowing, not wanting to see firsthand if they could cross water. Those arrows continued raining down. My arms were aching and heavy as lead, and my heart felt just about ready to stop on me. Even when I finally reached the side of the Mascis and the crew dropped ropes down for me to secure the boat I was in, I didn't allow myself to believe that it was done.

Like so many events of significance that had taken plenty of planning and preparation, it had been accomplished within no time at all. It was done.

*

Burroughs insisted that the war hammer be left in his possession, and I told him that wasn't going to happen. After that, he suggested it be placed in the cargo hold with two men constantly on watch. I told him that certainly wasn't going to happen.

"Right now," I said, "the crew is likely consisting of two types of men – those that don't have any idea to what we could have retrieved, and those that have made a deal to hand it over to some figure or other from the council, no matter the risk."

"You would dare imply a member of the council would commit such betrayal!"

"Yes," I said. "Would you be foolish enough to believe, without a doubt, there isn't a chance that one of them would consider doing that?"

Burroughs stared right at me. He wasn't used to such a lowly specimen refusing to bow to his commands. For a moment, he must have considered ordering the men to come kill me. Doing so must have been too much of a risk. If there was truth in the tale of what I was still claiming, they would have even less of a chance. And maybe it really did have to be me who handed it over to their visitor.

"Then what would you do?"

"I need a cabin," I said, "with a door that can be locked, and I need to have the only key to the door."

Burroughs laughed. "You expect to be given the captain's quarters? And how would that look, should another vessel happen to take an interest in us?"

"Why would they? We're just a simple trading ship, making its return to Stoneisle."

I was under his skin. He thought he was keeping that hidden, but the muscles twitching in his face gave his true feelings away.

"Then we shall share the room."

"Then you shall have to be tied up," I said.

"This is preposterous." He yelled, "Do you really expect me to agree to your demands on the matter?"

"I don't think you have any choice."

The captain, I forget his name, placed the key in the

palm of his hand. The look of him made me think this was the worst thing he had ever been asked to do. I thanked him because of that, headed into his personal sanctuary and slowly closed the door behind me. The last thing I saw was the look of sadness on the captain's face, and the annoyance on Burroughs'.

It was a good-sized room. No windows, which had me think how even the captain was tired of looking at the sea. The cot looked firm. I carefully placed the covered maul on top of it and finally examined my prize. The heat I had felt at times hadn't been in my head. Sections of the cloth looked to have been singed.

"What do you think you are going to do with that?"

I had my sword free before I had finished turning. There was nobody there, nobody at all… It's just that I had heard Jaxe.

"Do you think you can keep it from determined men such as me?"

I stepped back, sword ready, and surveyed the room. I even knelt down to check beneath the cot. No one. No one but me. But I had heard Jaxe, twice, and it didn't sound like he was behind the door or one of the walls.

"The only chance you could have would be by taking that weapon and raising it against me. You know that. You're old," he said. "You're powerless."

I rushed to the door, unlocked it and pulled it open. The corridor outside was completely empty. There wasn't a single sound or movement. I closed the door shut, locked it again. When I turned to look back at the weapon I had recently claimed, an explanation presented itself to me.

The war hammer had got inside of my head. It wanted to claim me, and the easiest way for that to happen was for me to remove that sacred binding and take the weapon in my hands.

I took a breath and asked, "Do you have a voice of your own?" on sheathing my blade.

Nothing.

"What if I threw you overboard? You could sink without a trace. You could sink to unreachable depths, and never be held again."

Nothing.

After a moment, I laughed at myself and took to filling my pipe. I had grown old and slow, but it was possible I had also lost my mind.

The sound of somebody approaching the door pulled me from my slumber. I got up as quickly as I could, took my sword and glanced to the hammer. Still covered. Still where I had placed it, which was out of sight, should anyone insist I open up.

The footsteps stopped. There was a knock at the door.

"Who is it?"

"The captain told me to bring you some food and drink."

I was hungry and I was thirsty. Could the hammer have reached out to others, or could it be somebody following the orders from a corrupt man of Stoneisle? I had never trusted Burroughs. I had no reason to trust the lord of Stoneisle or a single one of his sycophants. It's a sorry state of affairs when you're left trusting a man of magic.

"Go away," I said.

"I'll leave it outside."

"Take it away with you," I insisted. "Tell your captain, and tell Burroughs, that I won't be disturbed until we reach Stoneisle. Any man that chooses to ignore this order will be dealt with."

I heard hurried steps retreating down the corridor.

Time disappeared all over again. Without a single window, I couldn't see the rising or setting of the sun. But I came to be thankful there was only one way into the cabin. It meant the door was all I had to worry about. After so long, I still found myself checking for hidden trapdoors or other ways to enter. The emptiness within my stomach clawed at my insides. The idea of throwing the weapon out to the water returned. Instead, I crawled back beneath the covers.

There was the weight of somebody sitting at the end of the cot. Bleary eyed, I sat upright and reached for my sword, expecting a blade to find my heart.

My hand froze on reaching the hilt. I couldn't believe my own eyes. It was Yasmin, sitting before me. Her beauty had always been enough to freeze me in my tracks. When she smiled, I froze that little bit more. I took a breath to gather my thoughts.

"You're not here," I said.

She smiled, and she brushed a little hair back behind her ear. I remembered the times I had gently brushed my lips against that ear. Yasmin glanced to the weapon, then back at me. "Why are you doing this? Do you even know the answer?"

It wasn't Yasmin. That didn't mean I could bring my sword against someone, or something, wearing her appearance. I lighted my pipe with trembling hands. Whatever this was, it waited patiently for my answer.

"It's my noble deed," I said.

"No," she said, "you are doing what you have always done, you are following the decisions of another. I know you must have thought of all you could achieve with what you have, and instead you're taking it to be destroyed by a man you may never have met, but you have certainly encountered his kind…"

I smiled on hearing that.

"The Brothers Aeternal?" I said, "I never mentioned those to Yasmin. Not once."

I woke up.

There was no weight placed at the foot of the cot. There was nobody in the room but me. But the dream I had could have taught me a valuable lesson. Without getting up, I dragged my boot close and took the dagger from it. It could take me an instant too long to reach my sword. Having the dagger under a pillow could prove useful.

I slept on and off. Hunger came and went. The journey back seemed longer because of it. I considered unlocking the door and going above board but decided against it. I tried to remember if years of training had taught me how to measure the time in a situation like this, and nothing came to mind.

There was a knock at the door. I hadn't even realised sleep had reclaimed me.

"What is it?"

"We're approaching Stonisle," Burroughs said from the other side of the door.

"Let me know when we're ready to lower the

longboats," I said. "And I will cross the remaining water, alone, in the boat that carried me to Allsen."

"You surely can't be serious!"

"I take the possession over the water on my own," I said. "You can join me in the carriage once we're back on land, but I refuse to be in such a confined space with unknown men."

"How dare you! The men you insult were carefully chosen for this task, yet you insist on believing they will betray you at the first opportunity?"

"That's what plenty of men do," I said. "And you would know this, if you didn't keep yourself so far removed from them."

"And what if it is more than that? What if the war hammer is already influencing you, and you daren't risk being separated from it?"

And what if he was right? I had considered that myself. The thoughts and dreams I had already experienced did not feel as if they were of my own making. But then, I had surely resisted their calls? Could any of the other men aboard this ship? Could any of the men of Stoneisle?

"Answer me," Burroughs said. He had lost full control of his composure.

"You could have sent any man to claim it," I said, and on remembering Keely, added, "and perhaps you did. But I took it, and the responsibility of keeping it out of the wrong hands remains with me."

"And now, does a part of you wonder if you may have the suitable hands to wield it?" Burroughs asked. I could hear the smile in the sound of his voice. I didn't like it.

I silently approached the door, placed a hand against the smooth grain whilst also reaching for my sword.

"Who visited you?"

I didn't give him the chance to answer the question.

"Or whose voice have you heard? You know any of your archers could find me if I were to try rowing in any other direction."

"And any one of those same archers could find a man that may be tempted to try relieving you of the weapon," he said. "I see holes in your logic, can you tell me you do not?"

I swallowed, took a breath and said, "You have one chance to see this destroyed. Your one chance means doing it exactly as I say."

No response came. I stood, and I listened. It dawned on me that Burroughs could have been out there with a group of men, all ready to force their way in here. But there was no sound, and the locked door felt no impact against it. Still, I carefully took a silent step back and stood prepared. The silence remained unbroken. If they were going to come, they would have been pounding against the door already. I allowed myself to relax again, turned and saw her sitting at the foot of the bed, as if she had never left. Maybe she hadn't.

It wasn't Yasmin. I reminded myself of that.

"I'm glad you look like that," I said, taking my hand from my sword. I was exhausted. I wasn't here to fight, not now.

"It's good to see you, see *her*, this last time," I said, almost sighing. "My end is approaching… I can feel it."

"You cannot allow any of these men to claim it. You

know that."

"Do I?"

I took to filling my pipe.

"And you know you can never give it to the mage. How can you be so sure that his kin did not intend he be kept away from it because he is the one that is far too dangerous?"

"He said he wants to destroy it," I said, striking a match, "but he could be lying. His kind tend to do that."

"Then take it," she said, "and sail until you find a place where you can never be found."

"Maybe I could. I could bury it, too," I said. "And if it's found? I'd be long dead by then. So would the person you're wearing… If she isn't already."

"The knowledge of the gods is revealed to any man that claims the war hammer," she said, smiling. "You would know for certain. You could, perhaps, find me."

"I've heard the gods are dead," I said with a shrug. "I doubt there's anything of theirs I need to know."

"There are needs," she said, "and there are *wants*, and you could have both."

"And at a great cost," I said.

"You could go unchallenged. And have you not thought others will only know of what you have, if you allow others to discuss it? You are still to reach Stoneisle. Only one of those you sail with know of your trophy."

"Raen," Burroughs asked me from the other side of the door, "who are you talking to?"

Panic struck me. I looked to the door, then back to the cot. She was gone… Of course she was gone.

"I was just thinking," I said. "Let me get some rest. I don't want to be disturbed until it's time to lower the longboats."

This time, I heard him turn and walk away.

*

I woke coughing. Black smoke was coming from beneath the door, filling the air. The heat hadn't reached me yet, but I had experienced fires in the past.

Almost bringing my lungs up as I coughed, I took my sword and sheathed it, picked the hammer from the ground and rushed to the door. I was glad I had kept the key close. I turned it in the lock, took the doorhandle and quickly pulled my hand back. The heat had been too much. I tried to shake the pain from my palm, decided not to waste any time and brought my elbow down on the handle. The door opened. I pulled it wide with my foot and more black smoke flooded the cabin. The corridor outside was on fire. The floor had been claimed, and the flames were already running along the walls, brushing against the ceiling. It was difficult to see any more than a couple of feet ahead, but I made out the silhouette of someone moving. They were calm. They didn't care about the inferno.

The smoke parted for a moment. For a moment I saw the prisoner of Stoneisle. He looked at me. His expression was impossible to read, I didn't know whether he was bored or concerned. Then the smoke was drawn together like curtains, and he was gone. Even his silhouette had disappeared. Was he really aboard the ship?

I ducked down low, hurried through the burning corridor. I could feel the heat of the hammer, the heat of the flames combined. Flames were trying to claim the cloth that covered the long-hidden weapon. I told myself not to worry about that... Not yet.

Everywhere I turned had been claimed by the spreading flames. I couldn't see a single member of the crew, neither living nor dead. Hurrying up the wooden steps, all I could do was hope the flames hadn't weakened them too much. Hope that they wouldn't break beneath me. But I made it up on deck. As my lungs dragged in the cold air, I coughed more. Doubled over, saliva poured from my mouth. I could taste ash. I stumbled to my knees, reaching a hand out to keep myself from collapsing. The cloth against the hammer was darkened by the smoke. Small flames were spreading over it.

Still coughing, almost unable to breathe, I patted the flames out with my hand. I remained on my knees, greedily taking in the cold air. I could hear the crackling of the flames behind me, feel the heat they made coming through the gaps of the deck. When I was ready, when the coughing came in brief, short bursts, I forced myself up onto my feet. The Highsmith was close enough for me to see every man on board, and I recognised a lot of them as having belonged to the Mascis. I certainly recognised Burroughs. They all just stood in a line, staring right at me. At least a half of them were standing with bows.

And I felt my lips curl back, just like that of a wolf readying itself to attack.

I said, "What is this?" and somehow, they looked to have no difficulty in hearing the question.

"The war hammer," Burroughs said. "If you make any attempt to remove it from its covering, every archer will release an arrow with intentions of causing immediate death. I want you to know that, Raen."

"Understood," I said.

I wondered if it was just my imagination, or whether the feeling of the ground beneath me was quickly changing. Whether it would soon surrender to the heat and drop me into the waiting fires.

When I freed my sword, the archers readied their arrows. The sight almost made me laugh. I wondered what they could have thought I was planning to do. Even Burroughs gave a slight twitch, like he was tempted to seek cover behind another man.

"If you surrender the weapon to me," Burroughs said, "if you kneel and offer it, I guarantee that no harm will come of you."

"Why do you want it?"

"To bring to the prisoner," he said. "I want to know that it is no more. Look at you," he continued, "can you not see what it is doing to you? Can you not witness how it has already taken to corrupting you?"

"You're the one who set the bastard ship on fire."

He smiled. "You always wanted to know your surroundings," he said, "because you felt it would prevent others from gaining an advantage. Your surroundings are what I have insisted they be. You may have seen the battlefields, but I designed them."

I wanted my hands around his throat. I wanted to see the life vanish within his eyes. But I didn't show that. I took a breath, took in my surroundings as best I could. Plumes of black smoke were coming from the bowels of the ship. There was the Highsmith, and then there was nothing but open water. Despite his claims we were nearing Stoneisle, I couldn't see any signs of land.

And every man aboard that damned boat watched me. They did their best not to blink, for fear of missing some great trick. The majority of them were likely desperate for me to try anything that would be cause for my death. The rest, maybe even Burroughs? They wondered if they could claim the hammer from my dead hands, or whether it had to be surrendered. I wondered that myself.

I heard an explosion. The ship jolted and I almost lost my footing because of it.

"There is no other way out of this," Burroughs said. It almost sounded like he was pleading with me.

"Have your men lower their weapons," I said, "allow me to come aboard and continue for Stoneisle, and you have my word that no harm will come to a single one of you."

They couldn't bring themselves to quite believe what I had said. First one man laughed a little, then another. It spread almost as quickly as the flames beneath me. Soon, almost every man was laughing. The others, concerned, looked to Burroughs for guidance. Burroughs looked to me, narrowed his eyes, and tried to decide whether he had misheard me. He thought of what he had heard me say, and considered what I could have said, hoping I had tossed him something to work with.

I heard the sound of splintering wood. A deep crack was running along the floor beneath me. Smoke quickly began to escape from it. The floor could give way any second, and the flames below would be waiting to catch me.

"Raen—" Burroughs started all over again, but the sound of snapping branches pulled my eyes from him. The wooden boards were warping. I swallowed, tried not to panic, and looked back to Burroughs and the others. For a moment, I saw them as something else entirely. From their hooded robes and signet rings, I recognised them for what they really were – Brothers Aeternal. I knew some of their faces, because I had put them to death.

And strewn around their feet as well as my own, the men they were imitating. Even Burroughs wasn't too far from me, hands at the gaping wound of his stomach, as if he had died trying to return the organs that had spilled from it. The positioning of his fingers and the bloody flesh covering them made it easy to see he had removed them himself.

There was no smoke, there was no fire, only death.

The smoke and the heat returned, and the bodies disappeared. 'Burroughs' and the others still stood facing me from the Highsmith. I stared back at them, and I kept the hammer they desired in my sights.

"Raen," he said, and I didn't let him finish. I took hold of the hammer and ran back for the stairs leading back into the depths of the ship. Despite the calling of my senses, I knew my surroundings weren't really as I saw them.

"Prepare to go aboard," I heard him yell, "we can't

influence him, not whilst he is in possession of the weapon!"

I dropped down on the stairs. I ignored the heat, the smoke, and began to claw at the weapon's decaying cover. Brothers Aeternal could only ever be dealt with in close quarters. I knew that from experience, but I was outnumbered, and they were far too powerful.

I heard the sound of their feet hitting the deck. Whether they had simply jumped or flew, I had no real interest of finding out. I desperately continued pulling the material free, revealing ancient metal and—

There was a loud knock at the door. I took a breath, snapped out of it. I was kneeling beside the cot, in the process of removing the ancient artifact from its sheaving. Was this real?

Another knock at the door.

"I need to speak with you."

Burroughs.

I swallowed. It could be a trick, but it could also be what was real. It was difficult to tell.

"Give me a minute," I said, and I pushed the hammer beneath the cot, out of sight, before walking to the door. The handle wasn't hot to the touch. If anything, it was cold. I unlocked the door. Burroughs was standing in the corridor. "What is it?"

"It is fast approaching the time to lower the longboats."

"We've returned to Stoneisle."

"Yes. And I have thought over your demands," he said. "You may take your own boat, but I will be close by in another, and there shall be an archer keeping a keen interest in your every movement."

"I have no issue with that."

"There is more," he said. "I have already had signal sent to the men at Stoneisle. There shall be three carriages awaiting us. The first will travel ahead, with an archer at its rooftop and two men accompanying me within.

"You shall travel in the second, and despite your protests, you shall be accompanied by a carefully selected man that I will personally vouch for. The third carriage shall follow behind and, again, there shall be an archer on the roof and two men within. There shall also be a small band of men on horseback, maintaining a respectful distance accompanying us. All necessary of course. We cannot risk having the weapon claimed from us," he said, "should any other have learned of what we possess."

I didn't respond right away. I looked for any hint that this wasn't Burroughs but couldn't find one. But I could see how the way he looked at me had changed. He no longer believed he could predict my actions. Hearing me hold a conversation with myself would be an understandable cause – if that had truly happened. In the end, I nodded.

"I'll get ready to make my way back on deck," I said, already closing the door. "Be sure to thank the captain for his generosity."

He didn't try and keep me from closing the door, and he didn't protest as I locked it. With little time left, the first thing I did was take the hammer out from beneath the cot. I examined its covering. It had been loosened. I'd really been determined to get it free. A little embarrassed, I smiled.

"Quite a trick you played," I muttered, and I took to tightening the cloth all over again, hoping no one would notice how close I had come to removing it, "but you've lost."

Once I was sure it looked undisturbed, I placed it atop of the cot and took my dagger from beneath the pillow. As I was slipping it back inside my boot, I paused and reconsidered. In the end, I slipped it inside of my sleeve. The tightening of the material would keep it secure, as long as I moved carefully. Now I was ready. I filled my pipe, got the tobacco burning and walked out of the captain's cabin with the mighty war hammer in my possession. There was no heat coming from it, not now. It must have worn itself out.

Back on deck, I saw the pale night sky. The clouds above were thin and sparse, but cold rain was still falling. Straight ahead of us, Stoneisle. The lights of burning lanterns looked down on us. Burroughs looked directly to them. Even when I stood beside him, he kept his eyes on his homeland.

"We're quickly approaching our end," he said. "What do you intend to do once this is over and done with?"

"Drink."

They cautiously lowered the longboat. Four men to man the oars, another with bow and arrows at his feet, and Burroughs. Burroughs kept looking to me, thinking he was too subtle for me to notice. The man with the bow and arrows kept his eyes on me, kept his face right at me. He wanted me to know how he wouldn't be letting me out of his sight. It didn't bother me.

The longboat came upon waves that were turning excitable, and the knots were untied before the ropes were pulled back up. As those same ropes were fastened to the small boat I had recently put to use, the men of the longboat began to slowly move away from the Mascis. When the time came, I sat in the boat with the oars to my side and the hammer at my feet. They gently lowered me down to the waiting waves. Thunder rumbled overhead, but I couldn't see anything. Despite the rain, the skies still looked almost clear. I started rowing towards Stoneisle as soon as the ropes were unfastened. The longboat remained ahead of me, but only just, and the waiting archer kept his eyes on me. I don't think he even blinked.

Those stone steps that climbed Stoneisle were slick because of the rain. My legs ached from how cautiously I climbed them – one hand keeping a firm hold of the great weapon, the other on the rope beside me. Burroughs and one of the men from the boat walked ahead of me. The archer remained close behind, but not close enough for me to be able to turn and hit him. As expected, three carriages were waiting for us. I noticed a man on the roof of each one keeping low, as if told to keep out of sight. Not too far off in the distance, another four men watched us on horseback. Two men in worthless armour stood close to the carriages, waiting to greet us. The look on their faces was all I needed to know they were relieved at our return.

"Sir Burroughs," one of them said, "we are blessed by your homecoming."

I didn't tell them how he hadn't been the one to

make it back from Allsen.

"Good blessings follow good plans," he said. "Is Stoneisle secure?"

"It is," the man said, jowls shaking as he nodded. "We've men watching the full perimeter, and yours is the only ship to arrive."

Burroughs nodded, looked to the distance in silence as he considered something. "I'll lead on," he reminded me. With nothing else to say, he walked quickly to the first carriage with one of the men rushing ahead to get the door for him. Burroughs climbed within, the door was gently closed for him, and the loyal guard told the rider to get the carriage moving. I glanced back, saw the archer was still close by. He had kept his eyes on me. As far as I was aware, he still hadn't blinked.

"I take it you're coming with me?"

He slowly shook his head.

"Pity," I said, "I'm sure you could have told me all kinds of interesting things."

I walked over to the second carriage. Nobody hurried forward to open the door for me. I pulled it open, saw a man in yet more worthless armour sitting in there with a sword resting against his thigh and a carved dagger on his lap. He seemed a little nervous. I climbed in, pulled the door shut and sat opposite him. The carriage started moving at once. I took a deep breath, released it. My new companion swallowed and seemed a little more nervous. As I reached for my smoking pipe, he tightened his grip on the dagger. Even when he could see what I had been reaching for, he seemed uneasy. Whatever he had been told about me, it clearly left him with the idea I would suddenly make a move against him. I asked him, "What's your name?" as I was getting the tobacco burning.

"Gricious."

I started laughing. He swallowed, leaned back a little and tightened his grip on the dagger some more.

"Forgive me," I said, "but you share your name with an acquaintance of mine. Your father doesn't happen to be a sailor, does he? It's just you could have a brother you never knew about."

He looked a little offended at that one.

"I'm not meaning to upset you," I said, still laughing, "it just isn't a name you hear too often."

"It is a traditional name," he said, "one of nobility."

I laughed a little more and he looked a little more offended. A sound of rolling thunder kept anything else on the matter from being said. Rain started pounding against the carriage. My companion looked a little uneasy at the sound. He looked upward, as if he expected the rain to start falling on us and his eyes brushed over the hammer as he brought them back down. I wondered if he would be stupid enough to try something.

"Is it true," he decided to ask, "what people are saying… Did you really go to fetch something, for the prisoner?"

"Has anything happened in the time following our departure?"

"Yes," he said. "Things are back to as they should be. The crops are growing, and the milk is fresh, and the meats are without decay."

"Maybe you should just be thankful."

"But the prisoner remains," he said, quietly for fear

of being heard by another. "He has ceased his taunting of us, but he insists on remaining in his cell. Can we really rest, knowing he is satisfied at what you are bringing to him?"

"He won't have reason to stay any longer."

One way or another, I thought, my words were true. I could be handing him the most powerful weapon of all creation, why remain on an island like this when you could claim the world?

"But he could have plenty to return. We have showed him that we have no option, other than to appease."

We arrived at Stoneisle House, the door to the carriage was opened for me by a guard. Dripping wet and with his skin reddened by the cold, he didn't look too happy at having been told to greet me. Even the torch of his flame looked to be in the process of giving up.

I looked back, saw the carriage that had brought Burroughs was already heading elsewhere. The one that had trailed behind me was still approaching. Despite the darkness, I saw the men on horseback were maintaining a safe distance. I turned to say something to the guard, but he got in before me.

"With me," he said, and he headed towards his lord's home. I acted like I didn't notice how the few guards standing around took more interest in what I was carrying, than the scars on my face.

"I take it Burroughs has gone to gather the council?"

"Maybe," the guard said. "Or he's gone to make sure his ghoul has been treated well."

I laughed and went to reach for my pipe, before deciding the rain would render it useless.

"How does it make you feel," I asked, "seeing the people you know have died, wandering the fields?"

He came close to answering my question but decided against it. He stopped at the entrance, turned to me and said, "Sir Burroughs requested you meet him in the council chambers," and pushed the door open for me.

The hallway was illuminated by a mixture of burning lanterns and torches but appeared deserted. Only the mud and water recently walked in by Burroughs suggested there was anybody inside. I took one last look behind me. The third carriage had reached its stop, and the armed men it had brought stood looking at me, hands at their blades. The archers on each of the carriage rooftops were now kneeling, watching me with interest. I grinned, stepped into the property, and heard the guard close the door behind me.

The journey back to the meeting room was brief and peculiar. The only noise was that of my footsteps. I didn't see or hear a single person. Even the heavy door leading to the dungeon was without a guard. But the door to the council chamber was ajar. I pushed it open. Lord Stoneisle was standing at the far end of the room, with Burroughs close beside him and Kain close to Burroughs. A guard stood in each corner. The tables and chairs had been removed. The decorative change made the hairs on the back of my neck stand up. It was unlikely they had moved everything, just to mop up the rainwater Burroughs had walked in with him.

Stoneisle grinned and held his arms out like a welcoming father, but he didn't take a single step forward. "The noble hero of my homeland has returned to me," he said, "and I speak for all of my people, when I say we are most indebted to you. Come! Tell me of how you not only found what we have need for, but escaped the terror of Allsen!"

It would have been a smart idea to charge forward, handle the two guards and take Lord Stoneisle as my captive until I had secured my leave. The only reason I didn't do exactly that was my concern it was all the idea of the hammer. Like a fool, I offered something of a grin and walked into the room.

I hadn't gone more than four steps beyond the door, when a heavy hand landed on my shoulder and the point of a dagger was pressed to my neck. There wasn't any reason for me to turn, I already knew it was Campbell Hurley.

"Noble hero," he said, "how you honour us all, with your return."

Lord Stoneisle smirked. Burroughs sneered. Kain stood watching, mouth hanging open.

"What is this?" I said, "Where's your prisoner?"

Lord Stoneisle smirked all over again.

"In his cell," he said, "where I imagine he will remain, unless the weapon is brought down to him."

"I imagine that isn't going to happen?"

"No," Lord Stoneisle gloatingly said. "You are going to bring the weapon to me, and you are going to take to your knees and declare it is mine for the claiming."

"And why should I do that?"

"Because I meant everything I promised," he said, "of greatly rewarding you. I offer you it all… You may hold high rank in an unconquerable army, or you may simply live in luxury, for your remaining years. Or you can fall here, and bleed to death. And that's if you're lucky," he decided, smirking all over again, "I could have you experience new forms of pain for the rest of your pitiful days."

I looked to Burroughs and said, "This was your idea?"

"How dare you suggest I am so easily influenced," Lord Stoneisle hissed. "My blood is of a line free of corruption, and my actions are encouraged by a mind fed with the knowledge of the greats!"

"Then why do this? Why can't all you have be enough?"

"Because I should not accept having *enough*," he said coldly. "I was cheated out of my destiny long before I was born, but I shall reclaim it, with use of what you have to bequeath me. The gods must surely have brought the dream-reader to this island," he concluded, "just as they surely saw to your safe return."

I looked down to the hammer. When I looked back to Lord Stoneisle, I had a smile ready to show him.

"I want a palace of my own," I said, "and I want great riches, and I want to command your unconquerable army. But there is one more thing I would ask."

"Then ask."

"I want full ownership of Campbell Hurley," I said. "Campbell Hurley serves me, and he is to do it loyally and without question."

Burroughs laughed abruptly and was quick to regain his composure.

"Then I can assure you that he will serve you well."

"Then I suppose I should bring this to you," I said.

I moved forward, quick, but not too quick for any movements to appear sudden enough for Hurley to drive his blade through my neck. I knew he would be feeling sore. The idea of pulling me back and insisting I declare the weapon as his must have crossed his mind, but he resisted the temptation of doing so. Still, I like to think he was feeling a little broken hearted at that moment.

"That's enough," he said when I came within reaching distance of his lord. There was a lack of commitment in his voice. Even the hand he had placed on my shoulder as well as the knife pointed at my throat seemed to have lost the enthusiasm keeping them there. More than anything, he must have been praying that Lord Stoneisle would only betray me and reward him.

Lord Stoneisle was as good as bathing in the glow of his great victory. Burroughs looked just as pleased. And I smiled at them, to let them know I was pleased with my demands being met.

I placed a foot forward, planted it as if I were getting ready to drop to my knee and held the war hammer out as if it had been placed atop of my two open hands.

"Lord Stoneisle," I began, "it is my privilege to present to you—"

I pushed myself back into Campbell, knocking him off balance. I threw my head back immediately after, crushing his nose. Before he had a chance to recover, I tightened my hands on the weapon and turned at the waist, driving the covered handle into him. I couldn't be sure where it had landed, but I was certain I'd heard bones break. I didn't need to look back to know he had dropped to the floor and wouldn't be too much of a threat.

Burroughs' face was twisted with rage. The colour had drained free of it such was the shock at my daring to do this. Lord Stoneisle brought a manicured hand to his mouth, eyes widening in fright.

The two guards were useless. My actions had frozen them to the spot, but I knew it wouldn't last forever. I could take them, but doing so would waste time. Time could bring more men, some with bow and arrow.

I brought the head of the hammer against the jaw of Lord Stoneisle. The sound of breaking bone found the air again. My senses were so heightened, I heard teeth scattering across the tiled floor. His face was a bloody mess before he joined them.

Now the guards responded, but their first thoughts weren't of charging me, they were of checking on their injured ruler. Again, that could only last seconds. I turned and raced for the door, leaping over Campbell, his face contorted by rage and agony both, as he clutched at his hip.

"Kain!" I heard Burroughs cry out as I pulled the door open, "Kain! Control yourself!"

I couldn't resist the urge to look back. Kain had well and truly come to life, he was greedily taking bites from Lord Stoneisle's face. Panicked, the two guards desperately hacked at him with their dull swords until he turned his attention on them.

Campbell was either brave or a fool, although sometimes, there's no difference between the two. He was crawling towards the mayhem, not away from it.

Limited time was all I had. Once Burroughs had

recovered from the initial surprise, he would most likely take a blade and know exactly where to force it. With Kain no longer a threat, he would then call for more guards and claim his place as the new ruler.

Burroughs could never possess the weapon.

The door to the dungeon was locked. It wouldn't budge, no matter how hard I pulled at it. Taking a step back, I looked to the hammer I still possessed and considered swinging it with all my strength. But I didn't have to. I heard the lock pull back, then the door opened. Nobody stood waiting for me on those descending steps. The prisoner had proven useful, after all.

I raced down into the dungeon, more burning torches to hand than my last visit here. The reason was Lord Stoneisle had given order for the eight members of his council to be locked behind bars. They called out to me, begging for their release and making offer of great rewards. I ignored each and every one of them until I reached the cell of the prisoner that had brought me here. He was free of chains but remained sat behind the bars. As I came closer, he seemed to withdraw. The hammer. He couldn't stomach being too close to it, not unless it was given to him.

"What are your intentions?"

My question brought a smile to his lips. "I knew Lord Stoneisle would likely betray you," he said, "and believe it or not, that would be the finer outcome. Your actions have prevented another event from becoming possible, an event that would have seen many men—"

"I have the weapon," I said, "what would you do with it?"

The prisoner rose to his feet, keeping his back against the wall as he did so.

"I would take it far from here," he said, "and I would destroy its current form and send it to a distant plain, where it will one day become the possession of a deserving man."

"No man can be trusted with such power."

"But he must be trusted with some," the prisoner told me. "There is very little time to spare, and you have but one choice and that is to trust me. You know they are coming," he said, "and you know you will not overcome them all, not without truly claiming what you have in your hands, but what will become of you? And what will become of the lands if it is claimed by any other?"

I heard commands being called from above. I heard men baying for blood.

"Take it," I said, "I give it to you."

The gate to his cell was flung open by invisible forces. The prisoner didn't so much as walk out, as glide. The hammer escaped my hands as if it were repulsed at my touch, landing in his. He examined the markings on the old cloth and smiled to himself. "Remarkable," he said, "an enchantment in the language of the great Excalibur. I had expected as such, but to see it is something else entirely."

I watched as blue flame engulfed those markings and the material marked by them were turned to pieces of ash and the maul was fully revealed. It didn't look like it could possess such power, but sometimes simply believing in something is enough.

My hand was approaching my blade. If he were to

betray me, as so many had, there was surely no way to stop him – not now. All I wanted was for him to know I had been willing to fight.

Armed guards came hurrying into the dungeon. The prisoner looked away from his prize and appeared disappointed at having to do so. With a gentle hand movement, the guards that had come for us all dropped to the damp stone floor. I looked to them, then to him.

"They will live," he said, and he felt that was enough. The prisoner stepped closer and put a hand upon my elbow. He looked calm, without a care. I still prepared to take my sword from its scabbard. "We have no reason to be here, just as you need never to return here. It is time for us to leave, although I must warn you, it will be in a way I cannot prepare you for."

We were in a small rowboat, out at sea. The stale, stifling air of the dungeon had been replaced by cool winds. The sudden change of location had my heart freeze for a moment as I looked around me. Open waters, a dark sky filled with stars. The prisoner tried not to make his amusement too obvious.

"I am told there can be a feeling similar to being quite drunk," he said, and he took the oars and started rowing.

"How did we get to be here?" I asked, "Where are we going?"

"It seemed a less vulgar display of power to bring us straight here, than to render the men of Stoneisle completely useless. We must reach Allsen, where I can guarantee your safety, to see what must be done regarding the God of War's maul. And we must do it quickly, before my former brothers have chance to prevent us from doing so."

I sat back and brought a match to my pipe. "This may be a foolish question, but I'm hoping you will amuse me. Why didn't you take us right to Allsen?" I laughed, asked him, "Why the boat, if we're in such a hurry?"

"It would require too much energy, and energy is what I am going to need, and going straight there is exactly what would be expected of me. Make the most of the current calm," he said, "and be thankful I am old and wise enough to have considered the practicalities of a boat – this time."

I smiled, glanced to the heavens and saw a star racing across the sky before it suddenly vanished without a trace. It reminded me of my youth, and my training, and of the people I thought I had known.

"What you said, about Jaxe," I asked, "was any of it true, or were you saying what had to be said, just to get me to do all this?"

"Even the darkest hearts within the Brothers Aeternal would find it distasteful to bargain with Liberty Jaxe, but he is a master of gathering information and he would have learned exactly what was for the claiming, and who the Brothers had entrusted to uncover it.

"I witnessed countless potential outcomes, simultaneously, and within the blink of an eye," he said, "and believe me when I say I saw you fall on Allsen, to the blade of the man you once trusted more than any other."

"That isn't an answer."

"Is it not? Perhaps I can not assure you of your

future, but I can tell you of two paths before you. You can focus on Jaxe, and you will spill blood throughout the years until you are at last brought together again, or you can remain beside me and learn of things you could never have imagined. You could be wiser than you ever dreamed, and more important than you ever dared believe possible."

"I'll have to think it through," I said, emptying the smoking contents of the bowl into the sea, "but now, I need to rest."

I lay back and closed my eyes, then opened one to look at him on realising something.

"I don't know your name," I said.

"I have had many, but the name my mother gave me was Maerlyn."

*

We came to Allsen a little after sunrise. The place managed to somehow look a little charming. The rocks sparkled like jewels in the sun. Even the prison had something about it. But I kept my eyes open, expecting to see a revenant in search of shade.

I helped Maerlyn pull the boat onto land and as we dragged it inwards, I couldn't help but notice how few dead were to be seen. I had expected a pile of bodies with scorched flesh and arrows with long-since extinguished flames penetrating their bodies. It crossed my mind that they had stumbled on despite the wounds they had received.

"Here will be fine." Maerlyn decided once we reached a particular spot that pleased him. He removed his hands from the boat, took hold of the hammer and started walking, not once looking back to be sure I was close behind. "This could be a useful discovery to someone one day."

I took a last look at the boat and wondered why I felt strange. Then it dawned on me. Or I think it did, anyway. I hadn't been here during daylight, but I could have sworn the boat and where we had come to place it, was exactly where I had found a similar boat when I had last come ashore. I shook the idea from my head, told myself it couldn't be. Land like this, it would be impossible to be quite sure of your bearings.

I caught up with Maerlyn and followed him beyond the imposing structure of the prison. The metallic ground remained but, here and there, almost unnoticeable I caught patches of what could have been marshland. Even weeds growing from cracks within the unnatural earth.

And I saw the decomposing remains of revenants. Birds had been eating at their flesh. I looked to the heavens. The light of the sun was already becoming too much, but the skies were empty. There wasn't a single gull or circling vulture to be seen.

Maerlyn stopped and bowed his head. I stopped beside him and realised we had come to be standing in the centre of a stone circle. Ordinary rocks, not like the ones of this place, marked with ancient runes. I had never felt comfortable around magic or its markings. After a moment I took my pipe and started to fill the bowl with tobacco.

"If you're expecting me to assist in some ritual," I said, "I won't be comfortable with that."

"We shall soon be joined by another, and you must remain within this circle," he insisted, "at least until she has gone."

"Who is it you refer to?"

Maerlyn kept his silence, and his head bowed. With the hammer held loosely in one hand, he began to carefully move the other over it. I watched him expertly reshape it into something new entirely – a great sword. I had never seen such a display of power. He opened his eyes and examined the blade. There wasn't a single hint of emotion on his face. If he was proud at his creation, he didn't reveal it. Marelyn turned, looked back to the sea. I followed his stare against the crashing waves and saw no ship on the horizon.

"How long will we—"

The question went unfinished. Seeing a woman emerge from the sea, walking calmly onto land with the movements of an unquestionable ruler was all I needed to forget it. Making sense of what I was seeing was now my main concern.

She was attractive, though certainly not the most beautiful I had ever seen, and the blue dress she wore was of a material thin enough to be entirely transparent. It clung to her skin. My hand crept for my blade a moment before I realised this could all be an elaborate distraction, luring us into danger.

"She is capable of travelling from one realm to another," Maerlyn whispered quickly at my side, "and you have just witnessed that she can survive the very depths of the ocean pushing down on her, yet you believe your sword could cause her harm? You must trust me as I tell you she wishes you no harm, and you must not make a single movement against her."

"If that's true," I said as she continued with her approach, "why the circle?"

"She may be able to survive the poisonous environments of the worlds she has walked through," he replied, "but that does not mean we would, or whatever poisons she may unknowingly bring with her."

"Maerlyn," she said as she drew near. Her voice was soft, almost musical and her ocean-blue eyes were firmly on the dream-reader. "Has your task reached its conclusion?"

"I have done all that I can," he said. Maerlyn stepped to the edge of the stone circle and held the blade for her to tak, allowing only his fingertips to leave the ground he had claimed. "The fate of a realm is in your hands."

She smiled, claiming the sword. "Yes," she said, "I believe it is… I will give him the sword, and I do hope you have chosen wisely."

"I made no such decision," Maerlyn said, but she was already walking back to the waves. I watched her walk into the water, effortlessly submerging without a care until she was fully out of sight. Maerlyn turned and looked at me. He knew I had plenty of questions about what had happened, just as I knew he was satisfied at how taken aback I was at everything I had witnessed. "There are so many more plains, so many more lands, than those in the world we see around us," he said. "The sword shall come to belong to the best of men, and great deeds shall be accomplished because of it.

"And of us," he said, and now he was smiling, "the great things we do shall never see our names immortalised in song, but we do not require such acknowledgment. The path we follow—"

"I've done exactly what I said I would."

For a man that claimed to have seen every potential outcome, my words clearly took him by surprise.

"Heir of Caleb," he said, smiling at me like I was a child unable to understand the seriousness of a situation, "are you so willing to turn you back on great things, all to confront Liberty Jaxe?"

"You should already know the answer," I said.

"You could become a great man."

"I'd never want to be. But you were right about one thing," I said, "the boat would prove useful."

I turned and started the long walk back.

"Then it must not yet be our time," he called after me, "but fate will bring us together again, one way, or another."

I stopped in my tracks and slowly turned to look back at him. A smile flickered across his lips. He seemed only too willing to believe he had changed my mind.

"If it does," I said, "be sure you're not working against my interests."

STRANGERS

It was during my eleventh, maybe even my twelfth, summer. Sister Frances pulled me from the classroom and guided me through the corridors of the citadel without providing many words. She certainly didn't offer any information. Whatever was happening, it was serious. I soon reached the conclusion that I would be taken to Mother Lily, where I would be punished for a deed I couldn't recall. Or the deed of another. The citadel would punish an innocent over letting an act go unpunished. But I was led to a door on a corridor I had never been shown before, and Sister Frances tapped gently and rhythmically against it. If she were out of breath, she hid it well.

A man's voice told us to enter. Sister Frances stepped away from me and said, "Well… Go on."

I swallowed and took a hold of the handle, keeping my eyes on her. A part of me wondered what kind of trap this was.

"Quickly," she said to encourage me, "you shouldn't keep him waiting."

I turned the handle. Sister Frances smiled and nodded at that. With my eyes still on her, I nudged the door open and took my first step over the threshold. The second my eyes moved off her, she shoved me into the room and pulled the door shut behind me. The citadel held many luxurious rooms, but this one outshone them all. Stained glass windows displaying numerous gods and goddesses, from Destiny, with hair chopped short having her appear as a feminine, beautiful man, to Victor, with the war hammer he used to conquer nations and reshape their lands.

"You see how there is no image of their parents?" a bearded man asked from the leather chair he sat in. He was dressed almost entirely in a shade of green matching the containers of wine the monks were so reluctant to share. The sheathed blade he had resting upon his lap looked too heavy for any man to hold. Despite the signs of wealth, I still saw the thin scar against his throat and guessed somebody had unsuccessfully hanged him.

"You know why that is, don't you?" he asked.

My face turned back to the decorative windows. To Despair, tricked to remain forever imprisoned within a cage of his own making, as punishment for his selfishness and untrustworthy nature, to Devotia, her smile and eyes hinting at the love she could place between two people. I looked to those eyes and that smile and struggled to look anywhere else. A skilled artist must have driven himself to madness in his pursuit of perfection, but it had paid off.

"It is to show you that even gods may find themselves without their parents, but they are never too far from their siblings. They say you share this trait with them," he said, and he smiled, but so briefly you could have easily missed it. "Did the sister tell you of my name?"

I shook my head. My lips moved to respond but I didn't make a sound. My nerves had claimed me.

"My name is Ervin Caleb, and they tell me you are Raen. Is this true?"

My lips twitched. This time, I released a barely audible croak. His response was to loudly sigh by way of revealing his disappointment.

"They told me you were intelligent, that you excel in all of your classes," he said, "and they bring you here and you struggle to talk. Is this a trick of some kind? Did they think I would be softened at your condition and willing to take you from their possession because of it?"

I could feel my heart beating at the back of my throat. The citadel was filled with unwanted children, many parents claiming they were handing them over as a tribute and every single one of them eventually reached the age of understanding how you would leave. If you were a boy, and if you were a particularly lucky one, you hoped for a noble family to claim you and a life as a warden or a scholar – either one could see you earning a name. If this didn't happen, you were eventually sent to the capital to serve in the king's army. Lucky girls were claimed early, to be the playthings of much luckier children. If this didn't happen, they hoped a kind family would at least show an interest in their being a maid.

"No," I said, and even I thought the sound was pitiful.

"To all gods and goddesses to witness this, I wonder if you are even a child. You sound as a farmyard animal!"

For a moment, I felt as if I had been possessed. I rushed forward without knowing I had intended to and threw myself to my knees, my arms around his legs as I pulled myself close. Tears were streaming down my face. Emotions I'd known never to reveal now refused to be held back any longer, and it couldn't have happened at a worse time. The man could leave without me, and I could make a better impression on another, but what if the two knew each other? I pictured him recognising me and finding joy in telling others of this day.

The sound he made on taking a breath had me certain he was ready to pull me loose and throw me aside, but he didn't. He seemed to hold that breath for the longest moment. Eventually, he spoke.

"My son would be around the age you are now," he said, "and I am sure he would never shame himself with such a display as this. Get off me and stand, I won't tell you again."

The muscles in my arms tensed in wanting to pull me ever closer, but I separated the fingers I had entwined and released him from my grip. The simple action must have taken a matter of seconds, but it felt to have taken much longer. Keeping my head bowed due to my own sense of shame, I got to my feet and took a single step back.

"You're still snivelling," he said, "and someone of your years should have control over such basic emotions. Do you think my wife is nearby, that her maternal instincts will see her take pity on you? I can assure you that she has no interest in my returning with a weeping bastard. We are proud of our name, and we would not consider giving it to one who would ruin it."

I nodded to show my understanding; used the back of my hand to wipe the snot from my face, then put both hands behind my back.

"Be thankful we are under the gaze of the gods," he said, "for I will be kind enough to let you try again, because of it. I am told your name is Raen."

"My name is Raen," I said, hating myself whenever my voice refused to remain steady, "and I understand why a man puts such importance on his name."

"Do you really, or do you simply recite what you have been told? You don't have to answer that," he said, "not yet. Let us simply hold conversation."

He asked me of my studies, and I answered as best I could, even after it became obvious to me that he already knew much of my progress. And he seemed pleased to talk of my experience in combat and arms training, which I was happy to discuss at length, having been told I excelled at it. He often mentioned his son, and always in the past tense. The question I wanted to ask was if his son was dead or left unable to continue the family name due to injury. The question went unspoken, because I didn't want to risk provoking him, and our talking went well because of it.

"Do you believe you could honour my son," he asked, "and my name?"

"I would give my life to."

He looked to me and, after a moment, drummed his fingertips across the handle of his sword. He no doubt believed that my response had been another practiced recital. It wasn't. At the time, I had meant it. I was so desperate for purpose I had believed it.

His eyes returned to the stained-glass windows, as if he were in search of divine guidance. Just as suddenly, he was upon his feet.

"If you give me reason to regret this, you will learn that even the gods will not protect you from my wrath."

I followed him out of that room as Raen of Caleb.

*

Three carriages waited outside of the citadel. Despite the sword he carried, Ervin Caleb moved quickly and did not look back to be sure I was even following. He turned to approach the first carriage and I dutifully went to follow him. Another man hurried out of the second and grabbed me by the elbow with fingers stained by smoking. He was tall and thin as a rake, but there was great strength in his grip.

"You're riding with me," he said.

I looked to Caleb and how he was yet to look back. I watched the waiting horseman of that first carriage dutifully open the door for him to enter before closing it once he was within.

"I don't know what you're waiting for," the thin man said, releasing me of his hold, "we're riding back here."

I swallowed and looked to the man. There wasn't any emotion on show. He had the facts he had spoken and there was nothing else of interest to him at that moment.

"My name is Raen."

"Raen of Caleb," he said to correct me. "I'm Busch. Did Sir Caleb mention me?"

"No," I said.

"It doesn't matter, soon you'll know me better than you do your own shadow. But get in," he said, "we're just waiting for one more."

My heart froze at the idea of another boy coming with us. It wasn't unheard of, but it was rare. Two would compete against one another for the name. One would be forced to return to the citadel. Despite the cool air, sweat began to appear on my brow.

"And this must be her," he said as Sister Frances joyfully led a girl from the citadel.

"Will she be a maid?"

"You'll learn your only worry is displeasing me," Busch said. "Now, get your arse in the carriage and be thankful I'm being generous enough to tell you a second time."

I hurried into the carriage. Busch climbed in and slammed the door shut once he was placed beside me. The temperature felt to be rising and the contained air was pungent with the wax used to clean the leather padding of the seat and citrus. Our journey onward began almost immediately, and I longed to look back and stare to the carriage trailing behind us but knew it best not to. Busch would no doubt tell me what would be worth looking at.

"We haven't long to go," he said, rolling a cigarette, "just beyond Mealand. You'll be able to see the citadel. Let it remind you how quickly you can be back here, if you don't do what I say."

Sir Caleb had enough land to house his own farmers, and they stopped working the fields to respectfully stand as we passed them.

"If you aren't up to it, you could maybe end up as a farmhand," Busch said without a care. "Your failure could be used to motivate another into trying harder."

With no idea how to respond, I decided it best to remain silent.

"It interests me," he said, rolling another cigarette, "to know whether you will come to see my face on every farm animal you come to kill, or whether you will come to praise me for securing your name."

Of course, my years in the care of the citadel had taught me to be respectful. We had been told it would be the greatest privilege to be given the chance to earn a name, and how kind those that had come to claim us would be. Sitting in the carriage, I wondered if my experience was an exception.

"Lady Caleb hates the smell," Busch said, blowing smoke to the ceiling, "so smoking indoors is frowned upon. Of course, if it were up to me, Sir Caleb would take to reining her back in."

I looked to him and dared ask, "Do they have any children?"

Busch clicked his tongue, then shrugged his shoulders before answering my question. "Not in this realm," he said, "and I suppose you should consider yourself lucky because of it. They *did* have a son."

"What happened to him?"

"What do you think happened to him? He died, of course."

Removed from the farming land and the cottages of those working the fields, we arrived at the magnificent Caleb home. Small buildings placed nearby housed the families of his most devoted of sycophants. He did not insist on guiding me around the property. He stepped out from his carriage and quickly disappeared inside. Busch and I left our own carriage and waited for the last to stop beside us. A kind-looking governess stepped out, dutifully followed by the girl they had claimed from the citadel. That was the first good look I got at her… At Yasmin. Her brown hair had traces of blonde and her nose was noticeably slender. Having been kept from the fairer sex for so long, she shone to me like a star.

*

Busch reluctantly gave me a brief tour of the home, ending with what would be my room. When we first set foot in it, I thought there must have been some mistake. Yes, the room I had slept in at the citadel was spacious, but I had also shared it with several others. Now I had so much space to myself, my footsteps were most likely going to echo.

Busch walked over to a window and stared onto the land we had recently travelled. "Make yourself comfortable," he said without looking back to me, "and a maid will collect you when we are to eat. You can rest today, and become accustomed to your new surroundings, but do not think you are going to have it easy. With the sunrise tomorrow, your education by way of the sword will begin."

"I was one of the best students at combat lessons," I said.

"Then I'll be happy to learn whatever wisdom you have to share with me," he said, turning to me with an unpleasant smile.

A maid collected me some hours later and took me to the dining room. I followed her instruction and sat at the large table, made from the wood of a white apple tree.

"Rise when Sir or Lady Caleb enter," she as good as whispered into my ear.

"How will I know it's Lady Caleb?"

"You won't mistake her for help," she smiled, and she drifted silently out of the room, closing the door shut behind her.

I waited a long time.

Servants came and went, each bringing small items and dishes to the table. The most I received from any of these was a brief smile, a nod of the head, but no bow or polite introduction. When Lady Caleb at last entered, I knew she was not a hired hand. The jewels and fine garments she wore were dulled by the sorrowful expression upon her face. With her head almost bowed, she approached the table in silence, clutching a piece of faded cloth to her breast. Both nervous and unsure as to whether she was even aware of my presence, I cleared my throat in attempt to attract her attention on dutifully rising to my feet.

"Lady Caleb," I said, "I am grateful to be in your company."

She took her seat without a word or single glance in my direction. With one hand keeping the cloth to her chest, she used the other to pull a polished glass towards her, then a jug of wine. I realised as she was still in the process of filling her glass that she had no interest in telling me I could sit. As I cautiously lowered myself into my seat, I took a gamble in saying, "You have a wonderful home."

"I have no home," she said, guiding the wine to her lips. "This is a mausoleum, nothing more."

Sir Caleb entered shortly afterward, although it felt painfully longer. He moved so quickly you could have mistaken his walk for a run. All for show, of course. All to see how quickly I could get to my feet, and all to have the servants and maids desperate to keep up with him. As one man was pulling his chair from under the table, another was filling his glass as another filled his plate. One servant was placing cuts of meat on the plate in front of me, before I had been told to sit back down.

"You may sit," Caleb said as he gave me the briefest of glances. "And you, my love," he said, despite how she had remained seated. A maid refilled her glass and would have returned the container to the centre of the table, if it were not for Lady Caleb taking her by the wrist and guiding the jug to a resting place within arms-reach. With all plates filled with food and the glasses filled with wine, the waiting staff lined the walls and awaited the moment we may require something else. Of course, I wanted to ask of Yasmin, and whether she would be joining us. Only my desperation to remain here maintained my silence.

"Did they feed you this well at the citadel?" Caleb asked.

"We did not go hungry," I said, "but your cooks are more skilled."

My answer had been true, of course, and Sir Caleb seemed pleased by this. Throughout the entirety of the meal, Lady Caleb held the cloth to her chest and, over the years that followed, there was only one occasion where she did not keep it so.

Caleb took a napkin from the table and wiped the oils from his lips. "How do you find your room?" he asked, intentionally dropping the soiled napkin to the floor. A servant had raced over to collect it before I had swallowed the mouthful of food I had been chewing.

"Luxurious," I said. "I have never seen anything like it."

"It's not his room to have," Lady Caleb muttered, shaking her head as if disagreeing with the words of an invisible guest seated beside her. "We risk dishonouring the just dead if we are to say otherwise."

We ate until Caleb decided he had consumed enough. Once he had finished, the servants took to gathering all plates as he wiped his mouth, regardless of what was left before me or his wife. He left the room knowing the hands would clear up and, eventually, both his wife and I would make our own departure. As I recall, she left soon after him, muttering to herself, and I remained there, long after the servants had finished, awaiting instruction. Eventually, I took myself to my room in silence. I couldn't sleep, but I didn't want anyone to suspect that there was something wrong with me, so I extinguished the flame of the candle and sat before the window in darkness.

A carriage arrived late in the night. I watched Sir Caleb climb within the compartment; watched the horseman tug at the reins and take the vehicle out of sight. I would learn much later that he was often going to visit one woman or another, but I was certain he was running such important errands on that first night. Once the feelings of excitement and nervousness and wonder could no longer resist my exhaustion, I stripped and climbed under the covers of my cot. Sleep embraced me as an old friend. The following morning, I was awoken to a cold hand pressing firmly against my mouth. In the early dawn, Busch stood over me with a dagger placed close to my face.

"Had I chosen, you would have woken with your life gushing from your neck. I could have easily chosen for you not to wake at all. Look at you," he said, removing his hand and sheathing his dagger, "you're pathetic. What use could you be to any other if you can't be woken by someone approaching?"

I had no words of response, though Busch had clearly expected I would have. In a moment he grew tired of my silent stare and shook his head. "Meet me outside," he said, turning to the door, "we may as well see how poorly you handle your ground."

Outside, I found him waiting with another boy of my years. Busch introduced him to me as being Allen of Kerwynn, before explaining he was in fact the son of William Kerwynn, one of Sir Caleb's most trusted allies.

"William doesn't want a useless bastard of entitlement, and so his own son must earn his name," Busch said for my benefit. "If the two of you are going to be wardens and be worthwhile ones at that, you are to listen to my every word and follow my every command.

"Allen, you are to show Raen what I have been teaching you. Fight."

Allen required no further instruction. He struck my jaw before I could understand what was being demanded of us. Before I had a chance to get over the blow, he had taken us both to the damp ground and was placed atop of me, his knees pinning my arms down. His fists found my face and the side of my skull without challenge. Panic had gripped me so tightly I didn't even attempt to struggle free.

"That's enough," Busch decided, "both of you, get up and shake hands. You're to depend on one another, not grow to hate one another."

Allen was off me within an instant. He even helped me up onto my feet. My face was stinging, the sides of my head throbbing, and I had the copper-taste of blood in my mouth. Remarkably, with his knuckles red, he looked to me with something almost resembling concern as he offered me his hand. And of course, I took it.

"The two of you will have enough people wanting you dead," Busch said, "never forget that."

The days went on and Busch came to my room each morning. At first, I feared sleep and tried desperately to remain awake. After some weeks, I was able to slip into a deep rest the moment my head went against the pillow and awaken before he arrived. The weeks became months. Busch had us spar one another and introduced wooden swords to our training. At first, I was no match for Allen. Busch scorned me. He claimed the citadel had taught me not to fight, but to dance prettily with a sword. Busch insisted that no tactic could be described as being 'underhand' if it kept you alive and weakened your opponent.

The seasons changed and I changed alongside them, becoming as Busch wanted me to be.

And sometimes, I caught sight of Yasmin. She was always beside the governess or Lady Caleb; wonderfully dressed and without a hair out of place. Always beautiful. It confused me. I had believed she had come to be a maid, yet I never witnessed her perform any menial task. The learning I saw her undertake was of reading and writing. One afternoon, as Busch had Allen and I riding horses through the fields, I asked about her place in the home.

"Unless you're hoping she'll one day save your life," Busch said, "it's nothing for you to dwell on."

A year was gone, and another was long underway before I returned to the citadel with Allen at my side. We joined one hundred or so others, all gathered to swear allegiance to the royal bloodline and begin our service as wardens of the lands. King Selborne was in attendance, though he appeared to have little interest in being there. The one thing I truly remember of him was how he didn't resemble the image displayed in oil paintings. He wasn't as tall as he had been depicted, just as he wasn't as slender, and his jaw was certainly not as square, nor the flesh of his neck as tight. Once we had finished a promise to give our lives in defending his honour, he clapped without enthusiasm and told us the people of Sundeberg would see us as beacons of justice. As he walked from the stage, a member of his council dismissed us all without ceremony. Given no further instruction, we each accepted the fur-lined cloaks handed to us and began the journey back to our homes.

*

The meal was so extravagant, the servants had been required to bring another table into the room for all the food. William Kerwynn joined us that evening. I had seen him a number of times but had never asked his name or been told it. He was huge. His shoulders were like anvils. His red hair was tied back, his beard kept just as tidy.

Lady Caleb was not present, and that was of no concern to me. But I was disappointed. I'd assumed she would be there and, given the occasion, Yasmin would be with her. Yasmin had never eaten with us. I was convinced that they had deliberately kept us apart. But it wasn't to be. This meal was to be enjoyed by the men and the men alone. Lord Caleb, William Kerwynn, Allen and myself. Busch was noticeably absent.

Caleb was overjoyed as soon as we all gathered. Looking back, he was most likely already drunk.

"Look at you both," he said as the maids loaded our plates and the servants filled our glasses. "Two fine men of Sundeberg. Two of the finest, even."

William lifted his glass and sniffed at the wine. "Your real training is about to start," he said. "No more playing with wooden swords."

"Yes," Caleb said in agreement, reaching forward to pluck a handful of meat from his plate, "you're looking at more than a fracture if the next sword you're up against finds its target.

"And I've been thinking about your future," he decided to add. "I've decided it would be best if the two of you travelled north."

"North?" William said. Despite his success in containing his emotions, it was easy for me to see how Caleb had reached this decision on his own, and William was far from ecstatic about it.

"They are wardens," Caleb said, pushing food into his mouth. "It would be good for them to be far removed from the comforts of this place. Let them see the lands and her people, even her most savage and ungrateful."

"And where would they sleep?"

Caleb laughed at the question. "There are many outposts," he said, "many towns where they could ask for a room, or even beneath the stars. How many do you believe remain so close to home, on taking the oath? It is a rite of passage."

"As is spending time with a more experienced warden. And as a matter of fact," William continued, "I do have such a person in mind. I was talking with—"

"These two young men have undergone enough training," Caleb interrupted, "and under Busch, of all people! Are you now going to tell them that you have no confidence in them?"

William took a drink from his glass before answering the question. "You're right," he said at last, "as you always are. My wife, however," he reasoned with a smile, "will be saddened at the distance between her and her firstborn son."

Caleb laughed and reached for more meat while having his glass refilled. "You have another son to keep her distracted, but you could always make a third!"

That night was the first time I drank enough wine for it to take an effect on me, and I'm sure it was the same for Allen. The four of us enjoyed one another's company, and both Caleb and William were happy to talk of events from their own lives. The servants were constantly bringing new bottles of wine to the table and replacing plates filled with stripped animal carcasses for those holding freshly prepared meat.

The night, however, came to a sudden end.

"Raen," Caleb said, getting to his feet, taking a moment to stop himself from swaying. "Come with me," he said, and he turned and headed for the door. I dutifully followed him to his private study. I had never set foot in the room before. I had never seen the door open. His private sanctuary was so organised, so well maintained, I worried he would suddenly decide my being there was a mistake, or I would say something to ruin the moment.

There was a satchel of worn leather on his reading table, alongside a sword beside its scabbard. He lifted the satchel first and turned unsteadily, holding it up for me to see as if he wished to be certain the light of the candles would be drawn to it.

"This has been in my family for generations, and now I want you to have it. Go on," he said, "take it."

I accepted it with caution, merely staring at it. It was cold to the touch. It had been recently polished, and although there was little to no chance that he had done it, the thought was still there.

"Thank you," I said.

"Just take good care of it, or as good a care as you are able to on the road. Your life may come to depend on what you can carry. And this," he said, turning to take hold of the sword, "is something else your life will come to depend on."

The lights of the candles danced along the blade. There was no need for me to touch it to know how sharp it was.

"My brother served as a warden. How I envied him."

Caleb smiled as if remembering a cherished scene from his life. "My father would not allow both sons to serve, you understand? But take it," he said, "it has been waiting for such a moment, I can assure you."

I swallowed and carefully took the sword from him. Much heavier than the wooden swords I had spent so long with, yet the blade was much thinner. Caleb watched me examining it, almost proud at the sight.

"The scabbard is new," he said at last. "I had it made to your measurements – or as close to them as I could."

I was speechless. Such kindness had never been shown to me. The moment was destined to be brief. Just as suddenly, Caleb's show of pride was tinged by sadness, although he didn't want it revealed or acknowledged.

"You should go," he said, turning his back to me, "get some sleep. You will no doubt want to leave as the sun rises. Until you return, may fate be kind to you."

I wanted to say something, but no words would come. Eventually I nodded my head, though he didn't witness the movement, and left the room with blade and satchel. Allen and his father both had left the room where we had dined, and I saw a servant extinguish the last remaining candle. My thoughts had become clearer than they had ever been before, and the silence of the home was heavy as lead. Restless, I wandered out into the cool darkness and almost immediately caught the smell of burning tobacco. I turned, believing it would be Busch, but it was not.

Yasmin was standing close by, smoking a cigarette. Now, when I look back at that moment, the smell of burning tobacco is replaced by the smell of wildflowers on the instant she noticed me. I spoke her name and regretted it, realising the two of us had never been introduced. Attempting to have her overlook what I had just done, I quickly said, "I thought Lady Caleb doesn't approve of smoking?"

Yasmin glanced down at the cigarette and said, "She doesn't, but the governess does, and I spend more of my time with her."

Satisfied with her response, she looked back to me. She kept her eyes on me as she guided the cigarette to her lips and drew back on it.

"You are Raen," she said. "I am told you swore your oath today and will be leaving tomorrow."

"That's true."

"Will you be travelling far?"

"Yes."

"You may lose sight of the citadel," she said. "I feel I will always be in its presence."

"You have bad memories of the place?"

"I am thankful of the food and education provided," she said, "and I am thankful my time there led to my being here, but it is a constant reminder of the family I will never know… The family that deserted me."

"We will never know why our parents did what they did, but we can choose to believe they did it for the best of reasons."

She weighed my words for value before dropping them without further hesitation. "Come and walk with me," she said. "You could be gone for years, and this may be our only chance to ever talk like this."

I watched her walk away, never once looking back to see if I would follow, then I quickly caught up with her. I wondered if this was even permitted, whether the men on watch would report us to Lady Caleb.

"Are you afraid?" she asked. "You came here immediately after the citadel. Both places are guarded. Soon, you will be a guard."

"They are certain I am ready, all I can do is have faith in their judgement."

"How important, for you, is a name? If it isn't of great importance," Yasmin reasoned, "you could simply request Sir Caleb allow you to remain here, as one of his guards."

"No," I said, "I have spent my life preparing for wardenship. Tomorrow, it begins as I leave this place."

"Then take me with you," she said. I assumed she was joking, because, if I had believed her, I am sure I would have taken her.

"Give me time to earn my name," I laughed nervously, "and maybe then I will take you somewhere far from the citadel."

"I doubt I will be here when you return," she said, and she took one final draw on her cigarette before allowing it to drop free of her fingers. "I am already certain Lady Caleb intends to gift me to another home."

"What makes you say that?"

"Do you remember the Weetmains?"

"I remember their name," I said. "Banking family. They make great donations to the citadel."

"Lady Caleb has insisted that I accompany her whenever she visits them, which is often. They tell me how pretty I am, and how proper, and Lady Caleb always tells me of what a compliment this is."

"You could be jumping to conclusions."

"No," she said, "there is so much more than that; it's difficult for me to explain. They have even asked if I would enjoy living in a home such as theirs; and told me how it would be a delight to have me living with them."

I briefly considered what she had told me. "Maybe she intends for them to continue your education?"

"I doubt it. I—" Yasmin stopped and laughed. "We're walking in the direction of the citadel," she said. "At least if I am to live with the Weetmains, I will be far from here.

"I still think you're lucky," she said, smiling as she turned to face me. "You are free to go as far from here as you please, and never look back."

"What if there was something I would want to return to?"

Yasmin laughed again. "Here? You have already put so much importance on receiving a name," she said, "don't allow them to convince you that the purpose they put on you is your own."

"It's different, for you," I said, "being a woman… Honour and a name takes on a whole new meaning, for us."

"I know," she said, turning to travel back from where we had met, "and that is a shame, it really is."

I tried and failed to understand what she had meant on saying that, then I caught up to her side all over again. Together we walked back to the Caleb home in a silence that was only to be broken when we stepped through the door.

"I wish you luck, Raen of Caleb," she said, "and I will

pray to see you again."

She turned and walked on without looking back. I crept up the stairs and into my room, confused for reasons I couldn't quite grasp.

The scabbard Sir Caleb had gifted me had been placed upon my cot.

*

I woke as the sun was starting to rise. Tired, experiencing the hint of a hangover and remembering every word exchanged with Yasmin the night before. And filled with a nervous excitement, of course. The comfort of these four walls would now be something I would be separated from, and I couldn't be sure how long for.

I could have fetched a servant and requested they bring me warm water and prepare me something to eat, but doing so didn't feel right. I dressed quickly and took my sword and satchel before creeping out of the room, determined not to wake any of the household or see anyone of their employ. Creeping down the stairs, Yasmin's words returned to haunt me. I doubted myself. I doubted what I could be capable of achieving and allowed myself to dream of what the future could hold if I were to wake her now and leave this place with her at my side.

Allen of Kerwynn was already waiting outside, kneeling in the morning dew, and smoking a cigarette. I noticed how his hand trembled lightly as he moved it away from his mouth, exhaling smoke into the still air. Knowing he was nervous helped me feel a little better. When he turned to look at me, I smiled briefly.

"You wake early?"

"A little earlier than usual," he said, legs stiff as he straightened. I wanted to tell him all about me and Yasmin but decided not to. I'm not entirely sure *why*, I just wanted to keep it to myself.

"A gift?" he said, eyes drawn to the sword at my side.

"I hope I earn it," I said, hand brushing against the pommel.

"My father's," Allen said, hand patting the sword at his side. The two of us stood in silence for a moment, simply staring to one another as we truly began to realise the weight of responsibility that we had claimed. With little left to say, we took our horses from the stable and began the road leading out of the private grounds. The men that had stood sentry were extinguishing their torches, relieved to know that soon they could sleep. They were all too tired to look to us for too long. They offered a word or a nod with a brief smile, but that was all. They didn't wish us farewell or assure us we would be in their prayers until we returned. When Allen caught me looking towards the citadel, he asked me of my years spent there.

"It seems so long ago now, I'm not sure which memories are real from those that were dreamed."

"Don't feel sad," Allen said, "the road we are on will give us many memories... Our story will be shared by others."

We hadn't been on an open road for too long before we encountered fellow wardens. Older than us. Experienced. We proudly greeted them. One sneered at us, the other smirked, but both looked back at us with contempt.

*

We continued our way north. Later that day, we were fortunate enough to encounter an older warden who was willing to give us a chance. Nothing serious, just one farmer accusing another of stealing from him. We retrieved the stolen items without any hassle and gave the guilty farmer a warning. The local earl wasn't happy when we came to him for payment. He took a few small coins from the yearly allowance he had for paying wardens and claimed he could have seen it taken care of as he handed them over. His comment did little to dampen my spirits.

The days that followed were filled with other trivial issues. Allen and I tried to help out whoever we could, soon realising how other wardens had no interest in the little things, but we soon grew bored. After a while, we decided to start sleeping during the day and patrolling the roads at night, chasing off a couple of bandits and the like as our reward. When we grew tired of doing this, we went back to sleeping beneath the stars and spending days at a time in nearby towns and villages. We got to know other wardens, some friendlier and more trusting than others. The days became meaningless. Time itself became meaningless. Splitting up bar fights, warning others for threatening behaviour and stealing. We'd apprehended a good number of men after the best part of a year, but they had surrendered without a fight. Most tried to run, and the chase was the only excitement we had. I found myself longing for the chase. I had to try and hide my disappointment as they admitted defeat and held their hands in the air without even trying to get back to their horses.

After the best part of a year, a night of wild thunderstorms and torrential rain struck. The two of us took shelter in an outpost. The ceiling leaked and the ground was exposed earth. Allen managed to drink himself to sleep. I wasn't as lucky. On the pitiful cot I had claimed for the night, I watched the water pour in and pool on the floor. Listened to the explosive sounds of thunder. Eventually I gave up all thoughts of rest and slipped my boots back on and stood at the open doorway, which happened to be the driest spot. The rain was falling heavily, flooding the land. Blinding lightning flashes occurred regularly. Because of all these things, the man approaching on horseback appeared to come from out of thin air. The brilliant flashes continually stole a moment. One second, he was bringing his horse to a stop, the next he had dismounted it, then he was coming closer and closer. It was too dark to see his face, but the way he moved was instantly familiar. I thought he must have been a warden we had met on the road, but I was wrong. It was Busch. I wanted to rush out and embrace him, but I didn't. I didn't want him to think I had grown sentimental and weak during my time away, or I didn't want to admit it to myself.

"Busch," I said, laughing with excitement as I walked out to meet him. "What are you doing here? Come in," I insisted, "we have stew to share."

"That lodging is for wardens," he said, planting his

feet, "and I'm not a warden."

"But you're our guest!"

"It doesn't work like that," he said, shaking his head. "All part of wardens keeping their information secure."

"You would rather have us stand out here," I laughed, pushing wet hair out of my face, "than sit with us? It's our cabin for the night, I say we can do whatever we decide!"

He simply looked me up and down. "You're still without chainmail?"

"Money goes too quickly on food and places to sleep," I said, feeling embarrassed. "Even the outposts charge you for food and board and delivering news you send home! And chainmail is expensive – unless you settle for repaired chainmail."

"At least you're both doing well," he said. "Honestly, I thought you would have made it all the way to the Black Mountains by now."

"We don't just move on," I laughed, wiping rainwater from my face, "we spend some time in most of the places we stop at."

"As long as you are doing well," he said, glancing back over his shoulder. "I'd best get going, before the man in charge comes to check I haven't accepted your invitation inside."

"He's not like that," I said.

"They're *all* like that."

"But wait," I said, dropping a hand upon his shoulder to keep him there longer. "Is everybody well? How is Yasmin?" I asked. I hadn't thought of her since the morning we started our journey and within a heartbeat, she was the most important thing in the world for me. I missed her terribly.

"Yasmin is due to be engaged," he said, and I felt my legs grow weak because of it.

"Yasmin?" I laughed in disbelief, longing for what he had said to be little more than a joke. "Who is she to marry?"

"The Weetmain heir. It's taken a lot of planning, but the families are as good as agreed on everything."

I felt as if I were swaying, ready to drop.

"She must be happy," I said.

"I haven't inquired. But I have a long journey ahead of me, so I must get going."

I laughed again. "Without seeing Allen? At least wait for me to wake him!"

"No," he said, turning to leave. "Stop wasting your coin on places like this. You can sleep beneath the stars and hunt for food. And if you find you aren't needed somewhere," he concluded, "move on."

After travelling northwards for so long, the Black Mountains insisted you go no farther. Treacherous and believed to be entirely unconquerable with only the sea beyond them. We could have reached them so long ago and journeyed back. Instead, we took every backroad and stopped at every non-descript town. We spent even longer in the cities, and all because we wanted adventure and we longed to make our names on finding it.

And during this time, plans had been made for Yasmin to marry.

The thunderstorm ended, and I listened to the quieting of the rain. I watched the water pouring in through holes of the roof as it turned to a trickle and finally the occasional drip. I noticed the daylight creep beneath the gap of the door and the lighting of my room as a rooster called. I heard Allen waking on the other side of the wall, and I waited for him. It was a relief when he finally pulled himself from his cot and came to me, finding me fully clothed and sitting on the cot I had wasted good coin on.

"How long have you been awake?" he asked me, still rubbing sleep from his eyes. I could smell the alcohol and cigarette smoke of the previous night from where he was standing.

"Long enough."

"Have you eaten? We should have enough stew left over."

"I'm not hungry. Eat," I said, "and then we can move on."

I knew he wanted to ask me if there was something wrong, just as I knew he didn't want to ask me unless he really had to. "Can you remember the names of any of the nearby towns?"

"No. But I want to keep going until we reach the Black Mountains."

"The Black Mountains?" he said back to me. That was enough to have him set to rolling a cigarette. "Why would you want to go there?"

"Our ancestors thought those mountains were where the world ended," I said with a shrug. "I'd like to see them before we start making our way back."

"Back?" Allen lit his cigarette. "You want to return home?"

"Don't you?"

"I… Of course," he said. "I'm just as tired of the

beaten paths and worn roads as I am travelling through endless fields, hoping I'll find them."

"So why go on?"

"My father hasn't sent word to a single outpost," he said, "not one. We've had our share of scrapes, Raen, but we haven't done anything good enough to earn our names."

"We could have said we were unwilling to leave our luxuries behind," I said. "But we didn't. I've lost count of the seasons we've spent travelling. All those days and nights, and we haven't even reached the end of Sundeberg."

"You want for us to return home and admit as much?" Allen laughed. "You want us to say we felt we had struggled long enough?"

"Look at what we've been doing, Allen, we've achieved nothing. We're no closer to earning our names now, than we were under Busch's command."

I knew my words had pained him. I wanted to take them back, but I also wanted him to feel as bad I was feeling. Allen glanced at me, then took to considering thoughts he wouldn't say aloud. In the end, he nodded on reaching an agreement, at least with himself.

"I'll travel to the mountains with you," he said at last, "but I can't promise I'll return home with you."

We ate what was left of our stew in silence.

*

I punished my horse. I made sure it kept ahead of Allen, all so we could make good speed towards the Black Mountains. We raced through the small towns and villages and ignored roads leading off to others. After stopping long enough for our horses to drink, we started all over again. The setting sun came, and we stopped only because the night became too dark and the land too treacherous. Allen made a fire, and I caught two rabbits to cook over it. In the far distance, the lights of the nearest settlements called out to me, begging me to reach them.

"This meat is better than the stew," Allen said at last, bringing our uncomfortable silence to an end.

"Because the meat hasn't been left sitting in a pan for days," I said.

"I'd bet the outposts prepare enough for days at a time."

"I'd bet you were right."

Allen sucked the grease from his fingers and rolled a cigarette. "There's a village on one of the mountains," he said. "My father told me about it. It's nowhere near the summit, but it's high enough. He told me the villagers won't go any further, because there are ghasts in those mountains that will try and push you to your death."

"Ghasts?"

"They're a form of spirit."

"I know what they are," I said, "I'm just curious to what would have them so far up a mountain."

"Those mountains earned their name. Some dark rituals were practiced all through those valleys."

I plucked meat from the bone. "That was all a long time ago."

"Depending on *who* or *what* you are, time moves differently."

Allen came at ease beneath the night sky. We hadn't sat and looked to the stars for such a long time. We took to talking of home, and it became clear to me how much he missed it. He rolled another cigarette and said, "I wonder what they are doing right now?"

"Sleeping."

"You think?" Allen laughed. "I don't. My father is most likely taking his last patrol of the grounds, making sure the sentries are ready."

"Sir Caleb has probably gone to visit one of his women."

Allen laughed again. "How many bastards do you think he could have hidden away?"

"Enough for an army to rival King Selborne's."

I caught a hint of the smell a moment before Allen. It was the smell of old sweat and freshly disturbed earth. We turned and looked into the darkness to see an aged man coming towards us, his weight leaning against a staff of carved wood.

"Forgive me," he said as he came closer, "I didn't intend to startle you, but I didn't wish to interrupt. I'm just a wanderer who saw the light of your fire and would very much like a moment beside it, if that would not be too much for me to ask?"

"You can sit with us," Allen said, "although we have no food to offer you."

The man drew close enough for us to see the deep lines upon his face, and the knots and the dirt in his hair. "I thank you," he said, slowly lowering himself down to the ground, "and assure you that I am grateful. My name is Boram."

"I am Allen of Kerwynn, and this is Raen of Caleb."

"Wardens?" He said, taking closer examination, "We rarely see your kind this far."

I said, "We're headed to the Black Mountains."

"Of course you are," he said, and he looked glumly to the fire. "I am glad that you are finally taking an interest in the missing children."

Allen looked to me. I looked to Boram. "Missing children?"

"Yes," Boram said, expectantly looking to us both. "You must know about the missing children?"

"Forgive us," I said, "but we have heard nothing of this."

"Then the gods must have delivered you to me. Closer to the mountains," he said, looking back to the darkness, "we've had children disappear from the towns and villages. Every time a child goes, lights were seen near the summit of the mountains."

"How many children have gone?"

"Six," Boram said, "maybe seven, and all without trace."

Allen guided his cigarette to his mouth and said, "Then we will find these children, or what has happened to them."

"Forgive me," Boram said, "but age has stiffened my fingers… Would you be kind enough to share a cigarette?"

"Take it," Allen said, and he held the cigarette out for Boram to accept, which he did without hesitation. The old man pulled smoke into his chest and appreciated the feel of its weight before talking again.

"Were I younger, even if I were in the twilight of my youth," he said, "I would have climbed those mountains myself. Now, such notions are but the foolish ramblings of an old man."

"You have told us, and that is enough. How long do you think it will take us to reach the mountains?"

The old man brought more smoke deep inside of him and took to examining the cigarette as he considered the answer. "Departing at sunrise, solid riding without stopping, unless you absolutely have to… I'd say you could arrive within two days."

"And when was the last child taken?"

"Last night, or maybe the night previous," he said, "I saw those lights up at the summit."

"Then those lights shall not be seen again," said Allen.

I nodded and said, "We should get some sleep."

"I'll take first watch," Allen said.

Boram took a final draw on the cigarette and flicked what remained into the fire. He groaned as he struggled to his feet, leaning against his staff for support. "Rest well, and may you put the people you will encounter at ease," he said, "but I must venture on."

"It is late, and it is dark. You are welcome to spend the night beside us."

"I have too far to go," he said, "and too little time."

"Let him go," Allen said softly, "or else it will become our responsibility to see that he gets there."

*

I dreamed of fields of wheat, drenched in golden sunlight. I caught glimpses of divine beauty and heard her delicate laughter. Brown hair and lips that must surely taste as sweet as honey. Hazel eyes merely hinting at such a beautiful, intelligent soul.

And I woke feeling lightheaded and happy because of her.

The darkest point of night had come and gone. I sat upright and stretched the tightness from my settled muscles on doing so. Allen was smoking a cigarette, and the fire still burned. I looked to him and simply asked, "Anything?"

"Possibly," he said. "I may have spotted moving lights, but if there truly is a village up in the mountains, it could have easily been a villager on sentry."

I rubbed at my tired eyes. "Rest," I said, "I'll wake you when it is time to go."

Allen didn't immediately respond. He took a draw on his cigarette and held the smoke inside of him until he was truly ready to exhale. The act itself was leisurely. "If there is a village," he said at long last, "then at least one of them must know something. About the missing children, I mean."

"They may."

"Two of us, upon terrain we have never explored. Many of them could decide to act against us, and they would have the advantage if they did so."

"What are you suggesting?"

"We should ask any and every warden we encounter to join us," he said.

"Then we will."

"And if we risk losing control of the situation," he said, "we should make our way home and gather a greater number."

"If that is what is needed, we will do it."

Allen nodded and took one final draw on his cigarette before flicking it away from the campfire. For a moment I could see it burning on the ground, then the glow disappeared but the smell remained on the air.

"My father told me the people in the village were a strange kind," he said. "He warned me how, the farther north you travel, the less respect for the royal bloodline and our ways you witness. Raen, there are no settlements farther north than the village we intend to reach."

"Then we will tell your father how we commanded their respect."

"And if we first run, with our tails between our legs?"

"Not all retreats are cowardly. Sleep," I insisted, "exhaustion has you doubting yourself."

He didn't protest. Allen pulled the hood of his cloak over his head and got comfortable. He was fast asleep within moments, leaving me to stare at the Black Mountains and await the sunrise.

*

We charged our horses onward at first light, only stopping on seeing a well almost hidden by the tall grass, with thick vines and branches wrapped around it. Allen lowered the bucket into the cool darkness and had it return filled with ice cold water. We drank, then we splashed water over our faces. As Allen was in the process of lowering the bucket all over again, I became aware of a woman coming from the direction of the nearest settlement, a bucket in each hand.

"I can wait," she said, "you two got there first."

"We're just about finished," I said, and I pushed my hair from my face. Cool water ran down the back of my neck.

She smiled, looked to Allen and then back to me. "Are you two *really* wardens?"

"What else would we be?"

"I didn't mean to offend," she said, "it's just we don't see many wardens up here."

Allen said, "We're here because of the missing children."

"The missing ones?" She said, "I had heard something about that."

"The children from your town are accounted for?"

"Yes," she said with a nod, and she briefly looked back. "I heard two were taken from one of the next towns… Twins. A terrible thing."

"Yes," Allen said, and he quickly added, "King Selborne will not rest until they are returned."

She said, "I'm glad that he wants something done… A lot of people will be just as glad to hear this."

We rode on. Allen, having claimed we now travelled on King Selborne's orders, rode with unmatched determination. Our horses were displeased at having to work so hard, having spent so long at ease. I suspect they even took to hating us. There appeared a reluctance in following simple commands. Even when we granted them time to recover, they did not appreciate the apples we provided them. The night arrived and as we secured our horses to nearby trees, I was prepared for at least one of them to kick out in protest. Thankfully, that did not happen. Had our places been reversed, I surely would have done so. The journey was exhausting but as Allen rolled himself a cigarette, I looked to the Black Mountains and saw how close we had come.

I dreamed of her again that night, and accepted she was more captivatingly beautiful than I had remembered. She was fascinating to behold; her appearance deserving to be expertly preserved in stone. I watched her walk the corridors of the citadel as if they belonged to her, sunlight penetrating the stained-glass windows radiating her light brown hair. You would be blessed to give everything you were, and everything you could ever hope to become, to her.

I felt the cold, gentle rain on waking. I pulled my cloak a little tighter and looked to Allen on sitting. He glanced to me, then returned his gaze to the light of the fire. A cigarette was slowly burning away between his fingers. The horses remained where we had secured them.

"Anything?"

"Nothing I've seen," he said. "Mountains have been in complete darkness."

"Any travellers?"

"No."

I nodded and wiped a hand across my face. "Get some sleep," I said.

"I'm just going to finish this cigarette."

I looked to the mountains as Allen looked back to the fire. After a while he said, "Do you remember your dreams?"

The question startled me. It had me worrying how

I could have said something foolish in my sleep, but I didn't want to reveal anything unless I really had to. I wanted to keep all knowledge of the vision of beauty to myself, for as long as I could. So I decided to answer him with a lie.

"Sometimes I wake up and know something about the dream was unusual, but I can't remember *what*," I said. "But I forget about that, soon enough. Why did you ask?"

Allen took a draw on his cigarette before answering. "Just I had an unusual dream last night. And it's strange," he said as he gave an embarrassed smile, "because I've only really been thinking about it since it grew dark, but it's just got me feeling a little concerned."

"What was your dream?"

Allen smirked and shook his head, as if unwilling to make sense of his feelings. "There is little to describe," he said. "I saw mirrors hanging in darkness, and they were shattering as ringing bells could be heard. That was all. Or, at least, that's all I could remember."

"And you believe this means something?"

Allen laughed and took a draw on his cigarette before tossing it into the dancing flames. "My mother believes dreams could offer a glimpse of the future, or a sight of something transpiring that the gods decided you should know about." He briefly covered his mouth as he yawned, then looked back to me and said, "I'm not saying I completely believe her, but things have happened that I had dreamed about."

"We were taught of such things at the citadel."

"You don't think I'm mad?"

"No," I said, "but it is a rare gift, when it occurs. Be careful of following your dreams; they can turn the best of us paranoid or leave us longing for something we are never to have."

Allen laughed again, briefly, and lay flat on the ground. He closed his eyes and said, "I know it's bound to have no meaning… I'm just tired and hungry and I miss my home."

I took a breath and released it, deciding within that moment to be honest with him. "I've been dreaming of something, recently," I said, "or, I've been dreaming of someone. A young woman, to be precise. Beautiful. When I see her, I know how it feels to be in love, as foolish as it sounds."

Allen did not laugh at my confession, nor did he ask for further details. He had fallen asleep almost immediately after he had ceased talking.

*

Birds cautiously took to reclaiming the skies as they lightened. I kept my eyes upon the Black Mountains and saw no lights or smoke from a fire. No matter how many times my eyes slowly moved over the same areas, I saw no signs that there could be a village there. Unless, I had decided, it was hidden by one of the areas dense with trees. Eventually I caught a rabbit, skinning and cooking it over the fire before waking Allen. He took a breath and failed to recognise me for a second – long enough for his hand to find the hilt of his sword and then he laughed and fell at ease.

"Morning, already?" he said.

"Morning, already," I said. "Any dreams?"

"No," he said, and I was certain he was lying. "We seem a lot closer to the mountains now it is light… I think we could be there by nightfall."

"If we make good speed," I said. "At least we won't waste time catching our breakfast."

We moved on. Grey clouds covered the skies and the cold winds and falling rain became ferocious, but we didn't stop, even when we struggled to see what was right in front of us. I noticed the outpost when it was still some way ahead of us. I could see the holes in the roof a lot easier than I could see what remained of the beaten track leading to it. A quick glance would have been enough for me. I would have gladly judged it as being deserted and carried on.

"Outpost," Allen said from beside me, sounding as if he had been covering the distance in place of his horse.

"Deserted."

"I don't think it is," he said, "they're flying the flag."

My first thought was that they had forgotten to take it with them.

Allen said, "We need to stop there, just for a minute."

"We're making good time."

"A minute won't stop that," he said. "I want to send word of what we are doing. I want my father to know what is happening."

I felt that would be an unnecessary delay, then I remembered the key difference between us. Unlike Allen, I had no family. It was understandable that he would want to tell his father how he finally had a sense of purpose, following so long spent dealing with the intoxicated and their small acts of theft. In a decision still regretted to this day, I charged ahead.

"Go," I said, slowing my horse near the ruined path leading to the outpost, "I'll wait here."

Allen nodded, smiled, and kicked to the sides of his horse. I watched him dismount it as he neared the building, and I watched him hurry inside. He had never looked so young as he did at that moment before he fell out of sight.

Allen was readjusting his satchel as he hurried back out and mounted his horse. Despite his hurry, despite how little time he had spent in there, I couldn't help but feel we had wasted valuable time. I even considered racing on, knowing he would have to work to regain his place beside me. Instead, I said, "Are they sending word?"

"They are," he said, smiling as he placed a cigarette between his lips. "I got us some cuts of deer," he added, patting his satchel with an open palm. Coin and time had been wasted, but I said nothing. Perhaps thankful for the brief stop, our horses continued without protest. We travelled long after darkness had fallen, only stopping when the unknown ground became too dangerous to go any further. Despite the gentle rain, we made a fire and ate the first of the deer meat. When Allen volunteered to take first watch, I accepted his offer without hesitation, perhaps still a little annoyed at his sending a message. Or, annoyed at him for having someone to send one to.

And of course, I dreamed of her. My beautifully divine angel, still without a name.

*

The rain ended as Allen slept, and the clouds dispersed. Light spread over the lands and I looked to the Black Mountains. A part of me felt that I would touch them if I reached out my hand. I was certain I could smell the rain on the trees and hear the birds moving within the branches. The sight of such imposing formations was almost enough to keep me from noticing the travellers. Nine men and several women, some carrying children, moving southwards. Dirty, dripping wet and struggling to pull their carts along, it was clear they too had been sleeping beneath the stars. But what was the reason for their travelling, and under such conditions?

Nomads?

The citadel had taught us of such people. We had been told they had no desire to belong, for they were too scared to fight. We had been told they had no honour or value. They were lower than trained dogs – inbred and untrustworthy, but they were coming from an area we were yet to venture to. I looked to Allen. Still sleeping, I decided not to wake him and got to my feet, running through the tall, wet grass to meet the travellers. When I hurried out ahead of them, they stopped moving forward and took a defensive formation without hesitating. The men pulled hatchets and daggers from their belts; the women lowered the children and with blades of their own on display, placed themselves directly in front of their youngest. My hand had wanted to reach for my blade as if on its own accord. If any of the travellers noticed a flinch of my wrist, it was not enough for them to charge at me.

"I'm a warden," I said.

One of the men took a single step forward and looked to me from beneath his brows. "You're a lad in a fancy cape," he said, grip tightening on his blade.

"I want no trouble with you. My friend and I are travelling north. We've been told that children have been taken."

The man in the lead glanced quickly at those waiting behind him. Even with my eyes kept on him, I noticed the entire group responded. The men looked to one another, as did the women. But the women were different. They looked to one another with hope, or even relief. I seized the moment and said, "I only want to know anything you wish to share."

He considered my words and straightened his shoulders. He held his weapon in the air for me to see and then slipped it behind his belt. I nodded in understanding. The man started to walk forwards, as did I. His party remained back, remained prepared.

"Are you nomad?"

"Yes," he said. "You're looking for the children?"

"We are."

He nodded and looked to the side. There was every chance he was looking for another; a man in hiding with bolt ready. "You said you're with someone?"

"I did. He's nearby. Have you witnessed anything? Lost anyone?"

The man took a breath as he tried to decide whether his customs permitted him to hold such dialogue with me. He glanced back at his party. The sight of them was more than enough to lead him to decide.

"We were in a larger group, camping on ahead," he said. "Traveller crossed us some nights back, told us a couple children had been taken from nearby. You get children being taken, or you notice thieving or fighting, then my people are the first to be blamed. I said we should all get moving away, these are the only ones that come with me.

"The last night gone," he said, "we were resting around the fire, when someone came towards us, like he'd come from thin air. Drunk, maybe. He didn't seem in control of his words, and he stuck to the shadows. But he warned us of a giant figure of black furs, with its face covered by a horned skull of some kind. He told me this creature was responsible for the missing children."

"Did you ask how he knows this?"

The man laughed and looked back over his shoulder. "I woke the others," he said on turning back to me, "but he had disappeared as suddenly as he first arrived."

"Footprints?"

He shook his head and said, "Grass was too tall. And it was too wet and too windy. Without any hounds, we'd no chance of tracking him. So, all we could do was move on as soon as the sun was rising. But I tell you," he added in a hushed whisper, "when night returns, I feel he isn't too far. But maybe it would be a good thing if he is close? Now I know he's there, and he's real, perhaps he's here to watch over the children? And that's what you should do if you get the chance. No mercy should be offered to those taking little ones. You cut his tongue out if it looks like he will be given his time to talk at a trial."

"I'll see if there's any truth in what you were told," I said. "But what about you, where are you going?"

The man shrugged. "Just on," he said. "When you come across my people, it would be a kindness if you tell them what I was told, and that I'll be going straight until first sound of running water."

"I'll tell them," I said. "Travel well."

"Aye," he said as I turned to make the short walk back to camp, "and may you."

I caught sight of Allen crouched low in the tall grass, his face a mask of disgust, blade free of its scabbard. In case the nomads were still watching me, I acted as if I were brushing something from my cloak. Allen saw the subtle gesture for what it really was, that I was signalling him to move away. He seemed reluctant to do as such. He took a deep breath and kept his eyes on the travellers before finally pulling away, keeping hidden as he retreated.

"Well?" he asked once we were back at camp.

"He said he's been told of the person taking the children. Tall and in black furs," I said, "a horned skull covering his face."

"And you believed him?"

"He believes that's what he was told," I answered, mounting my horse. "But I wasn't there. He could have dreamed it and then woken, refusing to accept he had fallen into a deep sleep when he was supposed to be watching over them."

"Perhaps," Allen said. "How sure are you that those children they travelled with belonged with them?"

"I'm sure," I said. "It would have been easier for him

to try and cut me down, than to try and lead me astray with a lie."

*

We rode for hours. The sun had long reached its highest point and was starting its slow descent to the earth before we could smell wet ash and old smoke. We found what was left of those the traveller had left behind. Tents and carts had been set ablaze. Men and women both had been thrown onto the fires. Even the horses hadn't been spared. I looked over the mindlessness and knew it should never have been.

Allen was the first of us to speak.

"There are no children," he said.

"They would have ran."

Allen nodded and began to roll a cigarette. "Could be whoever did this decided to take them… To see if any of them belonged to the nearby towns or villages."

I recalled the towns and villages we had gone through. I remembered how the people stopped and looked to us as we went by. Some of those people must have known about this, just as some of those people would have played a role in it. Not one of them spoke up. Not one.

"This was no act of justice," I said.

Allen neither agreed nor disagreed. He lit his cigarette and tossed the burning match aside on breathing smoke into his lungs. "What would you have us do?"

I took a breath and slowly released it, facing the Black Mountains. They seemed to constantly increase in size, but the distance between us refused to shorten.

"There's nothing we can do for these people," I said, "not now. But we may still save others."

Darkness came and the air grew colder. I saw the light from occupied lands and tried not to picture how the flames brought to the nomads must have looked to these same people. I tried not to dwell on how they may have even heard the screams. But the anger would not release me from its grip. I tried to outrun it. I tried to race my horse into the ground as if it would be some act of penance and yet, suddenly, I found myself bringing my horse to a stop.

We had come to be at Abuscrombe, the small town standing at the very foot of the Black Mountains. It was so unexpected, so unbelievable, that I looked all around me as if searching for a sign that this couldn't be true. It was much darker than I had realised. My ragged breathing sounded as if it had been the horse controlling me.

"We're here," I said to reassure myself, "we've reached the mountains."

"We have," Allen said as he appeared beside me, relief upon his face. And it was funny, because I had to stare at him for a moment to remember exactly who he was. It was like I was meeting him for the first time.

"Allen," I remembered at last.

"Raen," he said, partly smiling as he rolled a cigarette. "What shall we do now?"

"Isn't it obvious? We go and get a drink."

You'll find that all inhabited places will have a place of worship and a tavern, and you know which is which because, when you're in need, there will always be a light at the tavern windows.

Allen quickly smoked his cigarette as we walked the flooded ground of the town, my eyes focused on the tavern. Something didn't feel quite right, and I realised what it was before we got there. The air was silent. No songs, no drunken laughing, not even a drunken threat. A couple of people had hurried out, their heads down low, but they weren't talking about anything that could have soured their fun.

As we neared the door, we both noticed a trail of blood leading out onto the mud. Only recently, someone had rushed out of here having suffered quite the wound. Allen flicked his cigarette aside and said, "Looks like there could be trouble."

"Only one way to be sure," I said, and I pushed the door open and stepped inside. There was still a good number of people drinking in there, but they all looked to be keen to keep themselves to themselves. A woman much older than she was desperate to look was collecting empty bottles and when she turned and saw us, she nearly dropped them in alarm.

"We don't want any trouble," she said, "we've already told your friend that we're not all like Garren."

"Friend? What friend?"

The woman turned and I looked to where she was facing. He could have been a little younger than I was at the time, just as he could have been a little older. The dirt on his face from a long journey made it hard to tell. But he was in good spirits, his fur-lined cloak draped across the young woman pressed tightly against his righthand side. The young woman at his left giggled as she guided a bottle to his lips.

I didn't give another word. Taking controlled, calm steps towards my fellow warden, I felt as if almost every other eye was now watching my every move. The only sound was the laughing of the two women and the young man enjoying his place between them. Eventually he looked to me, staring right at me with that wild smile.

"My name is Raen of Caleb, and this is Allen of Kerwynn."

He laughed and said, "This is Kara – or was it Tara? And this is Sheena. Or is it the other way around?"

The girls laughed along with him. I struggled to decide whether he was intoxicated or obnoxious.

"I'm playing," he said, "take a seat and talk with me. My name is Liberty Jaxe, and I'd bet we're here for the same reason."

His name was Liberty Jaxe. *His* name. There was a chance he was of money, but I didn't get that impression. So what had he done to earn his title, and so soon?

"Girls," he said, "I'm not going to say something better has come up, but it is more important. You're going to have to find someone else."

They didn't coo or tease. Their demeanour changed immediately. They quickly rose to their feet to go. They even looked a little relieved.

"I'm going to have to take that back," Jaxe said as he pulled the cloak from one of the two before slapping at her behind. The moving of the two had revealed he kept a small, curved blade at each side. His sword was nowhere to be seen.

"I think we've got our privacy now," he said. "Please,

sit with me."

I took hold of the nearest chair and had pulled it back a touch before he suddenly asked me to stop and reached beneath the table, pulling his sheathed sword into view. My first thought was that he had earned his name far too early. His sword out of reach and either one of the two girls could have easily claimed one of the small blades and used it to open his neck.

"Thank you," he said to me, and he placed the sword down upon the table. More needless boasting.

I said, "Are you out here alone?" on taking the chair from beneath the table. Allen dragged a vacant chair from nearby. We all sat together, as if we were friends or even equals.

"I am," he said, "and before you ask, I haven't sent any requests for support. By the time one of those greasy old men from the outposts had even headed out, I would be on my way back down already.

"And that is why you're here, isn't it?" Jaxe smiled and said, "You've heard of missing children and lights coming from the mountains? I can't think of any other reason for somebody to come way out to the end of the world."

"We've heard something else," Allen said as he took to carefully rolling a cigarette. "A nomad told us he had been told who, or what, is responsible."

Jaxe chuckled dryly and reached for his bottle. "Is that so? Tell me," he said, "did you check your valuables after he'd finished telling you that? Nomads are secretive. They're also sneaky."

"I have no reason to doubt him."

Jaxe stared right at me as he drank greedily from the

bottle. Once he was ready, he placed it back down in the centre of the table and took a breath. "I'll listen," he said, "what is it the nomad knows?"

"Tall man," I said. "Black fur, face behind an animal skull."

"Actually," Jaxe said, "that doesn't sound too far-fetched. Man must have thought you had an honest face. You venture up into these mountains, you're going to want to keep yourself from freezing. And any man stealing children is going to want his identity kept hidden."

Allen said, "Have you ever been in the mountains?"

Jaxe looked to him and smirked. "I've been about as far as I've needed to go," he said, "and that was far enough."

"Is there a village up there?"

"There *was*," he said, grinning wildly all over again, "and if it had a name, it's long forgotten. No one seems to know what happened there, but you won't find any villagers up in those mountains."

"A shame," I said. "We have no witnesses."

Allen struck a match and guided the flame to his cigarette with trembling hands. "It also means we won't have the risk of them standing against us. We should remain cautious," he said, "just to be sure, but the mountains now feel a little less dangerous."

"And I agree with that," Jaxe said. "You couldn't spare a cigarette, could you? The only problem is if we head up now, we'd most likely fall to our deaths. Why do you think I'm still here?" Jaxe laughed. "I've no intention to start making my way up before the sunrise."

"Could we travel by horse?"

"If we were careful," he said. "But we will reach a point where you'll want to feel the ground beneath your feet, so you know to jump before it gives way beneath you."

Allen gulped and handed him a cigarette. "The ground is so treacherous?"

"Most things will be," Jaxe said, "unless you're willing to believe you're capable of being much worse."

*

The tavern had no rooms to claim. Jaxe laughed off their news and told them we would be fine sleeping at the table. Open-mouthed, the owner tried and failed to think of a way to be rid of us. In the end, he walked away defeated. It didn't feel right to me, but I was tired. I was tired and I knew the safest way of venturing further was with Jaxe, because he had a knowledge of the mountains.

The locals began leaving one by one, all hoping that we wouldn't be there the following night. The owner and those under his employ took to gathering the empty bottles and tankards; sweeping up the mess and extinguishing the candles as they worked in uncomfortable silence. They didn't get too close to us.

"Have some bottles of water ready for our departure," Jaxe said loudly enough for them all to hear. "And we would like some eggs and bread to eat before we leave in the morning."

It didn't feel right, especially when my offer of coin for their trouble was refused. Jaxe said to me, "You have to be careful, your generous nature will leave you with nothing, if you insist on paying at every inn and town you come across."

"They work for it," I said.

"And we work to keep lesser men from taking everything they have worked for." Jaxe turned to Allen and said, "If you could spare another cigarette, it would be appreciated."

Allen nodded and, without saying a word, began to roll two cigarettes. Jaxe turned to me and smiled, believing a point had been well made.

"You see?" He said, "A polite word and an understanding of the help exchanged can be just as valuable as any coin."

We slept on the chairs we had been sitting. I was the first to wake. A young woman was creeping by with a few eggs balanced in her hands. She looked at me and expected me to yell about being disturbed.

"Good morning," I said.

"Good morning," she said quietly. "We've got your bottles of water ready, we're about to start your breakfast, if it isn't too early?"

"No," I said, "it isn't. Let me give you a little coin, for the trouble you've gone to."

"No," she said, shaking her head and quickly walking away. "No trouble."

I wanted to accept what she had said, but couldn't, so I took a few small coins and silently placed them under the table for her to find. Then I stood and stretched, trying to rid my body of the stiffness that had set in during the night.

"Allen," I said, placing a hand against his shoulder

and gently shaking him. He woke almost immediately and looked to Jaxe before looking to me.

"Is anything wrong?" he said.

"No," I said, and I smiled. "Nothing is wrong. I'm just stepping out for a little fresh air."

Allen nodded. "I'll come with you."

"You can stay here, if you like."

"No," he said. He got up, yawned, and then stretched. "A little fresh air will get my thoughts ready."

We made our way to the door, and I noticed the spill of dried blood on the floor that carried on as the injured party had made a quick exit. That kind of trouble is to be expected in any tavern, but I felt Jaxe had most probably been the attacker. If Allen had been paying the same attention, he didn't show it. He kept his eyes on the cigarette he had rolled by the time we stepped out into the early morning sun. The air was cool and despite the light, the skies were a dull grey. A few people were tending to their animals. They glanced in our direction before pretending they were too busy to pay any much attention. Allen got his cigarette burning and said, "Do you think you could ever stay somewhere like this?"

"I don't know. Why, do you?"

"I don't know," Allen said, "I was just thinking. A lot of wardens, once they get too old for it, pick a place to stay and uphold the law there… Even train a few fellas to work under them."

"You've got a home," I said, "and a family."

"I know that. It's just an idea."

Jaxe woke and we all three broke our fast together. Once he decided we were ready, we started on. The owner of the inn gave us our bottled water and cuts of meat. I didn't feel right accepting them, but I didn't want to cause any mistrust with Jaxe.

It was Jaxe's decision for us to make our way on foot.

"It looks like it's going to rain, and the path is going to be slippery enough," he said. "If I fall off that damned mountain, I'd rather my horse was taken by one of the people down here, not one of the animals up there."

Allen said, "What animals?"

"It's the wolves you'll need to look out for."

*

A heavy rain started to fall, making the slippery ground of the mountain even worse. Water poured over soil that couldn't absorb it fast enough. Soon, we had thick vines and exposed roots slowing us down. When we reached the trees, they were almost a blessing. The thick branches and leaves kept the worst of the rain off us. But it got a lot darker. The light must have been hidden by the clouds, and the trees were reluctant to show us any that was managing to break through.

We carried on up the mountain. Struggling to maintain my balance caused my legs to ache, but I didn't complain because Allen and Jaxe must have felt the same. After a while, we found the remains of the deer. Rainwater caused its exposed skeleton to almost sparkle. The stomach had been torn open, the entrails spilling out. The smell was terrible. After that, we looked for any other carcasses out of morbid curiosity.

A sight of splintered bones hanging from branches

caught my attention. I pointed it out to Jaxe and said, "From the days of the villagers, or something more recent?"

"Could be a hunter, trying to keep his bearings."

The trees moved closer together and had us having to turn to move ahead, so subtle at first it would have been easy to overlook. The woodland became increasingly dense, blocking what was in front of you from view, having you wonder if you would soon have no option but to turn back, and suddenly the trees were gone.

What remained of the village rested within a clearing. Decaying wooden houses placed on stilts of varying size and angles. Frayed rope ladders reached into the tallest points of giant trees, revealing more structures and unstable runways moving through the large branches. Everything I looked over appeared ready to collapse, and still I found myself worrying of archers hiding above us. Allen took in his surroundings.

"There must have been so many people here," he said.

"And now there isn't," Jaxe said. "Let's keep moving… This place never feels too right for me."

*

Cold rain was replaced by heavy hailstones as we continued. Despite the hoods of our cloaks, I felt the weight of each sharp fragment of ice as it struck my skull. The cold penetrated our furs. Our hands became red and numb.

"We need to find a place to shelter," I said. "We've

no chance of climbing in this, and even less chance of climbing if we can't feel our hands."

Jaxe said, "It could stop before we reach the rockface."

"And if it doesn't? We need to find a place to shelter," I said once again.

"Raen is right," Allen said. "It's wiser to find a place now, then to reach the rockface and have to turn back."

Jaxe shook his head but gave no verbal disagreement. He must have known I was right. We had long left the shelter of the trees; all we had now was protruding rocks and paths of waterlogged earth. If any one of us had been a little older, a little wiser, we would have known to stop within the treeline when we had the chance.

The hail stopped as we ventured on, but an impenetrable darkness fell long before we could find anywhere to rest. We moved cautiously, for fear of falling from a great height, and we talked constantly, to be sure we remained near. The sound of thunder rolling overhead was warning that rain could soon fall again. When lightning decided to strike, I was certain that Destiny had smiled upon us. I have no doubt that Allen and Jaxe must have been just as foolish.

That moment of almost blinding light revealed the open mouth of a cave, an old and twisted tree placed before it like a long-serving sentry.

"Did you see that?" Allen said into the darkness, his voice filled with hope. "Did you see that? Did you see it?"

"Cave," I said as I took a hold of his forearm, more fearful of losing him now than ever before. "We can shelter there."

I knew the direction to take for us to reach it, but fear claimed my thoughts. I was scared we would wander into the darkness and freeze to our deaths, salvation only a short walk away. I longed for lightning to light the path once more, but the sky refused to assist us. Of course, we all felt it the moment we took our first step within. The air became still and cooler. In the distance, a sound of running water. Jaxe said, "Wait a moment," and I heard him drop his satchel to the ground and rummage through it. The brief sparks of light as he took to striking two pieces of flint together were as magical as the previous display of lightning.

Jaxe had carried small branches in his possession. Far too small to be used as torches but, bundled together, could welcome a fire.

In what felt to me like another blessing, fire came willingly. I laughed. I laughed because, had I not, I would have cried.

*

We found a couple of dry branches scattered along the floor of the cave. Each of us claimed one and held it to the flames. Torches in hand, we took a good look around. The sloping ground was wet, but it would keep us from the worst of it. A weak fountain poured drinking water in one corner. We took turns, drinking greedily at it. It was cold and it tasted of old metal, but it was exactly what we needed. The only problem was once we had had our fill, we soon realised how hungry we were. We all felt it. Not one of us said it.

We headed back to the warmth of the fire. Each

one of us, dripping wet, was surely feeling the cold now. Allen wiped his hands as best he could against his cloak and took to rolling some cigarettes. He tossed one over to Jaxe before he even had to ask. Jaxe grunted by way of thanks, tried lighting it over the fire at arm's length and lost half of it to the flames. But he didn't complain. He happily started smoking from what remained.

"Getting warm, dry and rested should be our immediate priority," he said. "We can hunt something when it gets lighter."

Allen looked to me and said, "I think that's best."

"It is," I said. "We'd be fools to head back out there."

Jaxe blew cigarette smoke into the air. "We should decide who's taking watch, and when."

"I don't mind going first," I said.

"Fine by me," Jaxe said. "Either one of you can wake me when you decide it's my turn."

He took a final pull on his cigarette and flicked what was left into the fire. Without another word he placed his satchel down on the ground and rested his head on it, body curling up close to the fire. Allen gave me a pitiful look.

"Get some sleep," I said.

"You're sure?"

"I'm sure," I said. "I'll wake you when it's time."

"Thank you."

Allen smiled and repositioned his satchel. I'm sure he was asleep the second his head fell upon it.

For a long time, there was nothing but the sound of the winds rushing beyond the mouth of the cave. I threw some extra branches on the fire and the sound of crackling wood lasted a couple of seconds and no longer. Allen and Jaxe slept on, their chests rising and falling with each breath that went unheard.

When I first heard the muttering sound, I took it to being one of them talking in his sleep. It grew a little louder, still too low for me to make out what was being said and I realised then it was coming from one of the darkest recesses of the cave.

Nobody could possibly be there. We had taken in our surroundings and saw no one. There was no way another could have entered the cave without my noticing. But the muttering continued, and I stared at the darkness it came from, wondering if exhaustion was to blame, or madness.

He hurried out from the dark shadows and moved across the cave. Startled, I was on my feet and ready to strike before it dawned on me that he was quite transparent.

"I must tell you about Natalia," he muttered, looking at me for a second before he walked out into the violent winds. I watched him walking on, growing fainter as he did so, and felt the strongest desire to follow.

Jaxe's arm moved forward, his hand taking hold of my ankle. I looked down at him. Eyes still closed, he looked to be sleeping.

"Careful," he said on opening them. "Ghasts don't necessarily experience time as we do, and most are a little mad. He could have a warning that could save your life, but he could just as easily be leading you to your death."

Jaxe removed his fingers from my ankle and merely

stared at me. Whatever decision I was to make would be mine and mine alone.

It took me just a moment to get a torch burning, and another to hurry after the spectre. Those first steps I took on the frozen, solid ground sounded as if I were walking over broken glass. I stopped and blinked rapidly, the harsh winds feeling as if they were trying to pluck out my eyes. Mist crawled over the earth. The ghost looked to have disappeared and I found myself unwilling to accept that. Turning desperately, I caught sight of it wandering in the direction that we would be headed at first light. Already, the apparition was almost impossible to see. Not wanting to lose it, I gave chase.

The winds seemed all the more determined to keep me back. No matter how I struggled to move quickly, the distance between the ghost and me never seemed to change. Cold gusts pulled at my cloak in an attempt to lift me from the ground. Those same winds removed a layer of clouds from the crescent moon, and light found my immediate surroundings. The ghost of the mountain had simply disappeared. The winds, albeit briefly, were gone just as unexpectedly.

It was the newfound silence that allowed me to hear the low growl.

I turned slowly, without any sudden movements, and saw the mountain wolf. Almost as white as snow. The burning torch had its eyes look like they were made of solid gold. The beast released another low growl, lips curling back to reveal sharp fangs.

Busch had told me of these animals. He had claimed the fur at their necks was thick, and the skin excessive, and so you had to cut much deeper than you could imagine to seriously injure one.

He had also said, like most wild and savage animals, they feared fire.

"Back," I said, and I quickly swept the air in front of me with the torch as I gave the command. The wolf flinched but growled again and slowly edged forward, never taking its eyes from me.

"Back," I said again, cautiously moving forward as I made another swiping motion with the torch. The wolf growled all the louder, now baring every fang in its mouth, and prepared to charge. My hand took hold of the hilt, right before the wolf leaped at me. I barely managed to sidestep the animal and although its body was against my blade for only a fraction of a second, I felt the weight was nearly enough to push me off balance.

Turning on my heels, my heart froze as I believed myself to be slow. I turned, expecting the wolf to be upon me, jaws snapping. Instead, I saw the beast on its side, panting heavily as a deep wound across its stomach bled onto the ice. It was all so pitiful for that instant. Then the winds appeared to howl in protest at what I had done and reminded me of how unforgiving the environment was.

Hearing fast approaching footsteps, I turned in panic.

Jaxe. He was laughing, though it was almost impossible to hear him over the cries of the wind.

"Good work," he said, his arm going around my shoulders. "There's enough meat to see us through the next few days."

The wolf was heavier than I would have imagined. The icy ground made it difficult, but we managed to carry it back to the warmth of the cave. Allen was still sleeping.

"Get some sleep," Jaxe said as he looked the carcass up and down, "I'll get this done, then wake Allen so I can rest."

*

Everything within the cave was held in the glow of pure light when I woke. Allen, smoking close to what remained of the fire, smiled to me. "Some night I missed," he said.

I rubbed the sleep from my eyes and stiffly repositioned my body so that I was sitting. Congealed blood made a trail from where I had last seen the body of the wolf, leading beyond me. I turned my head and stood, looking to see where it led. The rocks nearest the fountain were almost black with the blood that had been spilled.

"We've got good cuts of meat," Allen said from my back. "Unseasoned, but just what we need. You're lucky you were asleep, it meant we couldn't put any in your satchel. I don't think me or Jaxe will ever clean the oils from inside of ours," he laughed.

I stretched and turned to face him. "Where is Jaxe?"

Allen laughed like a mischievous boy of half his years and glanced to the ground before looking back to me. "He's gone off to hang what remained of the wolf," he said. "He likes the idea of scaring whoever placed the bones you saw in the branches."

Jaxe returned soon enough. He was amused at whatever he had done, but I didn't mention it at all. I simply left him and Allen to their quiet chuckling as we continued moving on. Mist seemed to be coming from the ground and the rockface we were walking to. It curled and danced within the wind.

We had already noticed the vultures overhead before we made our discovery, just as we had seen them pecking at something before the rockface we would have to climb. Nothing could have prepared us for what it was.

A small boy, no older than six or so years. The birds had made a mess of him, but it was the fall that had killed him. Allen looked upward, then back down to the broken body at our feet.

"Some monster threw him to his death," he said, and he was so angry he was close to tears.

"No," Jaxe said, examining the body on his hands and knees, "he fell, but there's nothing to show that he was *thrown*. The dirt on his hands and under his nails says he was climbing. Damage to his nails could be a sign he lost his hold."

"Who was he climbing with?" I said, "To come all this way just to be left here…"

"We knew we would have to keep going," Jaxe said, "at least now, we know we're sure to find someone."

"And they'll die for this," Allen said, "I swear they will."

We climbed with a new sense of determination. The rocks were slick with moisture and the winds grew strong as we scaled higher and higher, but nothing would stop us. Nothing could stop us. Allen was determined to find his answers, to find his killer, and his ascension was reckless because of it. I could hear his ragged breathing, just as I could hear each and every time he had to quickly reposition himself to prevent a sudden drop to his own end. He ignored my calls to slow down, even when he caused stones to tumble down towards me.

"You're going to get us both killed!"

He didn't stop. Not for a single moment. He kept on moving higher and higher until he reached a ledge and pulled himself out of sight. When he didn't reappear within a couple of seconds, I started to panic.

"Where's he gone?" I said for Jaxe to hear.

"Stay calm and keep climbing; we'll find out soon enough."

Jaxe was the second of us to pull himself up. He turned back almost immediately and reached down, giving me his hand and pulling me onto the shelf. There was more than enough room for us to stand. We could also take another thirteen steps before we were against the mountain wall again. Allen had already taken some twelve steps. He was knelt near an opening that would be just about possible for us to squeeze through. I thought it was the hole he was examining, but I was wrong.

A fire had burned close to the opening, and it was the ashes that had captured his attention. Blue ash resembling chalk dust marked the stone ground. Charred bird bones and branches made a crude half circle. I thought Allen was focusing on it out of desperation, hoping to show some knowledge to rival Jaxe's after he had studied the dead child's remains. I was wrong. He knew exactly what he had found.

"A *summoning fire* was made here," he said.

"A summoning fire?"

Allen looked to us for the first time since he had reached this spot. "My father told me all about them," he said. "It's an old, old magic, mostly practiced by the nomads. It calls people to you."

"It could explain the lights people had seen," I said. "Maybe even the boy we found."

"Yes," Allen said in agreement, turning back to face the dark opening. "I bet, if he hadn't fallen, the boy would have crawled through here…"

He quickly tried to crawl through the space but was unable to because of his satchel. He briefly returned to his knees to remove the bag from his shoulder. Jaxe didn't ask him what he was doing. We already knew. There was no discussion to whether we were doing the right thing, no discussion on who should be leading the way.

Freed of his satchel, Allen crawled through the narrow space with ease, disappearing into the open mouth of darkness.

"Allen?"

"I'm still here," he said. "There's room to stand, room to walk. You need to see what is in here."

It was a spacious cavern. Stalagmites running in a curved line on the floor were matched, like a mirror reflection, by stalactites on the ceiling. Combined with the warm air circulating all around us, it gave the impression of being in the mouth of a monster.

"Look," Allen said as he pointed ahead, "over there."

A faint, almost invisible glow came from within a

narrow tunnel. It was an unnatural light. You'd be a fool to investigate it. I swallowed and took my first steps to it, hearing nothing but my own breathing. I took a breath before stepping into the passage and thought it would never leave me as I turned and saw what lay ahead.

Dozens of ghasts, one next to the other, running all the way to the end of the tunnel until it turned out of sight. More of them were possibly beyond the turn.

Their lips were still, but I could hear their whispering.

A hand fell atop of my shoulder. Gasping managed to pull me back from the edge.

Jaxe, wanting to know what had taken such a hold of me. He said, "I've never seen anything like this."

"No," I said, "I'll bet no one has."

Being reminded how I wasn't the only living soul in there encouraged my breathing to return to normal. Despite the trail of dead right in front of me, I was able to see things more clearly and search for the finer details… How the walls of the tunnel were covered by the outlines of hands. Outlines carefully traced with charcoal.

"Can you hear them?" Wide eyed, Jaxe said to me, "Can you hear their talking?"

"Yes."

He grinned, then almost chuckled. "It's good to know I'm not going mad," Jaxe said, and he slowly walked forwards, passing through the spectres as if he couldn't see them. The sight momentarily stunned me. Allen was right behind me, watching in his own sense of disbelief. If he hadn't been there, it's possible I would have made a run for the opening we had crawled in through like snakes. The way Allen looked to me, I'm sure I could have convinced him to come with me. I swallowed, looked beyond the ghasts and, once my eyes were on Jaxe's back, moved onward.

The first footsteps were the hardest. A breath was stolen with every cold ghast I walked through. My legs were heavy, and the whispers of the restless spirits became deafening until there was only silence. I focused on my own breathing. I tried not to look into the frozen eyes of every ghast stood before me. I tried to focus on Jaxe's back.

Jaxe.

A sudden hatred for him filled me. I couldn't understand it, but I didn't question it, not for a single moment. The dead were no longer there. All I could see was Jaxe, walking directly ahead of me, and my feelings were of hatred and betrayal. I felt my lips twitch, felt my face contort with disgust. I felt my hand take a hold of my sword. It would be easy to kill him. I was certain he deserved it.

Then just as suddenly, I caught glimpses of divine beauty and heard her delicate laughter. Brown hair and lips that must surely taste as sweet as honey. Hazel eyes merely hinting at such a beautiful, intelligent soul. I blinked a tear from my eye and quickly pulled my hand from my blade. The hatred had gone as easily as it had first appeared. The ghasts before me had also returned as had their tormented whispers.

Jaxe stopped for a moment, then turned out of sight. My heart froze and I hurried for him in a clumsy jog, desperate to reach him before he could be harmed.

I joined Jaxe in another spacious cavern. The walls

curved around us. Men had clearly taken tools to the walls, for the shape could not have been natural. Antlers with burning candles at their points hung from rusted chains attached to the domed ceiling. In the centre of the room, a domineering figure sat in a throne. Ancient skin beneath thick furs had become as leather or forgotten parchment. Eyes without a hint of colour. A sinister smile caused by age causing lips to rot away from the teeth. To the left of the throne, a double-bladed battle axe that looked too heavy to lift, a handprint of blue dust staining the haft. To the right, an animal skull of some kind, horns protruding from its sides. The bone was so polished, I could see the millipede crawling along it without having to take a step closer.

I said, "Whose throne room is this?"

Jaxe pointed up to the ceiling and I saw it was covered in ancient runes. Markings of the old tongue. I only remembered Allen had travelled alongside us on hearing him catch a breath at my back.

"We can't be here," he said in a panic, "this can't be real, I've seen this place in nightmares forgotten until now!"

Each one of us freed our blades as the archaic body on the throne got to its feet and looked over each of us. The first thing I noticed was how it drew in a breath and slowly released it. It was breathing. That meant it must have been a living creature that could be killed. The second thing I noticed was the palms of its hands were stained blue. My eyes flickered back to the axe, then quickly back to the creature. Whatever it was, it had been behind the summoning fires.

"Raen," Allen said, "you have to go. You have to run."

The creature returned to its chair and spoke in a hollow voice of age and ruin.

"You are no interest to my cause, and I am capable of granting mercy," it said. "Go now, and praise thanks to Despair for every breath you take from this moment."

My voice was cold and measured, despite the hatred that spilled into me. "The children," I said, "what have you done with them?"

"You have to run," Allen repeated. "Raen—"

The creature tilted its head towards me. "I gave them in Despair's honour," it said, "as I will many more, to see him released from unjust imprisonment in his sister's realm."

Jaxe denied me the courtesy of a warning of any kind. He charged at the black priest with his sword ready, and I wondered if that was the key to gaining your name.

Impulsiveness.

It took a heartbeat for me to see how we had underestimated our opponent. He looked like he was ready to crumble into dust, but he was on his feet before Jaxe was on him. There was startling fluidity in those limbs. In one movement he had plucked the horned skull from his side and slipped it over his face. In another he had kicked Jaxe back and rolled over the throne, claiming the axe from its resting place without difficulty.

"Raen," I heard Allen say, but it was too late. I was already lunging towards the creature. He deflected my blade at the last instant, but Jaxe was there immediately after, his own sword breaking the axe haft in two.

It didn't deter our enemy. He accepted having two weapons as easily as having one. Quickly stepping back, he found the time to slip under my defences and forced the pointed end of the haft into my side. Shock struck me before I could truly understand what had happened. Busch had told me being stabbed felt a lot like taking a punch. He had lied. I felt the object puncture skin and muscle. I felt it force its way *inside* of me, and I felt my body try to keep a hold of it as it was pulled free of the flesh.

I heard blood splatter across the stone ground.

I tasted blood in my mouth.

Jaxe hadn't noticed, or he didn't care. He went on with his attack as I stumbled back and released my sword. My hand clamped against my side. It was wet. Warm. I could feel the weight of the blood pumping against the palm of my hand. And I could feel my legs trembling, preparing to drop me. Allen took a hold of my elbow with a strength I didn't know he possessed and turned me to face him. I didn't even recognise him.

"Go," he said, "run! We'll keep it from you."

I rushed for the tunnel without hesitation, not once looking back to see how my companions were coping. All that mattered to me at the time was my survival.

My shoulder connected with the wall of the tunnel. Pain shuddered down one side of my body. There was one second where the pain didn't matter, I thought I was free.

I only remembered the ghasts when I lifted my head and saw them all. I saw them all turn and look at me with a hungry interest. They came moving towards me, reaching out to touch me.

And I laughed.

I laughed at my own defeat as their coldness smothered me. I laughed even when I dropped down onto my hands and knees, cold fingers reaching for my mouth. Dozens of words being spoken all at once.

Low to the ground, I realised how it was littered with bones. The bones of many children. I clutched my bleeding wound and rolled onto my back and tried to focus on the dark ceiling as the ghosts swarmed all over me. All talking. All reaching for me, as if desperate for my undivided attention.

"You should know Natalia—"

"—requests, and what is to become—"

"You're gonna come around—"

"Demanding the shadows—"

I recognised the plant that flowered in the darkest crevices above me. The citadel had warned us all about it. About how it could cause hallucinations that pushed the strongest of minds to temporary insanity. And I was laughing all over again. I was still laughing as the light of a sun began to fill the tunnel. I laughed, thinking if this was to be how it ended, then it could have been a lot worse.

There was the blinding light, and there was silence.

He came to me as an outline, a silhouette walking out from the great light. His voice was low. He spoke quietly, but every word was clear as polished crystal.

"A follower of old magic, hoping to free an ancient god, by use of sacrifice," he said. "He may have proven himself successful, but we needn't worry about that. Not now."

He knelt before me and placed a hand gently on my cheek. Even inches apart, he was nothing but a living silhouette. I felt his eyes move over my wound.

"This will not do," he said, and there was humour as gentle as his touch in those words. "You deserve a greater destiny than this.

"You know the stories of the gods, of trickery and betrayal," he said, "and still man tries to prove he is beyond such acts. Such notions of nobility have caused the deaths of many good men. You would do well to remember that, Raen Caleb. A wife and child may come to thank you for it."

He moved back an inch and was gone, along with the light he had brought with him. The tunnel no longer looked so special. Even most of the ghasts had deserted it, and those that remained seemed to have no interest in me. I looked up to the plants hidden along the ceiling and smirked. How much of my time here really happened? How much of my time out of here really happened? Was I really a young warden in search of a name? Had I really been raised in the citadel? Did the citadel exist outside of my own mind?

Water was dripping somewhere. Once I acknowledged that sound, it was easier to accept the sounds of metal striking metal. Of Exhausted grunts. I looked to my hand. The palm was smeared in blood and wet earth. I examined where the wound at my side had been. The skin was bloody but, underneath it all, there was nothing but a painful-looking bruise.

I pressed my back against the wall, got to my feet by digging my heels into the ground. I looked for my sword and remembered I had discarded it in the chamber. Jaxe called something out, but I didn't hear what.

Jaxe and Allen were still in there, still fighting that black priest.

I made my way back to them all.

Allen was bleeding from a small cut above his right eye. Jaxe was now carrying his blade in one hand and one of those curved daggers of his in the other. Their opponent was toying with them. Removed from the action, it was easy for me to see that. They were constantly on the attack and their enemy seemed to be in retreat, but they were humouring the creature.

And not one of them had the time to notice me.

I got down low and hurried into the cavern, scooping the weapon I had dropped from the damp ground in silence. My sounds were easy to ignore. And I remained low and silent as I crept through the shadows, waiting where the monster they fought would eventually come.

I didn't have to wait too long.

As the creature came backstepping in my direction, I hurtled through the darkness and plunged my sword into his back. Blood, thick and black as tar, trickled out of the wound. Beneath its helmet, the monster may have even gasped. Even Allen and Jaxe both looked surprised, and who can blame them? They looked to the blade that had seemed to burst from their opponent's gut, then they looked beyond him and finally noticed me.

Jaxe grinned and cried out as he moved forward, severing one of the child-killer's hands from the wrist. He didn't stop there. He took another step, turned and forced the blade of his curved dagger into its side. Once the creature had dropped to its knees, Allen took the opportunity to plunge his blade into its chest. All four of us, as still as stone, panting for breath. My eyes moved over each of the mortal injuries we had made. Each one, slowly releasing that foul blood.

"You," the creature struggled to say, "you have no idea what you have done. Despair would be our only hope, and now he will remain imprisoned."

Jaxe laughed and gave a flick of the wrist before dragging the curved blade upwards. The monster would have slumped forward, if it hadn't been for the weight behind Allen's blade keeping it up. I took my opportunity. Stepping back allowed me to pull my sword from it, then my blade cut through the air and severed the head from the neck. Allen swallowed. He withdrew his own blade and our enemy hit the ground. We had slain the killer of children and now, we didn't know what to do next. The three of us stood in stoney silence, first looking to the body at our feet, then to one another. I looked to Jaxe and said, "Have you ever encountered something like this?"

"Once," he said, "another nameless figure that claimed to have sworn a pact of allegiance to some power or other. They're most likely exaggerated claims and boasts to try and scare men of the blade from challenging them."

Allen looked to me. "Your wound," he said.

"Not as bad as it looked," I said quickly. "You're bleeding."

"Yes," he said, and he briefly held the back of his wrist against the cut over his eye. "He caught me with his elbow."

Jaxe got down on his hands and knees to examine the two halves of the battle axe. "It's always an idea to look for items of value during the peace that follows," he said. "Treasures. Weapons. The rulers of the towns will often trade good coin for something they can use to tell a tale."

"Does the king have no claim to these?"

Jaxe smiled. "The king doesn't know about them. To me, that means he mustn't care."

Jaxe got to his feet, leaving the shattered weapon where it had fallen.

"Our work is done," he said, "we may as well start back."

*

Sleet travelled on the cold winds. We journeyed back down the mountain in silence, each of us deep in our own thoughts. I considered all that Allen had said, his talk of nightmares and of how much importance he found in my having a way to escape and wanted to ask him about it. For a reason I couldn't quite explain, I didn't want Jaxe to hear the discussion. I held my tongue because of it.

We claimed shelter in the same cave we had used before and washed the dirt and dried blood from our bodies in the spring. The wound I had suffered remained just a painful-looking bruise, and I caught Allen looking at it with an interest that rivalled my own. As the chill and ferocity of the winds increased, we decided it best to spend another night there.

The fire we built rid us of the worst of the cold, but silence refused to abandon us. We smiled and joked but such displays were only brief. I don't think any one of us slept. Come first light, we were moving all over again. We passed the old village and found it exactly as we had fist found it – in utter abandonment. Still, I found myself expecting to see someone step out from one of those huts, or placed on a runway high amongst the branches. But we saw no one until we reached the burning torches of Abuscrombe at the foot of the mountains. The people glanced at us in passing but quickly looked elsewhere. Not one of them offered a greeting or asked what we had encountered. Jaxe made it clear he intended to claim his horse and be gone. I said, "Won't you be drinking with us?"

"No," he said, and he smiled. "We have returned from the end of the world, and I intend to celebrate it with a woman of quality you won't find in a town like this."

The insult had been spoken loud enough for those passing to hear, and I knew it had been intentional. Of course, the most he achieved was a few quick glances followed by hurried steps.

"Until we meet again," I said.

"Yes… I'm sure we will. In time."

Jaxe took his horse and rode on. Allen rolled a cigarette and released something of a sigh that had me wonder if he disliked Jaxe. It reminded me of how, when in the presence of ghasts, I had felt a deep and unexplainable hatred for him. Enough for me to consider running my blade clean through his back.

"Let's get a drink at the tavern," Allen said, "and rest

at the fire. Maybe even see if we can find a maid almost capable of reaching Jaxe's impossible standards."

I laughed at that one.

"I think a drink and a little company is what we need."

We made our way to the tavern. The trail of blood that had been spilled out of the door had been cleaned away. Inside, we got a couple of drinks and a table. The mood of the other drinkers was more joyful than it had been during our last visit. A couple of drunken men with instruments performed songs and were applauded by those nearest. It all put Allen and me at ease. We laughed and we joked about old times. Whenever I remembered his talk of nightmares and how he had told me to leave him and Jaxe to face the creature in the mountains alone, I pushed my concerns to one side and focused on the joy. I could ask him for all the details when we were travelling between towns. As he took to rolling another cigarette I said, "How long should we stay here?"

He shrugged. "The night, at least," he said. "Jaxe may have made a tall claim, but he's probably going to find a room at the first town he comes to."

"No," I said, "how long should we stay in Abuscrombe? One week? Two?"

Allen pulled smoke into his lungs and slowly released it. "I can't imagine anything ever happens here," he said. "It's a farming town leading onto nothing but cursed mountains."

"Exactly. Maybe we could make the most of the quiet for a time, before moving on. Spend a day or two here and there as we make our way home."

Allen said, "You still think it's time to return?" on bringing his drink to his lips. The look on his face betrayed him. It showed me how he wanted to return as much as I did.

"Don't you? It could be what we need, just to spend a week in our own beds and eat good food."

Allen considered it, or pretended to, and nodded his head. "We conquered the Black Mountains and killed a creature of magic," he said proudly. "We may have earned our names."

I heard the barman over the laughter and the music. I heard the dread in his voice as he said, "Martyn, don't!"

A tall, wiry man in furs headed our way. He didn't care how he barged by people trying to enjoy the night. As he drew nearer, I saw the snowflakes in his matted hair and how the cold outside had turned his skin red. Allen was sitting with his back to him, still enjoying his time, until he caught sight of my face. He turned in his chair to get a good look at what had captured my attention. The man, Martyn, stopped close to us, eyes fixed on me.

The mood in the tavern had changed. People had fallen quiet. Most lowered their heads. Almost all of them tried to hide the fact they were now looking towards us with interest. I returned Martyn's gaze as Allen stubbed his cigarette out on the table. Despite how angry our new arrival was, I smiled at him and tried to present him with a cheery disposition.

"Evening," I said, "friend."

He kept his silence. He didn't even blink. But I noticed the movement of his fingers... How he kept making and releasing his fists. Martyn wanted trouble, and I was young and foolish enough to think I could talk him out of it.

I almost laughed at the situation, and I knew that only made it worse.

I said, "Can I help you? Would you like to join us?"

"You're wardens."

"Yes," I said, and I nodded. "We've sworn allegiance to the king, and to his people."

"We had a warden come through here a couple of nights ago," he said, and I knew full well who he was speaking of. I remembered the trail of blood that had covered the floor on the night we arrived. "The son of a bitch went for my brother."

Allen took his tobacco pouch from his satchel and started rolling a cigarette. He must have thought it was a good idea to show he didn't intimidate easily. I knew it was the wrong play to make, and that it would be for the best if I held Martyn's interest. Before I could say anything else, Allen looked to him and said, "Was he defending himself?"

"Defending himself?" Martyn said, "All he asked was the bastard's reason for being here, and a wound from the blade was his answer! He suffered for days and nights before peace came to him!"

"There must have been more to it than *that*."

Martyn had heard enough. He had pulled Allen to his feet and close towards him in an instant. I was on my feet, freeing my blade and clambering over the table. It had looked like he was punching Allen in the body as Allen tried to push him away. Women screamed. Men tried to place as much room between them and us as they could.

When Allen fell onto his back, I saw the blood at his mouth. The delicate splashes of blood across his pale face. I saw the bloody knife in Martyn's hand, blood running onto his skin, and froze. Even Martyn seemed unsure of what to do. He was breathing heavily, shoulders rapidly falling and rising again, with his crazed eyes on my fallen friend. The attacker looked to me as if he had only just become aware of my presence. His eyes flickered. For an instant, he had considered dropping his weapon. Of course, it wouldn't have mattered to me if he had. I kicked Martyn in the chest. He fell back into a group of drinkers wishing to have no association with him and what was to follow, so they pushed him back towards me. I stepped to the ground and swung my sword as he was still stumbling forward. The blade cut deep into his neck. He turned still. His eyes widened as he began to convulse, choking on his own blood. He pressed his hand against the wound as soon as I had freed my sword from him. Blood hurried from between his fingers until he lost the strength needed to keep them there. Martyn fell face-first to the floor and died without attempting any last words.

"Allen," I said, releasing my sword and dropping to my knees. Lifting his head only caused the blood to run from his lips a little faster.

"Raen," he said, and he sounded as if he were falling into a dream, "I know it now, I know it's all about faith. The dreams, the nightmares…"

"Allen," I said. He was dying. I knew there was no hope of saving him, and all I could think to say was his name.

"Every step reveals a new path," he said, and he was gone.

I knew all eyes were on me. The people were too scared to risk enraging me by trying to leave. Tears appeared at my eyes. I closed my eyelids tight, until I was certain they were gone, and then I slowly lowered Allen's head to the ground and rose to my feet.

"I want him prepared for burial," I said, "and he is to be brought to the lands of Sir Caleb."

Not one person made an attempt to move. Breathing hard, I lifted my sword and looked over them. For a moment, I considered cutting them all down, one-by-one, and I don't doubt they were aware of this.

"I said he is to be prepared for burial and taken to Sir Caleb," I said. "Do any of you challenge this decision?"

One woman hurried forward, quickly followed by another and another. Calls were made for clean cloths and water. Those that weren't seeing to Allen lowered their gaze and kept their silence. The barman looked to me and took to pouring ale into a tankard with a trembling hand. "A drink," he said, "in honour of your friend…"

I caught sight of someone taking hold of Allen's satchel and snatched it from them.

"Forgive me," they said, "I thought he could have personal items to be bound with."

I sheathed my blade and flung Allen's satchel over my shoulder before taking hold of my own. Drinkers desperately tried to move aside as I made my way to the bar, claiming the jug instead of the tankard. The barman apologised to me as I stepped out into the cold night air.

A party of four left on horseback the following morning with Allen's covered body on the back of a plain cart. Martyn's remains may have gone, left on the floor of the tavern. I had resisted the urge to go back inside for more ale and spent the night sat atop of a small fence. I had watched people hurrying to their homes, desperate not to make eye contact with me.

I watched them take the body out of the town, then I looked over my hands. They were filthy again. Dried blood and dirt. It had become a common sight. I looked to them and knew it was the blood of a dead friend, as well as the blood of a dead enemy, and opened the satchel.

Wolf meat. Bundles of matches, bound together by thread. A fold of striking paper. A pouch of tobacco. I moved everything but the tobacco into my own satchel. I knew the nearby outpost would be happy to trade good coin for the satchel and tobacco, not to mention Allen's horse. They would pay significantly more for the matches, but they were too valuable for me to part with. Eventually, the barman stepped outside and came towards me. He had a dirty cloth at his side, as if it were his attempt at displaying a white flag.

"I'm sorry for what happened," he said, "and I hope you won't judge us all on Martyn's actions. You won't find a man or woman saying he didn't have it coming."

His words were nothing more than a plea for mercy. He wanted me to thank him; to tell him how I knew Martyn had been dealt with, and the good people of Abuscrombe had no reason to fear me. I left him standing there as I claimed my horse and rode on.

*

I traded Allen's possessions at the outpost we had visited days earlier. I didn't get as much as I had expected, but I didn't argue. And they didn't ask what had happened to my companion, although they found out as soon as I dictated the message for them to take to Sir Caleb. I said Allen had been crucial in defeating a being of dark sorcery in the Black Mountains, only to be killed by a coward in the town of Abuscrombe. And of course, I said the coward in question had been dealt with.

I wasted a couple of days in the outpost, handing back coin for a damp room and the occasional bowl of tasteless food and watered-down ale. Once I had grown tired of my own pitiful company, I moved on to a nearby village, finding the fight I searched for in good time. I continued south at a leisurely pace. Home, or what I considered to be home, was the intended destination. That didn't mean I was in any kind of rush.

Martyn was dead, but I hadn't rid myself of the anger he had awoken inside of me. I spent my nights drinking in one nameless location after another, looking for any excuse to pull my blade on those I considered worthy. In my eyes, any man capable of even a small act of theft could easily become capable of killing a warden. My days were spent recovering the night previous. If I had the energy, and I rarely did, I would move on.

I lost track of the days and wondered if Allen had been buried… Whether my letter had reached home.

Then, one night, I dreamed of Allen. We were out in the open, sitting near a fire. I knew he was dead. I didn't want to mention it in case he didn't. Without a care he struck a match and brought it to the cigarette dangling from his bottom lip.

"We have an alchemist to thank for matches," he said once the cigarette was burning unaided. "He was hoping to discover how to turn lead into gold, and he grew tired of the process of making a flame. He felt he was constantly wasting precious time."

"I was there when Busch told us that story."

"Do you ever wonder what was more valuable, in the end?" he said, holding the match upside down as the flame moved towards his fingers like a living thing. "Instant fire has more uses than gold."

"You're right. But that alchemist still longed to turn lead into it."

"And he never succeeded," Allen said. "But you can't deny his discovery changed the way we live, even if it was entirely accidental."

"Is this really why you come to me," I said, "to speak of the creation of matches?"

Allen tossed his match into the fire, where it was immediately consumed. "No," he said. "I came to remind you of what I said, of how every step reveals a new path. Without intending to, you can come to be where you need to be, without even realising."

"Then you came to discuss fate?"

Allen smiled and took smoke into his lungs. "Fate

shows a number of paths to take," he said, "but you alone decide which is best to take. Maybe I shouldn't have tried to reason with Martyn, maybe it was for the best that I did?"

"Then you know you're dead?"

"Yes, I remember it well. What happened after my last breath had been taken," he said with a smile, "is a mystery even to me. But my end and what occurred following it is not important. Not really. I have no more paths to take, yet you have many. You must believe in yourself if you are to choose those that will lead you to where you need to be."

Allen smiled and briefly looked back to the fire. It was a smile that had me doubt I was quite understanding the importance of what he had to say. He looked back to me and opened his mouth and I had no doubt that he was ready to tell me something crucial.

*

Strong hands pulled me from the cot and tossed me to the ground. It was dark. I could smell damp air, just as I could smell stale alcohol on me, but I had no idea where I was or how I had come to be there. I remembered drinking and travelling, but then what?

The hands of the intruder roughly lifted me. I stood for a moment, then I was being pulled back, my heels dragging across the floor, an arm at my throat restricting my breathing. I tried to pull the arm free and failed.

"Drink doesn't suit you."

I had heard that voice before, I just couldn't recall

where or when. My attacker kicked open a door at his back and pulled me out into the pouring rain. I tried desperately to dig my heels into the mud. A flash of lightning claimed the sky and momentarily blinded me. I was still blind as I was pushed to the wet ground. Still blind as I tried to wipe rainwater and dirt from my eyes. Still blind as I felt for my sword and realised it was still in the room I'd been unceremoniously removed from.

Still blind as I was shoved onto my back.

The icy rain continued to fall on me. I heard the roll of thunder and saw another flash of lightning from behind closed eyes. There was no fight inside of me. I didn't even have enough left to look my attacker in the eyes and tell him to get it over with.

"Open your eyes and get to your feet, boy. I spent far too much time in your company for you to die drunk and in the rain."

Busch.

It wasn't easy, but I did as he commanded. Unsteady but on my feet, the sight of him was almost enough for me to lose control and embrace him. Almost, but not quite enough. I stood swaying, suddenly certain I was about to bring up the beer and food I had consumed. Busch stared back at me, emotionless.

"You've paid coin for a roof over your head and you have us standing out here in the rain."

"You're the one who used to say you wouldn't enter any outposts," I said, and I turned to return to the pitiful cabin I couldn't quite remember paying for. Busch had shown me one more thing, I'll give him that. Here I was, staying at an outpost and not one warden had noticed him coming here and dragging me from my cot. Not one person had come to my aid.

The roof was leaking, and the floor was dirt and stones. The bad smell turned a lot worse once Busch had closed the door behind him. There was a table with two chairs. A chipped plate on the table held the remains of the watery stew I had eaten; an upturned jug on the floor had hopefully been drained of all the alcohol it had held before I'd dropped it.

I sat at the table and came close to falling back to sleep. Busch stared at me for a moment, considered taking the free chair and decided against it. "How much did they charge you for this?"

"I don't recall."

"It doesn't matter. Whatever it was," he said, "it was too much."

"Did Sir Caleb show you the message I sent?"

Busch took a breath before responding. "He told me what you had to say. Allen had already been put to the ground before it arrived," he said.

"Have you come all this way to tell me that?"

"No. I've come because Sir Caleb wants you back in time of the next full moon," he said. "Yasmin's engagement to the Weetmain heir is to be made official, and you are expected to attend a private dinner to celebrate their union."

Yasmin. I couldn't remember the last time I had even thought about her. It was hard for me to even picture her, but knowing she was to be married only managed to make me feel a lot worse.

"Allen told me he'd been having dreams," I said, and I could have said it to try and distract myself from the news Busch had just shared, but I could have said it just because I was still a little drunk. "He'd been having premonitions."

"He got that from his mother."

"Is his mother a seer?"

"No. Not truly, anyway. If Allen had been capable of seeing what was to come," Busch said, "he'd still be alive."

I pushed myself back from the table and got back on my unsteady feet. I reached for the blade and realised it wasn't even at my side. I felt foolish. I also worried a little at what Busch would do to me, because he must have known what my intentions had been.

"Never look for signs or dwell on your dreams," was all he said, "there is no order or guidance for the chaos of our lives."

The jug on the ground was empty. I knelt down anyway, picked it up and hoped there was somehow something left for me to drink. Of course, there wasn't a drop.

"We never did get chainmail," I said.

"I saw his body. Chainmail wouldn't have made any difference."

I looked back to him, needing to know whether he had said that to make me feel better. He was unreadable.

"And chainmail is no match for a man prepared," he said. "It's false confidence for a man with doubts."

I nodded; dropped the empty container and reclaimed the chair at the table.

"You are not to blame for his death," Busch said. "The blame falls over two people, and the man in the tavern is buried deepest."

"You're blaming Allen?"

"He must take some responsibility, yes. Allen allowed a nameless bastard in a tavern get close enough to wound him. There was no long game played," he said, "no battle of wits underway. He was bettered by the anger of one man and nothing more."

I smirked and shook my head. "I'll return for the full moon."

"You could return alongside me."

"No," I said, "I still have a couple of things to see done."

Busch nodded, turned and opened the door. He froze for a moment and looked back. "You think my thoughts on the matter are harsh, but I was fond of Allen," he said into his shoulder, "and that is why I worried that unless someone came at him with their metal unsheathed, or unless he was given a command to attack, he would try and reason with the unreasonable."

I reached for the empty jug again, longing for a remaining mouthful somehow overlooked.

"It sounds like you should take some of the blame for his death," I said.

"If that's what it takes for you to learn from this. At the very least, your opponent should be disarmed and on the ground before you make conversation of what's to be done."

The jug was empty, just as I hadn't wanted to admit it was. I took a quick sniff at the neck before placing it down on the table. "There's no drink left," I said. Truth be told, I was probably hoping Busch would suggest we get some to share.

"There are only two reasons to drink." Busch said, "To have people know you've reason to celebrate, or reason to give up."

I took a breath, released it and leaned across the table, just so I could knock the jug back onto the floor. A small part of me had been eager to blame Jaxe for Allen's death. I'd never wanted to spend too long looking back. Back at how I had known Martyn had meant him harm. Jaxe hadn't been there. The man might have thought Jaxe had given him a reason, but only Allen had given him a chance.

I had blamed Allen's murder on Jaxe without difficulty. I had reasoned my unexplainable hatred for Jaxe in the heart of the Black Mountains had been down to a part of me knowing he was no good. During the following acts of violence I had later committed, particularly those when I was drunk, I imagined I had been striking him down.

Busch had me question my thoughts without breaking into a sweat.

Sitting at the table in the dank cabin, I listened to the rain come to a halt. After a while, sunlight began to creep through the gap beneath the door. Allen and I should have followed Jaxe's lead and rode on from Abuscrombe. We should have kept with Jaxe.

That's what I thought back then, anyway.

Sometimes I wonder how differently things would have turned out if it hadn't been for Busch. I'd have never gone on to find Jaxe. Never befriended him the way I did or earned my name following what transpired in Collison. We may never have gone at one another like we did.

But I guess I'll never know. Not now.

Sitting at the table, I felt like I owed him an apology.

When the outpost keeper let himself in and said I would have to pay extra if I was planning on staying any longer, I gathered my things and rode on. There was still plenty of time before the next full moon, and I intended to find Jaxe before I returned home.

I stopped drinking and took to feeling a lot better because of it. I was sure my thoughts were my own again. Really, I was most probably trying to think how Busch would. Instead of paying for poor accommodation, I returned to camping beneath the stars. The only reason for me to enter inns or taverns was to apprehend wanted men. The only reason for me to stop at an outpost was to see if Jaxe was there or whether anyone had any idea where to find him. A few wardens told me they had seen him, but never recently.

*

I arrived back home in time for the full moon. Some of the men working the land nodded to me as I travelled the long road up to the house, but no one seemed too enthused by my return. No one I recognised, anyway. There was a new maid. We'd never met, but she knew all about me.

"Raen, just look at the state you're in," she said. "Undress and bathe before you present yourself to Sir Caleb. I'll have those filthy garments you are wearing cleaned. You're simply filthy! How could you ever let yourself get like this?"

I didn't protest. I went straight to the room that had been mine, discarding my clothing at the door. A hand gathered them soon enough. I heard talk of somebody drawing a hot bath for me to soak in, but I crawled beneath the covers and fell into a deep sleep.

*

It was dark when I woke.

The bedside candle was burning, and Sir Caleb was sat in a chair at the foot of the bed. It could have been a trick of the light, but for a moment it looked like he was smiling. I sat upright, rubbed sleep from my eyes and yawned without knowing I had been about to. After so long away, the man was an even bigger mystery to me. I wondered if I should apologise for the yawn because of it.

"Welcome home."

"I'm glad to be home."

I know for certain he smiled at that one.

"You say that because you are still relatively young. I have told you how my own father," he said, "had my brother become a warden. At the time, I believe he hated most of it. But when he came of age to marry and start a family, he confessed how he began to miss the long periods from this place. He missed the rush of excitement before and following a fight. He wanted nothing more than to return to the road. Even before he departed this place, I knew he would rather be free than seemingly imprisoned, forced to rule inherited land. But of course, my father had made him swear he would remain with his wife and eventual children. That's how my father was, you see? Determined to guarantee the survival of his name and his bloodline."

I lowered my head and softly said in remembrance, "Allen earned his name."

"And I am sure as many men would agree with you as they would disagree with you," Calcb said, "but the decision was for his father to make, and his father decided Allen did not."

The words struck me like a blow. It seemed impossible that he could make such a judgement.

"Allen killed a creature of sorcery," I said as if to remind him.

"That he did. But he was slain immediately after, and under circumstances his father would rather not have associated with his name."

"Then what now?"

Caleb shook his head. "He has another child," he said, "Stephen will be given the same opportunity to earn his."

"No," I said, "what about the marker to Allen's resting place?"

"It states that a *good son* rests there, and very little else. You may find this harsh, but each father holds his own standard. And sometimes, we should be thankful for that," he said with a laugh, as if a change in the mood could be so easy. "Busch told you of Yasmin. The celebration is to take place tomorrow evening. A small affair, but to confirm it."

"Yes," I said, now as confused as I was tired. "Long ago, I had thought Yasmin was to be a maid."

"She could have been," Caleb said, "but she proved

herself and became a Lady of Caleb. Her marriage will forge a great bond between our two families."

"Was that your reason for taking her from the citadel?"

"It was my hope, and I'm delighted that it was the Weetmains she so delighted. And, you should know," he said, "when the time comes that you have earned your name, you will have opportunity to marry those from other noble families."

Learning I hadn't earned my name was another blow being delivered, all over again.

"But rest," he said on getting to his feet, "I have such plans for tomorrow. Have food and drink prepared if you hunger, have a bath drawn should you long to soak, but rest."

*

There was nothing but utter silence and darkness when I next woke. No burning candle, and a quick glance out of the window showed clouds hiding the moon and stars. But I was starving, and I felt dirty, so I dressed and crept from my room. The thought of waking a servant of some kind crossed my mind, but I decided against it. Downstairs, I helped myself to cooked meats and thick bread. I prepared a bowl of steaming water and was so sure that nobody would appear, stripped naked and washed myself. Even in the light of a single candle, it was easy to see how filthy the water became. I had to empty the bowl and refill it two more times before I felt clean. Once I was dressed, I noticed a pouch of rolling tobacco in the kitchen.

The sight reminded me of Allen and saddened me. I opened the pouch and smiled on recognising the aroma, then I dug within the dried leaves and found rolling papers.

"Here's to you, Allen," I said, and I started to roll a cigarette. Despite how often I had watched him doing it, it was harder than I had ever thought. The finished cigarette wasn't as slim or as tight as Allen's had been. It bulged in parts and was noticeably looser in others. The sight of it had me chuckle to myself. With no matches to hand, I took the cigarette to the candle and brought smoke into my lungs for the first time as the tobacco was encouraged to burn freely. I coughed, sputtered at the new sensation. The taste was far from rewarding. If I hadn't dedicated the act to Allen, I would have tossed the cigarette out. But I finished it for him, despite how it made my legs feel weak. My temples were pounding. I made my way back to my room because of it, stripping again before climbing back onto the cot. Now that I was clean, I could feel the old dirt and grease I had covered the sheets with.

*

It was the sound of the hired hands that next woke me. They crept along the stairs and landing and communicated in brief whispers, but it was loud enough to retrieve me from my dream of the Black Mountains. The rising sun provided the room with enough light for me to see. I contemplated sleeping a little longer but knew my mind was too alert now, and that my body awaited instruction, so I got up and dressed. Looking out the window, I saw men with swords patrolling the grounds as farmers went to work. Some of these men could have been former wardens, others would have been trained by them. It crossed my mind that it could one day be my responsibility to train them, or at least see that they were up to scratch.

The maid I saw on making my way downstairs greeted me in passing, but she kept her voice low to avoid disturbing the master of the house. Stepping outside, I thought for a moment that Allen would be waiting for me. His death seemed to trouble me in a whole new way, now I was back. I tried not to dwell on it, and looked at the men whose work was already underway. There was nothing for me to do here. Sir Caleb had been on to something when he said you missed the road. It dawned on me how it could be an idea to leave the next morning.

I turned on hearing the door being pulled open behind me, was surprised to see Caleb stepping outside. My first thought was that he must have taken to visiting his various women during the early hours of morning.

"I thought you might be awake," he said. "The staff were too loud for me this morning, and it has been years since that was the case! You've awoken the sense of adventure in me."

I didn't know what to say to that, so I smiled at him like I understood him perfectly. I understood him so well, nothing else needed to be said.

"Come," he said, "let's go to the stables and we can go for a ride."

I nodded and fell in at his side without protest. The

workers were surprised to see him so early, especially those at the stable. They seemed concerned that he intended to go out without having breakfast. With Caleb present, I was simply overlooked. They only became aware of me again when he refused the company of guards and insisted that I would be more than enough to handle any situation.

"He returned from the mountains with barely a mark on him," he said. "You would have to be insane to confront him."

One of the men looked to me with undeniable resentment. I looked back at him until he finally averted his eyes and turned away.

Amongst the wildflowers at the very edge of the Caleb land, there was a large slab of rock. Rectangular in shape. A marker made of stone had been placed at one end of it, and carved into it were the words:

HERE RESTS A GOOD SON
VIOLENCE IS A FORM OF REASON

We didn't dismount our horses. Caleb and I looked down at the stone, at the marker. For a time, our horses did the same. I looked out over the sea of flowers and couldn't see another grave. It was like they had put him far out here, alone, because he didn't deserve the honour of being with those that were named.

I remembered the drunk that had claimed his life, and I wished I could go back to that moment and do it all differently. I thought of meeting that man near the door and cutting his throat in front of everybody.

Caleb looked to me and said, "What are you thinking?"

"That he didn't deserve the end he had. We'd made

it through the Black Mountains and killed something beyond an enraged man with a grudge."

Caleb nodded, as if there was any way he could understand, and he sighed. "As a warden, such events are a part of your learning. You should always remember Allen."

"I will."

There wasn't any doubt that he had wanted me to say a little more, but I kept my eyes on the rock and my tongue still. Caleb looked back to the stone. We stared in silence, until he decided we had been silent long enough.

"Allen had stated you were with another companion."

"We were," I said. "We travelled alongside another warden. Liberty Jaxe."

"Jaxe?" Caleb considered the name. "Jaxe as in *Lawrence* Jaxe?"

His question made me feel hopeful.

"Lawrence Jaxe," I said, "who is he?"

"A man of nobility. Land to the north." He said, "I had been told Lawrence has a number of sons, some a little less illegitimate than the others. I suppose Liberty could easily be one of them."

"I would like to see Lawrence Jaxe," I said. "I would very much like to try and find Liberty. There could be much we could learn from one another."

Caleb nodded again, more confidently this time, as if he truly could understand.

"Busch will be able to assist in the matter," he said. "Even if Liberty is no relation of Lawrence Jaxe, Busch knows enough wardens and their kind to find anyone at all."

"When will you speak to him?"

"Soon. First of all we must prepare for tonight's celebratory dinner. And tomorrow," he said, "I will have Busch share all he knows with me. If I must, I will even have him locate Liberty Jaxe on your behalf."

*

A maid drew me a hot bath. I closed the door, locking it out of habit and stripped before slipping beneath the water. Within seconds I felt more relaxed than I ever had before. Even with the sound of hands coming up and down the stairs, of constant movement coming from the kitchen, I began to fall asleep. I felt tears stream down my face, but couldn't explain their appearance, so told myself it was just the steam of the water. Finally, my eyes closed and remained shut. Yasmin's planned marriage shouldn't be a concern, I didn't really know her. She could bring the two families together and I would explore the roads. I could earn the right to my name, without question.

Looking back, I wonder how differently things could have been if I had kept to that plan. The Weetmain heir may not have died at my hands, and Yasmin could have still had a husband beside her. Jaxe could have been stopped before he went too far. Many good people could still be with us.

But these are different stories, and I am running out of time.

THE GREAT UNKNOWN

My mind registered the cold.

For a moment, I was tricked into thinking I had spent the night beneath the stars. Then I fully came around and realised such nights were long behind me. It had been another night in the room I was paying for. It was cold and it had a damp smell about it, but it was the best I could get.

My body took to complaining as soon as I started moving. Dull aches and pains that had been with me longer than I cared to remember. Bones scraped against one another. I reached an aged hand out and placed it atop the cabinet next to the cot. The skin was wrinkled. Loose. Pale, too. Occasionally, I'd still catch sight of a part of me and be a little surprised. The bulging stomach was something I would pretend not to notice.

I got to my feet, weight leaning against the cabinet and involuntarily groaned. Every inch of me protested against my movements. Old age was the true Realm of Damnation. It was the time to envy those you knew that were fortunate enough to die young.

I had dreamed about Allen. I was certain of it. I couldn't remember the finer details, but I examined my sides. Fat skin. A couple of small scars. I could swear that – some days – quite a large scar was there. Those days, I remembered how the black priest wounded me. Other days, I remembered how a lot of my memories of what took place back then were likely to be hallucinations.

There are days when I don't remember any of that. I don't even look for the scar.

I took a step forward and managed to kick the bedpan. Cursed myself for forgetting I had placed it there. Nothing spilled. The contents looked a little bloodier than usual. I looked away; walked over to the moth-eaten curtains and pulled them open. Grey skies over the stone streets of Harlow. No, not Harlow. Harlow was by the sea. This was Mealand. The district of Harcourt, to be precise. Harlow/Harcourt. No wonder I was confused.

My pipe, a pouch of tobacco and a couple of matches were on the window ledge. I packed the bowl. Unsteady hands dropped loose strands of tobacco on the dusty floor. I told myself I could pick it up later and watched the people out on the street. People looking to be left alone, people looking for trouble. They were all lumped together, with not enough space to move. A couple of wardens walked by, and I swear they are getting younger.

I struck a match, got the tobacco burning and started coughing as soon as the smoke neared my throat. Tears streamed from my eyes. Doubled over, I placed the pipe back down on the ledge. My lungs felt like they were trying to jump out of me. The coughing became so bad, I wondered if it would be the cause of my death. It kept me from breathing. There are names I hear from time-to-time. Men I had known. They had died young, and they were still remembered. Noble ends. No one would write about me dying of old age in a place like this. It was unlikely anybody would even notice.

I wiped the tears from my face, turned and made my way back under the covers. When I woke again, the streets sounded a lot busier. I struggled out from the cot a second time. Dressed, I stood and wondered where my blade was. Then I remembered my sword was long gone. It's not like I would have the strength or speed for it, anyway. All I had was the dagger beneath the pillow, where it always rested close beside me. I slipped it behind my belt; tried and failed to remember the man that had put it to my throat a long time ago.

Downstairs, Leonie was reheating stew. She took control of the property following the death of her husband. The only thing worse than her personality, was her looks. She could drain the colour from a summer violet. Squat, with a bulbous forehead and chunky forearms. Sometimes I found myself wondering if she could be the daughter of Arthur Yorn. Other times, I wondered who she reminded me of. I was glad she was willing to accept my coin. Despite her flaws, some lodgers found a way to pay her without finding themselves relieved of coin.

Leonie looked at me and said, "Where is your cane?"

She didn't have any care in her voice. Not about me. The only concern she had about my health was down to her worrying I would no longer be around to pay for the room.

"Cane? I don't use a cane."

"You do," she said, angered in the blink of an eye. "The big staff you use for support!"

The staff had been used briefly. The last winter, I had taken a fall on some ice. Once I had recovered, I traded the staff for something. I can't recall what.

"I don't need it."

"Of course you do," she insisted. "Look at you, you can barely stand upright! And what if you're attacked? You could keep them away with the staff; what chance have you got with that dagger?"

I felt for my pipe. It wasn't on me. It must have been left beside the window.

"Well, I'll be," she said on noticing my searching, "you've actually remembered I'm due payment!"

I was sure I had paid her. Her comment only made me question *when*. Days ago, or longer than that?

"I'll get you your payment," I said, "I have to go to the bank, first."

"I know you have to go to the bank," she said, angrily taking the ladle from the pan and using it to point at me, putting emphasis on her words. I watched thick gravy slop to the dirty floor beneath her. "Any other would have had a warden remove you already! You should think about that next time you take advantage of my kindness."

"A warden will cost you more than I ever could," I said and turned to the door to leave.

"A bounty hunter, then! See if they will show you the same courtesy!"

I smiled at that one. There is only one difference between a bounty hunter and a warden, and that is a bounty hunter is expected to prove they got the right person.

*

The entrance to the bank was guarded by three of Prince Selborne's finest. I usually caught sight of at least one archer on the rooftop. The same wardens circled back on the opposite side of the street. One way in, one way out. Not a single window. It still made sense the place was receiving a little extra attention, the young princess was scheduled to marry King Charles II of Stoneisle. They couldn't risk anything of value falling into the wrong hands.

I thought of the last Lord of Stoneisle and wondered if he was now serving his king in one way or another. As I neared the bank, I thought of the Weetmains for the first time in a long time, and my mind wandered to Yasmin because of it.

One of the guards didn't look the like of me. He stepped in front of the door as I got close, looked down at me with contempt. I had to tilt my head back to look him in the eye. He was big, but he wouldn't have been any trouble if it hadn't been for the years between us. Even now, plenty of ways to get him out of the way came to mind. It was the mind that wanted to do just that, it was the body I couldn't rely on. Too slow. Too sore. It would take me too long to get a good hold of him. My fingers would still be trying to secure a good grip and he would be bringing a solid fist to my gut.

"You're in the way of the door," I said.

He smiled. It wasn't a nice smile. It showed me he was glad that someone had been foolish enough to challenge him.

"Let him through," one of the other guards called. "Look at him, you really expect him to be any trouble?"

That hurt more than any physical blow would have. I'd become a figure of pity. I was too worn and old to pose any serious threat. The guard in front of the door looked to me, smirked, and stepped aside. I didn't thank him. The door was heavy, but I got it open without too much of a struggle and stepped into the bank. Dimly lit and cool. It reminded me of the place of worship on Allsen. I thought back to the hammer I had briefly claimed and wondered how different my life would have been if I had kept it. Would I have still been strong? A little younger?

A lantern was lit. A tall, slender man behind a large table had been responsible. He could have done it to snap me from my thoughts, he could have done it to try and be sure my eyes were only on him. It wasn't enough to keep me from noticing the guards that were sticking to the gloom. Large men, entirely in black. They even wore executioner hoods. They stood still as stone. If you gave these men reason to move, you wouldn't be walking out of here.

I walked over to the table. Knowing I had so many eyes on me and wanting it to appear I hadn't noticed, made me aware of every movement I made. I felt stiff. Unnatural. The man at the table took a fine quill and dipped it in an ink pot. When he realised it was going to take me a little longer to reach him than he had thought, he dabbed his tongue at his lips, trying to decide if he should smile or ask for my name already.

I took the folded scrap of aged parchment from my pocket and carefully unfolded it as I neared the desk.

Nine symbols, five marked out. My wealth had come down to four boxes. I hoped they were better than the previous five I had already emptied.

"Good day to you," he said. "Sir...?"

"No title," I said. "I want you to grab a box of mine," and I placed the piece of paper down in front of him for him to see.

"Of course," he said, and his tongue dabbed at his lips again. "And which can I get for you?"

I looked to him like he was stupid, then down to the meaningless markings that symbolised all I had left. Any could be just as bad as the next. I threw the choice to the dead gods and pointed one out at random.

"This one," I said.

He looked to the symbol for a couple of seconds, then back to me and smiled again. "And may I have your name?"

"Raen."

"A moment," he smiled. He took the lantern, turned and walked away with it. Darkness approached as he drew further away from me. He could probably work fine without the light, he wanted me to see the two guards at either side of the door he was approaching. A solid door of thick iron. I heard him turn a key he could have taken from any pocket. With the door unlocked, he pushed it open and walked into an adjoining room. The solid door closed behind him, and the room became as a moonless night. My ears pricked as I heard the subtle movements of a guard. There was a chance they were trying to get me scared. There was just as much of a chance that one of them was scratching at an itch.

Cold air raced into the room as the solid door slowly opened. Light spilled into the darkness. The keeper returned at a respectful pace with the lantern in one hand and the secure box fate had chosen in the other. It wasn't particularly big. The steel it was made of wasn't particularly thick. The look of it caused me to feel a little disappointed.

He placed the lantern down on the table, then the box beside it. With both hands, he turned the box, so the lock was facing me. The key was already in the lock. He looked up to me, dabbed at his lips once again and smiled. "Your item, Raen," he said. "Would you like for me to turn around?"

"I'm not getting undressed," I said, pulling the box a little closer as I turned the key. It jammed halfway, then completed its turn with a little applied force. I heard worn springs pull free in the mechanism. The lid lifted a little. The man looked to the box, then excitedly to me, then back down at the box. Even the guards were probably a little interested at what it contained. "Let's see what we have," I said to the keeper, and I pulled the lid free. The contents looked a lot more impressive than they really were. Quite a few coins, which I was thankful for, and some precious stones, which were worthless to me. I didn't know anybody that would be able to buy them, not for a fraction of what they were worth, anyway. I couldn't even remember how I came to own them. There was a chance I stole them from somebody just to prove a point. Making a good point can be invaluable – until it isn't.

I looked to the keeper. His eyes were still on the sparkling stones. Given the chance, he probably would have eaten them. I decided to gamble, said, "You happen to know anybody looking to buy these?"

"I," he said, "I'm afraid I wouldn't know where to begin!"

"That's understandable," I said, filling my pockets.

"What would you like me to do with the box?" he asked as I made my way back to the street.

"Reuse it," I suggested, "or melt it down. I won't be needing it," and I stepped back out into the blinding sunlight and came close to drowning in the noises made by a city of fools. Instinctively lowering my head to give my eyes a little time to adjust to the light, I started my way to the nearest tavern.

*

I was sitting in a nameless tavern. It was a place that attracted souls so bad, even the women wouldn't come here in search of a business transaction. It had grown dark outside and I had grown drunk. I thought of the precious stones in my possession and wondered if Leonie would accept them. She would never find anyone to sell them to, but she could be foolish enough to give me my room until I died. She could maybe even give me the entire building. I could see out the rest of my worthless days, offering cramped spaces for those with little possessions.

I patted myself down for my pipe, realised I had forgotten to bring it with me and patted myself down some more anyway. I grumbled, reached for my tankard of something nasty but wet. The man sat down beside me so quickly, I hadn't realised until he was there. He hadn't even asked if I would mind. When I noticed he was rolling a cigarette, I decided that was probably for the best.

"Cold nights we're getting," he said and once he had finished rolling the cigarette, he placed it down on the table and pushed it towards me. He didn't look up. Not yet. He took to rolling another. I may not have seen his face, but I noticed the grey in his hair. He couldn't have been too old. His fingers moved too quickly, and without error. Age hadn't taken to claiming his joints. "I can't remember the nights ever being so cold," he said, and he finally raised his head to look at me once that cigarette was finished. There was something vaguely familiar about him. The eyes, maybe. It's just I would have known them on a younger face. The face he had now was lined by the years, but I found myself suspecting he was a lot older than he looked. The grey stubble looked like something you could cut your hand on.

I lifted the cigarette he had provided and asked, "Do you have a match?"

He smiled at me. He knew I was struggling to place him to a point in time, there was no doubt about it. "Of course," he said, and he struck a match against the table. He used the flame to get his own cigarette burning, then he held the match out in front of me until I had no use for it. I coughed a little as the smoke troubled my lungs.

"All these places," he said with a smile, smoke leaving his mouth, "and all these people? There must be a reason why they are all blending into one and the same. I mean," he continued, "look around you. Just *look*. We trick ourselves into believing things change, but they remain the same. The change is all within us."

I kept my eyes on him, but he didn't seem in any hurry to lose the grin. I blinked, stared at him a while longer, and slowly looked over the people filling the tavern. And he was right. I hadn't noticed it before, but I did now.

The young apprentice sorcerers, arguing over a game of chance.

The man sitting with a large hound beside him. It looked a lot like the wolf I had slain in the mountains. It looked at me with such hate behind its eyes, I felt certain it could have been.

The giant of a figure with furs draped over his broad shoulders and a heavy maul at his back.

A group of men that looked like farmhands of Sir Caleb, and they hadn't aged a day.

Strangely recognisable faces hidden between them all.

"We invented time, because we couldn't cope with the idea of living forever," the man beside me said. "Now, we all convince ourselves that our lives are of the most – or deserve to be of the most – importance. But there are only so many stories that can ever be told. We're just variations of countless people that came first.

"We have aged more than the great heroes of old ever will. We have left them as children to us."

I looked back to him and was about to ask him his name. When he called out for two more drinks, I decided I would ask him a little later.

*

The two of us stumbled out of the tavern. It was late into the night. Thick fog had settled. You couldn't see a thing because of it. Just the damp, heavy mist and the coldness it wrapped around you. The man kept talking. I was too drunk for any of it to make much sense. Too drunk to ask him what he was talking about, or to even ask him to be quiet. Whenever I felt ready to challenge him in any way, he handed me a cigarette. Always something to keep me quiet, or to keep me from thinking too hard. His words went on washing over me.

The fog began to disperse. I saw trees ahead of us. The stone ground had been replaced by tall grass. It was enough to return me to my senses. Not fully, but enough. I wondered how we could have travelled so far.

"Wait," he said, and he held a hand at his side to keep me from taking another step forward. I reached for the dagger at my belt. "There," he said, "you see them?"

I saw them. Seven or eight travellers, huddled around a fire. Only one of the men was keeping watch. I watched them a moment longer, removed my hand from the dagger and said, "They're of no concern."

The man beside me quietly laughed to himself. "This must be the time," he said. "Stay here and watch this…"

Before I could say another word, he silently hurried forward. My hand went for my dagger, just in case the man on sentry could turn violent but quickly pulled back. I told myself that whatever happened would be nothing to do with me.

As he came closer to the group, he started staggering as if he were exhausted or maybe injured. His clumsy movements captured the attention of the man on watch who quickly got to his feet and took a hatchet of some kind from his back.

"It isn't safe here," the man from the tavern called. "The man of the Black Mountains is claiming children, and he will have no problem claiming yours. You will know him by the black furs he does wear, and the horned skull of a beast lost within the darkness that covers his face!"

I couldn't work out the importance of what he had said. Dumbstruck, I moved forward, looked northward and couldn't believe what I saw. The imposing Black Mountains were practically on top of me. Taking a breath, I looked back to the group of travellers. The man that had brought me here had vanished, and the sentry was desperately waking members of his party.

He froze, slowly raised his head to look in my direction. I quietly stepped back, hoping to find myself returned to the sea of fog, and woke on my cot. The room was dark, but I could make out my surroundings. Memory of the dream remained with me. I felt for my dagger and found it behind my belt. It took a second for me to realise why I had done that. Hearing the sound of movement, I sat upright and looked to the door. It was gently closing. Feeling at my pockets, I found the precious stones and coin remained, though some had spilled across the covers. If someone hadn't come to rob me, what were they doing here? I got to my feet as quickly as I could manage and rushed to the door, pulling it open. What I saw took my breath away.

The corridor stretched out for eternity. The walls, the floor, even the ceiling, looked to be black glass. I stepped forward. Reflective glass. I saw myself at either side, rolling back over and over again. I looked at my feet. It was the same. Finally, I looked up and saw my aged reflection looking down at me. Could this still be a dream? It certainly didn't feel like one. Bringing my gaze down, the reflections disappeared. Now, behind the glass, I saw swirling tides of grey mist that reminded me of my journey with the stranger. Poison, or dark magic, seemed the likely explanation.

I cautiously moved forward, unable to tell whether I was dreaming or hallucinating. It was hard to tell which could be more dangerous.

The mist to one side of me began to separate, revealing a brief glimpse of the citadel, and then it was covered all over again. Moving at a snail's pace, I tried to keep my eyes straight ahead, but it was hard. Quick glimpses of different locations were revealed and taken away just as suddenly.

Two young wardens travelling on horseback.

A glow near the summit of those bastard Black Mountains.

An army of revenants charging the last line of men.

It took my foolish, old mind a while to realise I was witnessing scenes of my own life. My younger self appeared, sleeping soundly in a ship's cabin, and remained for me to examine. Open-mouthed, I watched myself for a while. Reaching out, preparing for the sight to vanish at any second. I placed a hand against the glass. It cracked at my touch and the break spread in the blink of an eye, until it appeared I was standing within the heart of a spiderweb.

The floor shattered beneath my weight, and I fell into the night sky.

I woke, rolled onto my side. There was the briefest memory of a dream before it was lost. I was in my cot; in the pitiful room I was using. Looking to the window, I saw it was still night, and a crescent moon was looking down on the land.

The bedside table was missing.

Confused, wondering if I had come to be somewhere unexpected, I sat up and saw it. I had pressed it against the closed door, to prevent any intruders. I couldn't remember doing that, but there was an increasing number of things I couldn't remember doing. The precious stones were piled on top of it, alongside a handful of coins. My dagger was placed beside them.

Every part of my body complained as I forced myself out of the cot and approached the window. My pipe was on the ledge, where I had foolishly left it. I got the tobacco burning and looked down at the streets outside. They looked deserted, like I was the only living soul residing in Harcourt. A fox caught my eye, then something else but the coughing fit started before I could truly see what it was. By the time it had stopped, by the time I raised myself from my knees and wiped the spit and the blood from my chin, the street was empty again.

*

Leonie was skinning a rabbit. She didn't look happy, and she didn't look pretty. Her lips tightened as if she had tasted something bitter when she noticed me. She placed the knife and rabbit down on the block and stood with her hands at her hips.

"The noise you made last night is not acceptable," she said. "There are other guests here, and you should count yourself lucky that not one of them decided to pay you a visit."

I remembered coughing, but I couldn't remember getting back here. Either one of these could have disturbed someone. The thin walls and groaning stairs wouldn't have been any help.

"Well? Don't you have anything to say? The way you just stare, sometimes," she said, "is like you have gone off to another place."

I remembered the precious stones and thought about offering them to her all over again. And I might have, if a young child hadn't entered the room and stood close to Leonie's side. The girl silently looked at me with wide eyes. I had no memory of the girl. Leonie's daughter? I should have seen her before now, surely.

"I need to go out."

Leonie picked up the knife and pointed it in my direction. "Drinking again, I bet! If you make half the noise you made last night," she warned, "I'll have you on the streets!"

I went from one tavern to another. There was a feeling I was to find someone, or something, but I couldn't recall *who* or what. I saw men with familiar faces but forgotten names. Young and experienced wardens too keen to let their blades do the talking. One woman said – for the right coin – she could make me feel young and handsome again. I kept drinking, kept moving on from one place to another, even as they became increasingly disreputable. There was someone, or something, I had to find. I was sure of it.

The man approached me in The Swan. He approached my table with caution, waiting for me to look up from my drink before talking. "Excuse me," he said, "but it is Raen Caleb I see, isn't it?"

"That depends," I said, and I had to close one eye to get him into focus. "Are you going to claim I owe you coin?"

"I would never do such a thing," he said. He was as good as mumbling, like he was scared our conversation could be overheard. "You may not remember me, but we fought together, at the Siege of Newcombe."

Newcombe. The name was familiar. Something that occurred years after Stoneisle, but the details were not there.

"You do have something about you," I lied. "What is your name?"

"Darson," he said. "I represented the House of Chinaski."

"Darson," I lied all over again, "I remember you. Sit. Have a drink. Let's talk about our lives, or more cheerier things."

He took a seat with me and started with an apology. "I'm sorry, but my reason for approaching you is not joyous," he said, "although, despite appearances, I am willing to provide coin for your assistance."

Even with him sitting so close, I had to keep one eye closed to focus on him.

"Then what is your reason?"

He took to rolling a cigarette. "There is a whoremaster in the Flesh Quarter you may have heard of, he calls himself The Dragon?"

"Look at me," I said, "do I really look like a man that ventures into the Flesh Quarter?"

"You are old, I do not deny that," he said, "but I am betting you are still of your talents. In fact, there is no other I would rather have beside me at this time."

I drank from my tankard and returned it to the table with more force than intended. "You have decided The Dragon is your enemy? And what is it he has done?"

"He cut at the face of my woman," he said, "disfiguring her."

"What had she done to deserve that?"

"Nothing," he said, "not a thing, and you must believe me. But he took a blade to her face, and I cannot risk confronting him alone. I would need assistance, just in case any of the men he pays to watch over him should get too close.

"And so, I would pay you as handsomely as I can to help me. We would go into the Flesh Quarter and when the opportunity arises, I will make him pay. I believe that it could be easy enough if we are careful. But my eagerness to claim justice could see getting in and out difficult. That is where I would appreciate your expertise."

"Tell me, why was your woman in such a place?"

"How do you mean?"

"Why would someone so innocent, particularly a woman, venture into such an area?"

"I assure you, she didn't," he said. "The Dragon rode out from his den of sin, wanting to harm a man he felt had wronged him. My beloved was caught in the violence that came with him."

I looked at him and asked, "Were you the man he was looking for?"

"I assure you that I was not," he said, striking a match for his cigarette. "I doubt he even knows my name, but I guarantee he will."

I nodded and checked how much of my drink remained. I didn't feel like finishing it.

"Do you know how many men he has to hand?"

"I imagine as many as require coin," he said. "But I have been watching him. He has confidence in the Flesh Quarter… Arrogance. He often walks without a companion, certain that no one will dare challenge him."

"Then I really can't see why you would need me."

"I hope I won't," he said, "but I will still pay for your time. All I ask is you tell me when the best opportunity presents itself and to keep others from preventing my business with him."

"I'll consider it," I said, struggling to my feet. The tavern swayed around me. It took a moment for me to right myself. "And I will be here, tomorrow, with an answer."

"We could go now."

I laughed.

"We could," I said, "and we wouldn't stand a chance. I'll have your answer for you, tomorrow. You're free to look elsewhere."

"Then I will wait until tomorrow," he said.

I staggered out of the tavern and onto the street. The air increased my drunkenness. Someone had collapsed on the floor. I stepped over him and carried on walking, leaning against a wall for support. A warden looked at me and came walking over. My first thought was he was going to give me the choice between a night in a cell or handing over whatever coin I still held onto. My jaw clenched. As he came closer, rage began to fill me. I kept my eyes straight ahead, like I hadn't noticed him. When he placed an open hand on my shoulder, I was close to taking the dagger from my belt.

"Raen," he said, and he smiled. The anger was replaced by mild confusion. "Raen Caleb," he said, "I never thought I would see you again."

My confusion disarmed me. He spotted that quickly enough and smiled all the more.

"Raen," he laughed, "it's me – Stephen Kerwynn!"

"Stephen," I repeated, because I could think of nothing else to say. Now I knew who he was, it was hard for me to understand how I hadn't recognised him at once.

He laughed again as he embraced me. "I haven't seen you in so long," he said, "I thought I might never see you again. I haven't seen or heard a word from you, since—"

"You're looking well," I said, preventing him from digging up graves I'd rather see forgotten. "Tell me, why have you remained on the road, when you must have earned the right to sleep soundly under your roof?"

Stephen laughed briefly, giving the impression he was regularly asked the question.

"My father remains of sound mind and good health," he said, "meaning there is nothing for me to do at the home, no matter how he tries to convince me otherwise. I wanted to believe I could be of some use, but I didn't want to be too far from him, so I have settled here, in Mealand. I may not have the same level of comfort," he laughed, "but I do have a cot of my own."

I nodded to have him think I could understand. "I've settled here myself. My wandering days are long behind me."

"You have earned your peace. But I can't believe I have found you here," he laughed again, "and after so long. To think of how often we may have missed one another by a moment. What are you doing now?"

"Gathering information," I said, not wanting him to know how I had long become nothing. There was also a chance he could prove useful. "Can you tell me if the Flesh Quarter is as bad as I have heard?"

He took a breath that implied delivering the answer he knew could hurt him.

"It could be worse than that," he admitted. "If enough good men were gathered, we could go in there and get it under control. The problem is, and you are most likely aware of this, there are far too many wardens who are comfortable with the rewards they can receive for sharing information. Because of that, many won't go there. There are even rumours of prices being placed on the heads of wardens. And the king's advisers? It may be a cruel place, but it brings in coin."

"Can you tell me anything about a whoremaster? He's known as The Dragon."

"His isn't a name I have heard," Stephen said, "but it is a long time since I have discussed the place."

Two men coming from the tavern were in disagreement. I was certain it wouldn't lead to anything serious, Stephen wasn't. He looked beyond me. I could see he wanted to march right over to them and send them in separate directions. I took it as my cue to leave.

"It was good to see you, old friend, but I don't want to keep you from your duties."

"No," he said, "one moment, and we can eat together, and talk of our years apart."

He said it, but his heart wasn't in it. Neither was mine. I wanted to remember him as a good man. There was a chance he had stopped being that a long time ago, and I didn't wish to hear the details.

"Another time," I said, "we're sure to meet again."

*

Rabbit stew was simmering over a fire when I returned. Leonie wasn't around. I helped myself to a generous bowl. When I turned, the young child was at the doorway. Silently looking at me. I stared back for a while. No memory of her surfaced.

"Do we know each other?"

She didn't open her mouth. She didn't blink. She just went on looking at me.

"Where's your mother?"

No change. I finished the stew and made my way for the stairs. The girl stepped aside to give me a little space; turned on her heels to watch me. I stopped at the stairs and looked at her again. Whatever secrets she may have held, she wasn't about to share them. I made my way to my room. There was a faint smell of incense in the air. I wondered if Leonie could have been preparing to offer my cot to another.

"Damned woman," I muttered, forcing the window open. Cold air entered the room with the sounds of nearby drunks. Both were preferable to the smell of incense. I kicked off my boots and got onto my cot.

*

I may have woken, but I may not have.

I opened my eyes. It was dark. Silent. The window remained open. The room must have felt colder than it did out on the street.

I looked to the door. Open, but only just. I didn't see or hear a soul, but it felt as if someone had just walked out of it. The dagger was at the bedside table. I took it in a feeble hand and groaned on getting to my feet. Old, old man. Weak. My feet were clumsy. If anyone had just left, they would have heard me following. That didn't stop me.

The hallway stretched out to eternity. The walls, the ceiling, all black, cracked glass. Pale mist looked to be trapped within. A thin carpet of that same mist looked to cover the floor. Looking to it for a moment, I saw that wasn't the case. The mist was coming from a hole in the ground, the same I had fallen through. I stepped out onto the landing, because I was too old to have anything left to lose. It sounded a lot like I had stepped onto the surface of a frozen lake. Standing still, I listened to my own breathing and looked around me. Countless scenes, transpiring all around me, between the cracks.

I saw myself on a throne, a crown of antlers and bone on my head, and the great war hammer in my possession.

I saw myself cut down a drunken fool before he could brutally murder my best friend.

I saw Yasmin and me, happy, my handsome face without a mark.

I struggled to take my eyes from that one.

And I saw Jaxe bring terror to those he thought could challenge him, and I fought loyally at his side.

I stepped back, closed the door and rested my forehead against it a while. When I was ready, I returned to my cot.

*

Leonie wasn't to be seen. The young child sat at a table with a plate of cooked meats and bread in front of her. She stared at me in silence, as I had come to expect from her. I took a handful of meat from her plate and was chewing it as I cut myself a piece of bread.

"Where's your mother, child?"

She didn't respond.

"Your name?"

I ate the bread without hearing an answer to either

question. I took one of the precious stones from my pocket and placed it down in front of her. Her eyes never left mine.

"I believe this is priceless," I said. "Always believe that you are the same."

I made my way through the city, and I rid myself of the jewels I had claimed along the way. I dropped some into the tins of sisters collecting for the children of the citadel and was gone before they had noticed my donation. I discreetly dropped others on street corners, hoping fate would see them found by those most needy. Some I tossed to pigeons, as if they were breadcrumbs. And I reached the inn before Darson. Requesting a drink, I smiled on seeing how few coins I had left to my name. I took to a quiet booth, took hold of my pipe and looked to it for a moment before placing it on the nearest table, along with my tobacco and matches. Darson appeared before I was a good way through my drink. He saw me right away, hurried over with a cigarette burning away between his fingers.

"I'm glad you're here," he said, sitting alongside me. "I wasn't sure if you would come."

"Where's your weapon?"

He reached around his side and patted his lower back. "Out of sight," he said. "Some places in the Flesh Quarter will have you hand them over."

"Is the blade strong? If The Dragon has allies to hand, you won't want the blade snapping, or separating from its handle."

"It's not a blade," he said.

"Then what is it?"

"A light club."

I laughed at that. The way he looked at me had me think he required an explanation.

"It could be you don't want to kill him," I said, "but a blow from a club can kill – believe me. Or they can lead to a pitiful existence."

He seemed to think over what I had said, then he started rolling a cigarette.

"Don't be thinking this is any different to meeting someone on the battlefield," I said. "Any man you go for will fight like his life depends on it – because it might. Especially if he doesn't know you. The Dragon will be prepared to kill. If he really doesn't recognise you, he's going to think you're nothing more than a competitor. And if you let him live? You should hope he never finds you."

Darson got his cigarette burning, took a long draw on it and looked at me. "Sounds like you're trying to turn me against the idea."

"Not at all," I said.

"Good," he said, "because you won't."

I nodded and downed a little more of my drink. "You have time for one," I said, "if you need a little extra courage."

"I don't need it," he said. "I'm ready to leave as soon as you are."

We left soon after. When I signalled for a carriage, Darson didn't hide how he disagreed with my decision. "What are you doing?" he asked as the driver came closer. "He'll recognise our faces!"

"And?"

"I don't think we should travel by coach," he said,

lowering his head from the driver's gaze.

"I'm not walking all the way there," I said to him, "and, so there's no confusion, I'm not paying for the journey."

I looked to the driver as I pulled the carriage door open. "Take us to the Flesh Quarter."

"I'll take you there," he agreed, "but I'm not travelling through it."

"We'll go as far as you're willing."

Darson's mood didn't improve as we sat in the carriage. His face reminded me of boys in the citadel, when they were being punished for something they may not have done. He shook his head and rolled a cigarette.

"What's wrong?"

He said, "I don't think we should have got in."

"Then you should have brought a couple of horses. Your woman," I asked him, "how is she?"

"As well as can be expected," he said, refusing to even look at me. Even the way he blew smoke from his mouth was enough to show he was angry.

"Does she know you're doing this?"

"No," he said.

"You should have told her," I said. "That way, at least she would understand if you don't return."

"I'm tired of how you are talking," he as good as snapped. "I think you want me to be as scared as you must be!"

The driver stopped a matter of streets from where the Flesh Quarter officially began, and Darson paid him for his time. As we walked to the overcrowded district of loud drunks and observant women, I glanced around for any wardens. Two stood nearby. They watched the streets of the Flesh Quarter, but they didn't venture too close to them.

"There's an inn, not too far from here," Darson said, picking up his pace. "I hear it's a good place to start."

"From whom?"

"People I trust," he said, "and that is all you need to know."

It reminded me a lot of a place I used to go to. Sawdust was regularly being thrown on the floor. Some men collapsed from fighting, others from drinking. Darson sat smoking. I sat with an untouched beer he had bought me. At one point, a supposed magician performed acts of magic for us to observe.

"Drink up," Darson said, "we're wasting our time. There's another place I was told about."

A woman stopped me as we neared the door. She actually held a hand against my face and looked me in the eyes. She must have earned some coin, just for that.

"Your friend seems a little frustrated," she said. "Maybe I could make you both feel a little better? One at a time, or both together. Whatever you would prefer. It will cost the same."

"We don't have time for this," Darson called from the street.

I saw the flash of anger directed at Darson on her face, gently removed her hand from my own and smiled. "Another time," I said, and took to following the man responsible for my being there.

"I should have known the two of you were looking for boys," she called at my back. "You would need a third friend to even come close to being enough for me!"

One tavern followed another. The day moved on. The men became more violent, and the women, too. There was no law here, no order. Some crawled through the streets, too intoxicated or injured to stand. Men and women alike begged in the roads. Some, missing limbs, claimed to have been hurt in battle. I wondered how it had been allowed to come to this.

And I grew tired, but I remained with Darson.

We were sat within another tavern when he muttered, "There he is."

His words were exactly what I wanted to hear. Since we had claimed a seat, I had lost count at how many fleas I had been scratching at.

"Where?"

He discreetly pointed towards an unremarkable-looking man. Slender. Not particularly tall. Beardless. Hair shaved short. Interestingly, free of any companion.

I said, "Are you sure?"

"That's The Dragon," he assured me.

"He's alone," I said. "I could hand you my blade, and you could end him in the blink of an eye. You would be out of the door before he or anyone else had even noticed."

"No," Darson said, "I want to take my time with him."

"You mightn't get a chance as good as this."

"No," he said, "I'll take the chance that's given."

We sat, and we waited. After a while, The Dragon got to his feet and left. Darson quickly went to follow. I took a hold of his arm and kept him in his place.

"Not yet," I said.

"We could lose him."

"We could be drawing attention to ourselves, right as he is meeting others."

"And? That's why I brought you!"

"I thought I was here to keep you alive?"

He pried my hand from him and rushed after his target. I considered remaining where I was, but soon got to my feet and followed. When I stepped out onto the street, Darson was rushing ahead. I had lost sight of The Dragon. Darson turned a corner. I moved as quickly as my aching bones would permit, not wanting to lose the two of them.

A drunk came at me from the side and said something I couldn't make out as he grabbed at me. I pulled the dagger from my belt and quickly slashed at the back of his hand. The drunk yelped, staggered back clutching at his wound. I kept walking, turned the corner. Darson was still hurrying on. I saw The Dragon not too far ahead of him. Calling Darson would only get The Dragon's attention. I cursed under my breath and carried on after them. The Dragon headed down a backstreet. Darson followed. Neither one of them looked back, not once.

I reached the backstreet, looked down it and saw a wall straight ahead. Moving forward I turned into another dead end, turned to make my way down a longer stretch. No sign of either of them. I kept moving through what felt like a labyrinthine maze. My lungs were burning, and my legs were trembling, through adrenaline or exhaustion. This was a place to become lost, or to escape.

Then I stepped out into a large, open square, just in time to see Darson fall dead onto the dirt floor. Blood flowed from his mouth. His hands were pressed tightly to his side. Blood ran from between the fingers. The Dragon stood at one of only two ways out of the square. Two men stood over Darson, one of them holding a bloody weapon. It wasn't your standard blade. It looked a lot like something you would use to poke at the burning coals of a fireplace. Much easier to conceal. He was the first to look in my direction. His accomplice followed his gaze to me and briefly considered rushing over. The Dragon slowly raised his head and looked to me with mild disinterest, once he was certain Darson wouldn't be recovering. I realised how ragged my breathing was. Realised how I was still holding my dagger. I looked down at Darson, then back to the others.

"That man owed me coin," I said, struggling as my lungs tried to claim enough air. "All I ask is you let me go through his pockets."

The Dragon titled his head to one side and said, "I saw you with him."

"Possibly," I said. "He cheated me at a game. I just want what I'm owed."

The Dragon smiled and said, "Give him what he is owed."

I hurried back and waited behind a turn. The first to scurry out in front of me was the man with the weapon. He had just enough time to register I had taken a hold of his wrist before I plunged my blade into his side. Four times in quick succession. He stumbled, and he brought me with him. I landed on top of him. Even as I stabbed him again and again, he wouldn't let go of me.

The second man pulled me from him like I weighed nothing and shoved me into a wall. My head struck it. Dazed, I had just enough sense to try and slash at the air and hope for the best, but my dagger scraped against the wall I had been put against. His fist struck my jaw. My back went against the wall, knees bent to try and keep me from dropping. He kicked a foot out from under me, stomped on my hand to have me release the dagger. I felt bones break as he did it. Once he had kicked the weapon out of my reach, the kicks and the punches came raining down on me.

After a while, I still felt them landing, it's just there was no pain. Flat on my back, my eyes focused on a patch of sky. He occasionally came into my line of vision, a giant standing over me, as he kicked at my fragile ribs and stomped down on my broken body. I took it, and I waited for death. When he stepped away, I thought he would be picking up the weapon of the friend I had killed. But he didn't. He didn't return. And I didn't try and get to my feet. I was sure that this was the end. As my eyes closed, I even felt relieved.

*

But I woke some hours later.

The skies had darkened. A light rain had started and had most likely stirred me. I rolled onto my side and lost my breath to pain. The skin on my face felt cold, and stiff. I didn't need a mirror to know dried blood was the cause. Every part of me was in agony. With each movement, broken ribs prodded and stabbed at my insides. My right hand was swollen and bruised. It took more attempts than I'd care to admit to get onto my feet. My left leg was almost as good as useless; as I tried to make my way back out onto the streets, it dragged behind me. Thunder rolled overhead, and the rain grew heavy in an instant. The ground of the backstreets and alleyways turned to mud. Soon, it lay in wait beneath the deepening puddles and tried to keep my feet from lifting. I found the streets to be a lot quieter. The rain had chased most people in search of shelter. People crowded into taverns so full, it was hard to tell the sounds of anger from the sounds of joy as I walked by.

I stopped and leaned against a wall, hoping my strength would return. The rain was so bad, I had to wipe the water from my eyes. Eye. One of them was swollen over. At least I hoped it was. The thought dawned on me that I could have lost it. Those same ribs struck again as I tried to take a deep breath, and I cursed my sorry luck for keeping me alive.

A group of drunken men came tumbling out of a building. From the noise that was made by those still inside, it was safe to say there had been trouble. The three men shouted back, but it was all for show. They kept walking, coming in my direction. My good hand felt for my blade and didn't find it. I had left it behind. The shape I was in, it wouldn't have been much use. As the men neared, I readied for them to take their anger out on me. They didn't. They gave me the briefest of glances but kept on walking. Kept on repeating how someone-or-other would be sorry.

Glancing back over my shoulder, I saw them turn out of sight without a second look. I was beneath them. Too old. Too broken. Too little of a challenge.

I made myself start walking all over again.

The only light on the streets was coming from lanterns placed behind nearby windows. I heard someone ask me for coin but didn't see them in the darkness. It was hard to keep moving. Eventually my legs buckled, and I fell flat on my face. The rainwater on the ground began to flood my nostrils. I didn't try to reposition myself – I just accepted it. I closed my eye and expected a sensation like falling asleep.

Running footsteps. I expected it to be the sound of somebody running for shelter, but I wasn't so lucky. Hands took my shoulders and rolled me onto my back. My eyelids fluttered, then closed again. I didn't protest.

"Raen!" a voice yelled.

I opened my eye. When it adjusted, I saw it was Allen kneeling over me. He wasn't how I had known him. He had lived. He was much older. I smiled because of it. I said, "I'm glad it's you that come for me," and I slipped back into the welcoming darkness.

*

Incense was burning.

I opened my good eye as best I could. A small room. Unremarkable, but clean. A few candles were burning, probably just enough for someone to see me without any difficulty. I could barely move, but I knew I had been stripped and bandaged. Whoever had placed me in the cot had put a lot of cushions behind my back, to keep me sitting. Most likely to help me breathe. There was a small window on one of the walls to the side of me. I could see it was stained-glass. The god it depicted was a distant memory to me. It didn't matter. I'd long accepted that we had been left behind by the gods that hadn't died.

I closed my eye. The smell of incense remained. I could hear my breathing. It didn't sound too good. With a little effort, I could hear the winds blowing outside. I concentrated on them until sleep reclaimed me.

Allen was sitting in a chair beside the bed. When my thoughts had gathered, I realised it wasn't Allen at all. It was Stephen. It was Stephen that had found me close to death. I tried to talk and made a faint croaking sound. To my surprise, it was loud enough for him to hear.

"Raen," he said. He got to his feet and reached for something out of my sight. A jug and a cup. "You're awake!"

He poured some liquid into the cup. Something had changed, but I couldn't be sure what. Candles were still burning. It was a struggle to say a word.

"Don't talk," he insisted, bringing the cup to my lips. "Just drink. It will help with the pain."

I drank. I hadn't realised how dry my throat had been until the fluid touched it. A familiar taste. Something prepared by the wise men of the citadel. When he was sure I'd drank enough, Stephen removed the cup from my mouth. He even dabbed at my lips and chin with a cut of folded cloth. I swallowed, took a breath and readied to talk. He didn't try and stop me. This time, he patiently waited.

"You brought me here?"

I'm certain he heard the humour in my voice. It just wasn't the good kind of funny.

"They don't know who you are," he said in a hushed tone.

"How long have I been here?"

"This is your third night," he said.

"I don't know what you might have told them, but now I have woken, they won't keep me here. They'll throw me alongside the other worthless men they're tending to. Someone is bound to recognise me."

"My father will allow you to return with me," he said, and it sounded a lot like he was trying to convince himself as much as he was me, "he just needs a little persuasion."

I smiled to myself and nodded, allowing Stephen to believe I could imagine that happening. I was smiling because it was nice of him to put the blame entirely on his father. William Kerwynn – Sir Kerwynn, as he was now known – most likely would permit me to return. Natalia was a different story. If there is one thing a woman will hold onto with more determination than she does coin, it's a grudge. Still, I couldn't hold it against him for trying to cover her.

"It would be nice," I told him, "to see the place again," and I tried to lay back as best I could, despite the gathered pillows. My ribs tried to stretch out alongside me, even with the tight bandaging I could feel keeping them in place.

"You're tired," Stephen said. "I will leave you to rest,

and I promise you I will return at first light, but before I go," he asked, "who did this to you?"

I smiled as best as I could manage. "I was drunk," I said, "and I stepped out in front of a horse."

He didn't believe me. I saw that in his eyes. He smiled anyway.

"Rest," he said, "you were truly blessed to survive."

He stepped out of a door I couldn't see, and I heard his footsteps lead him further away until I could hear him no more. It was a little unsettling, knowing anybody could walk through that same door, and I wouldn't know until they were right on me. It just wasn't enough to keep me from trying to get a little more sleep. I closed my good eye and focused on the sound of the winds blowing outside and falling rain gently tapping at the stained-glass window.

Things change.

*

The rain was hitting the window with noticeable force. I heard the difference in the sound and knew that I had slept a little. How long, I had no idea. There was a roll of distant thunder. I opened my eye, saw only two candles remained burning. One at either side of the room. I doubted anyone would even see me if they went by. Despite there being only the small window, the room was illuminated by a flash of lightning. It was during that moment I saw Maerlyn standing in the shadows. I recognised him straight away. He hadn't aged at all. He was in the same clothing he had been wearing so many years ago.

"Funny," I said, "I hadn't expected to ever see you again. Hadn't even suspected that it would be one of the Brothers come to take pleasure through my demise, but stranger things have happened."

He silently moved closer to one of the candles. There wasn't much light, but it was enough to see his face. There was no malice there. Busch had once told me you were more likely to receive a quick death if the man looked angry, but that wasn't always true. A lot of angry men had ordered the slow and painful death of others. It all came down to how willing you were to get your hands dirty.

"You think your appearance will impress me?" I smiled. "I never intended to live forever."

"How long has it been," he asked, "since you last saw me?"

"Too long to keep count."

"Not for me," Maerlyn said. "You turned away from me on Allsen a matter of minutes ago."

I nodded, quite unsure to whether I should believe him.

"I remain unimpressed," I said.

He stepped back into the shadows, came closer to the cot and pulled the available chair with him. No rush in his movements. He sat down and looked to me. It felt as if he was looking at me, anyway. All I could see was his silhouette.

"Those few times you encountered me," he said, "I wasn't the same person. I was older, even younger. I came and left Stoneisle as I pleased. I would be focusing on matters of another time, another place, and another version of me would come from another time, and another place to be ready for your arrival, and your return from Allsen."

"Well," I said, "it was good of you to come and see me again."

"You're close to death. You would be lucky to see one final sunrise."

"Is that a threat?"

"No," he said. "It is simply truth."

I smiled. "It has been a long time since I watched the sunrise," I said, "I won't be too upset if I miss another."

I felt his silent stare on me all over again. Neither one of us said a thing. I saw it as a challenge, that he wanted me to break the silence. It could have been with him seeing time so differently. He had all the time in the worlds to choose his words.

"There are key events that have to happen," he said at last. "The Revenant War is one such example. I have witnessed and learned so much, yet I have barely even scratched the surface. It can be prevented, but it must happen sooner or later. The potential outcomes were worse than what you experienced."

"I doubt that."

"What else do you doubt? Your decision to walk away from me," he asked, "do you regret that? You should know I never lied to you, Raen. We could have done so much good together, and your life could have had so much meaning."

I smiled to myself, though I was certain he could see it.

"Another time," I said, "but not mine."

"And what if it could be? What if I were to tell you it wasn't too late? That you did not have to turn and walk away from me at that moment?"

"Impossible. My entire life from that moment would change."

"It would," he agreed, "as would the lives of so many others – even those you will never have met. What you have experienced was but one story, and I swear there are so many more, just not quite written. But they can be, and I promise you that it is not impossible. It's simply a matter of choice. You would be young again, with all these years before you."

"Memories of a future I had already lived would drive me insane."

"In time," he said, "you would forget them."

I laughed, shook my head and looked away. It's just there was nothing for me to look at, only darkness.

"I do not come with false promises," Maerlyn said. "I will not say that I promise you will live eternal, nor will I say your time will not come in a cot such as this. But I can promise your end will not be in *this* cot, at *this* moment. You stand before two paths, and one brings you to your impending death, whereas the other? Raen, it can lead to so many different roads for you to take. I will not beg you, nor will I corrupt your thoughts. The choice is entirely yours," he concluded, "but you are running out of time to make it."

I looked back to face him. Of course, all there was for me to see was his silhouette. The flame of the candle behind him seemed brighter than it should have been. It was blinding.

"Give me until the sunrise to make my decision."

THE END

MORE FROM
sci-fi-cafe

Available to buy in paperback and eBook from Amazon and other good online stores. Scan the affiliate links in the QR codes to find out more about each book.

Look out for our Audiobooks on Audible and Amazon too

Transplant
Greenways
The Tribe
The Seed Garden

Our Paranormal and Paranormal Romance books are all set in the same world and can be read in any order or separately.

The Threads Which Bind us
The Wolf Inside us
Into Dust
The Calico Golem

A Sun Going Down

Amidst talk of an uprising on a distant island, the young warrior Jonas Rowan encounters a deadly assassin within the great walls of Lawtone Castle itself.

If the warmonger referred to only in whisper as Kortahn believes even the tides of the Leonard Ocean are unable to keep him from claiming the throne, then the great kingdom must send her finest to extinguish his threat. Travelling alongside his fellow brothers of the blade, Rowan carries the burden of knowing he alone must also locate and judge Siersa, the pale bride of Kortahn himself.

A Sun Going Down captures the legend of heroes during their darkest hour.

The Wolf Inside Us

Jake is a reclusive genius shut away in his penthouse apartment where he draws his award winning zombie comics. Kat is one of his biggest fans. She's also his publisher's office manager and each week gets to visit Jake to see his latest work.

Over the years, Kat has developed a soft spot for Jake, so it's not surprising that she's completely thrown when he suddenly disappears. But stranger still, why did he leave a tiny puppy behind, all alone, and where did he get it?

Kat's relationship grows from more than simple puppy love in this sensual werewolf romance where life throws all it has at this girl and her dog.

Content advisory: Mild sex and fantasy sex references, alcohol, mild fantasy violence.

ISBN 978-1-910779-97-2

Into Dust

Ryan Malin had made a name for himself as the author of a very successful series of guidebooks on supposedly haunted houses. But there was always one that had been off-limits to him – Hewitson Cottage.

That was until he was approached by the alluring Kelley Stranack. She and her fellow university lecturer promised a whole weekend of exclusive access, all expenses paid. Naturally, he jumped at the chance.

Of course none of the places he'd written about were actually haunted, but this place... well, it had a history worth investigating.

But why had a cash-strapped university chosen HIM, paid all his expenses and who had paid for the cottage to be refurbished for their trip?

ISBN 978-1-910779-05-7

The Girl from the Temple Ruins

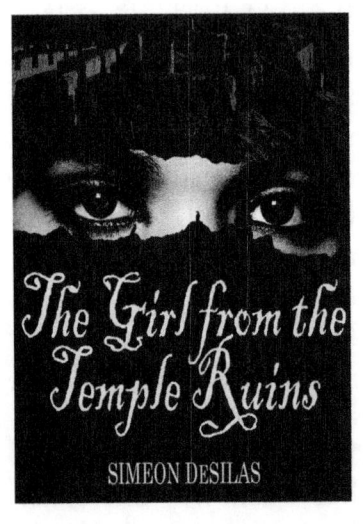

A temple to the goddess Amalishah lies in the remotest wastelands of Assyria. She is their protector but to others she is known as The Monster.

The Hittite prince Artaxias visits the Palace of the Goddess to implore the temple priests to free prisoners captured from the border. He knows their fate, the appalling human sacrifice that will be made to the goddess who must feed on human blood.

Four thousand years have eroded the memory and the evidence of these events until British archaeologist Michael Townsend discovers the subterranean lair of the goddess. Michael is visited and instantly captivated by a mysterious and beautiful woman. The Hittites called her monster, a creature now called vampire.

ISBN: 978-1910779-41-5

City of Storms

When top foreign correspondent Sean Brian flies into Manila in the Philippines, a typhoon and a political revolution are uppermost in his thoughts.

But what also awaits will turn his already busy life into a roller coaster of romance, adventure, elation and despair.

At the centre of this transformation is an infant boy child, born, abandoned and plunged into street poverty in the grim underbelly of an Asian metropolis.

This is the catalyst for a story ranging from the corrupt, violent world of back street city sex clubs and drug addiction, to the clean air of the Sulu Sea and the South Pacific; from the calm safety of an island paradise to the violent guerilla world of the notorious Golden Triangle and the southern Philippines archipelago.

As we follow the child, Bagyo, into fledgling manhood, we can only wonder at the ripples that spread from one individual to engulf so many others – and at the injustice that still corrodes life on the mean streets of the world.

ISBN: 978-1908387-99-8

Printed in Great Britain
by Amazon